...be in a day or two ...
I Hollande ...
... me to all your ...
to Batavia — I should so like to
... all again — I ... happy
... among you in Paris —
... spell has been over me
... my return — ... tell Alfred
... dream of the Pyramids
... of mine (with a wife my
... friend) is ... d'affaires
... to Naple — another
... is Prime Minister at
... — another of my early friends
... the writer at Palermo — ...
... make such a delight
... !
What a grumbling wretch
... me! Ever y... M. Whittle...

THE FORGER'S REQUIEM

BRADFORD MORROW

A NOVEL

THE FORGER'S REQUIEM

Atlantic Monthly Press
New York

FIRST EDITION

Published simultaneously in Canada
Printed in the United States of America

This book is set in 10.7-pt. Berling LT
by Alpha Design and Composition of Pittsfield, NH.

First Grove Atlantic hardcover edition: January 2025

Library of Congress Cataloging-in-Publication data is available for this title.

ISBN 978-0-8021-6415-5
eISBN 978-0-8021-6416-2

Atlantic Monthly Press
an imprint of Grove Atlantic
154 West 14th Street
New York, NY 10011

Distributed by Publishers Group West

groveatlantic.com

25 26 27 28   10 9 8 7 6 5 4 3 2 1

For Thomas Johnson & Lawrence Bank,
and for Cara

. . . when falsehood can look so like the truth,
who can assure themselves of certain happiness?

—Mary Shelley, *Frankenstein*

THE
FORGER'S
REQUIEM

We all die alive. That's what the earth said. Or so the buried man thought as he coughed into consciousness, unable to breathe or move. He was drowning, but in the land, not the sea. His legs and arms, the curled length of his body, were lodged in the ground, and his chest was compressed like a flattened bellows. Frantic, choking on grainy dirt, he tried to stir but could not. Tried to open his eyes but saw only darkness. He had no idea how he got there, or why. Had no memory of who he was. The crown of his head throbbed with each beat of his struggling heart. His face stung and his tongue tasted of bloody mud. A pitiful moan caught in his throat, muffled by the heavy shroud of earth that encased him. Otherwise, his world was silent. When he tried to scream, his screams were just ideas of screams.

This was neither a nightmare nor some delirious fantasy. He was interred in very real dirt shot through with ragged shards of rock and severed roots. However long he'd lain there unconscious in this makeshift grave, petrified as some latter-day bog mummy, it was clear he had little or no time left to save himself.

His lungs were hungry and the dank pocket of air that had kept him going was all but spent.

Gasping, he found he could bend his wrist and the crabbed fingers of his right hand. He fidgeted them sideways, up and down, frantic against the chafing soil, wincing with keen agony. A surge of adrenaline, blue and silver flashes of light, seized him while he heaved with all his strength against the leaden ground, his flesh and nails shredding as he scraped at the weight that held him down. Fist now clenched, he punched upward and out. Clawing at fallen leaves and branches, his hand at last punctured the surface crust, like a bloom of Xylaria polymorpha, a fungus known as dead man's fingers. His right arm and shoulder breached next, then his naked head broke through. He spat and dry heaved, settling his cheek on the forest floor while he drank the open air, panting like a thirsty dog. Nauseated by the sudden late-day light, he began to quake and mutter nonsense.

Minutes passed, more minutes. Nobody was around.

Once his limbs stopped shaking, he fell mute. Maybe fainted, he couldn't be sure. When he stirred again, he tried hard to remember how he'd gotten into this predicament, but it was lost in a haze. Pulling himself together as much as he could, he set about extricating his legs, after which he collapsed with a groan and rolled painfully onto his back. His vision was blurred at first, images doubling and wobbly. He blinked and did his best to make out this quiet woodland glade, which he recognized even as he found it utterly foreign.

Maple leaves flickered in the dusky breeze. Mustard yellow and rusty brown, they rattled like death charms. Their colors meant it must be autumn. Early fall, judging from the warmth. High pink cirrus clouds flew in tatters above, catching what looked like sunset light. A family of chickadees whistled their names, darting about in the branches overhead. One of them cocked its head to turn a bright black bead of an eye on the unfamiliar creature who had just emerged from beneath the forest floor. It made a series of sharp chipping sounds, then jetted away, leaving a springing limb in its wake.

No, the bird seemed to have told him. This was not a dream, even if he wished it was. Not even a nightmare, it was a waking horror.

He touched his bloodied face with fingers that reeked of charred skin. The back of his head smarted more aboveground than below. Hematoma?—the term came unbidden. A ghost of wind and it seared like flame. He remembered then, or believed he remembered, that he had tripped headfirst into a fire. He'd been grasping a knife, he was pretty sure. Had waved it at a man who stood across from him, face lit up with hostility and fear, before an unseen accomplice bludgeoned him from behind. Whoever these would-be murderers were, they'd failed to check his pulse before burying him alive. He winced as he sat up, resting on bony elbows, and saw the firepit full of ash, a thin whisper of smoke still rising from orange coals. He suspected that he himself had lit it. Maybe he'd even provoked the fight.

Evening had begun to establish itself over the forest. He needed to get moving. But where? A lone hermit thrush made a fluting call, and, after a moment, another, deeper in the tangle of woods, echoed in response. Mates, siblings, singing to each other. The man's eyes were abruptly wet with tears. Whether his weeping was from despair or the grit that scratched his corneas, tears were alien to him. Whoever he was, he was damn well not given to crying.

If only he had water. A creek nearby from which to drink. Instead, his elbows gave way as he turned on his side and dry retched again, his cheek plastered with leaves, loam, bits of club moss. He knew his life was in jeopardy. That he badly needed help. But he sensed he was behind enemy lines and had no friends in this strange place. He would have to gather up his broken body, force it to stand, and, if possible, walk to safety.

It had been a shovel, of course. He'd been clouted on the back of his head with the same shovel they used to bury him. And while he wasn't sure how he understood such a thing, he knew that the deficits a victim can suffer from such a head trauma often resemble those of a stroke, though minor residual deficiencies and even full recovery are possible. Strangely, he knew this in so many rote words, book-learned words. Which led him to a sideways thought of how the incarcerated—himself among them?—who found themselves in the joint on a violent-crime conviction sometimes became expert in the art of diagnosing wounds and forming prognoses. In idle hours—ergo, most hours—they might trade obsessive notes with fellow inmates and read medical texts. Whatever gets you through the stint.

So who had hit him? And did they live in that house he saw through the trees, a farmhouse cresting the top of a long grassy rise? He would get answers once he was able to process what had brought him to this degradation. For now, he crawled onto his hands and knees and tried to get up, only to collapse in a heap. Fainting, no doubt, was a symptom of his injury too. His breathing sporadic, he rested several minutes before attempting again to stand, but once more his legs scissored shut beneath him.

When he next woke it was full dark, and lights from the house on the hill shone like backlit amber. To survive, his only hope was to reach the margin of these woods, and crawl, stumble, drag himself toward those lights where there was water, food, medicine—everything he needed to hydrate, treat his wounds, collect himself, figure out what to do. And because the people in the house were likely dangerous, all this needed to be done in stealth for fear he might end up permanently back in the same hole he'd just escaped.

He willed his way forward on sore hands and raw knees. Every few yards, he lay on his flank for an ambiguous stretch of time before forcing himself to continue. Overhead, a bound-less array of stars in a blue-black sky gazed at him with serene indifference. But then some key detail changed as he struggled up the hill. The lights had multiplied. Upstairs and down, they punctuated the night. Though the heavy grasses into which he'd waded partly obscured his view, he could see the silhouette of one figure moving between downstairs windows, and another on the second floor. Could the person in the higher window see him, or was he cloaked by the darkness? Breathing uneasily through his mouth, he froze in place, waited until both silhouettes withdrew from sight.

Behind him a barred owl hooted but roused no response. Crickets sang.

Somehow—he would never remember just how—he managed to trek through a maze of sharp skeletal wildflowers and bristling orchard grasses, past a vegetable garden where he scavenged the last unharvested withering tomatoes and ground-rotting zucchini, to reach the house. Its lights had long since been extinguished, its inhabitants gone to bed.

During his trudge through the field, a healthy paranoia had begun to roil his gut. He found a hose by the garage and dared to turn on the water. The cool trickle smelled of rubber but he was able to rinse his burning eyes, wash the wounds on his hands and stubbled face and shaven head, and drink. God, though, was he famished. He was half tempted to pound on the door with what rickety strength he could summon and beg for help, come what may. But a deeper desire to protect himself, remain dead and buried to those who'd stuck him in that shallow pit, won the night. And so, belly filled with well water, he closed the spigot and floundered about, directed by some vestigial memory of this place. Soon enough, he found a spot to hide behind a thicket of andromeda along the far side of the detached garage. He arranged himself as comfortably as he could on a bed of spent foliage, woozy and drained, and fell into heavy sleep.

Morning light, filtered by the shrubbery, burned his photo-sensitive eyes. He'd been awakened by muffled voices of a man and—young?—woman on the other side of the garage wall from where he lay, followed by the sound of a car engine. A surge of dread ran through him as he froze in place and remained still as a hunted rabbit. Movement, then. The car backed out, pea stone crunching under its tires, and drove away. Sparse birdsong rose from the woods. The mewling of a cat he couldn't see. A welcome calm settled over his private world.

Here was his chance. Squinting against the sun, he crawled from under the bushes and staggered to his feet. Inexplicably, his left foot was bare, while his right was clad in a black leather shoe that was soiled but otherwise looked like it had recently been buffed to a spit shine. His outstretched palms were scraped, his wounds inflamed. He blundered around the end of the garage, leaned against its white clapboard long enough to situate him-self before picking his way to the rear entrance to the house. However wary he felt, however worried that somebody might still be inside, he was too desperate for food not to take the risk.

Peering through the unwashed windows of a set of French doors, he saw a printing press and other equipment, as well as a wall of books behind, which he recognized, however dimly, as being meaningful to him. The studio doors were locked, so he moved farther along the building to the back porch. Here he cupped his hands against a glass pane and gaped at the kitchen. This door was locked too, as were the adjacent windows. At wit's end, he cried out for help. Preposterous, he knew, futile, but time was wasting, and no better ideas presented themselves. If someone was home, dangerous or not, maybe they would take pity on him.

No one was and no one did. He caught the reflection of a mutilated face in the glass, the long field and curtain of pastel autumn forest mirrored behind, and quickly looked away.

Persuaded that the house was vacant, the man got into the garage through an unlocked side entrance and rummaged around until he found a shovel that had been freshly scrubbed clean. Surely the murder weapon, he thought, had there been a murder. Using it as a hiker's staff, he made his way back to the porch and, gripping tight the burnished handle, swung its blade as hard as he could against the pane. The sound was excruciating, as were the shock waves that raced through his eggshell bones. It took him three tries before he succeeded in cracking the glass, and several more before it broke. He reached around inside, undid the deadbolt, opened the door, and toppled a chair as he lurched toward the refrigerator. Standing before it, he ate a wedge of cheddar and some smoked salmon, tasting nothing, grunting like a beast, then drank more water straight from the kitchen faucet. Still famished, he rummaged through cabinets, fetched down some almond biscuits and a tin of sardines, and devoured them along with a mouthful of flat champagne from a nearly spent bottle he salvaged out of the recycling bin.

Despite his efforts to pull himself together, he slid to the floor with his back braced against the dishwasher and sat with his legs splayed, not quite passed out but not quite awake. A dizzying nausea rose into his throat and mouth from having gorged himself, though he managed not to retch. He felt like a marionette whose strings had been cut by his spiteful puppeteer as he stared ahead at glass shrapnel winking on the floorboards near the broken window. How he wished his legs and arms were made of a puppet's wood instead of the flesh and bone that bristled with burning pain. He fully passed out, then came to, disoriented for long minutes before remembering he was here in this house.

Whoever *he* was. Wherever *this house* was.

The medicine cabinet in the downstairs bathroom yielded some ibuprofen, of which he swallowed a fistful. Revived by the food and water, a little buzzed by the champagne, the man crawled on hands and knees up the oak stairs to the second floor. On finding the master bathroom, he filled its tub with warm water, pried off his one shoe, stripped away his grubby black shirt and jeans, and, teeth gnashing, lowered himself into the water. His thoughts, call them that, ran in circles as he tried hard not to pass out again. Once the wincing pain subsided, he carefully rinsed the burns on his face and scabbing bruise on the crown of his head. Before long, the bath looked like tainted swill, so he emptied the tub, ran more lukewarm water, washed a second time. All of this was accomplished in the slowest of slow motion. After gingerly patting himself dry, the man dabbed aloe on his face and fingers, and first-aid cream on his head. He pulled back the coverlet on the bed and sorely laid himself down, naked as a mandrake root, then fell into a dreamless sleep.

"You can't be here" were his first words to himself on waking a day or maybe two later, hard sunlight drilling his eyes, though the words raised the questions afresh—where was *here* and who is *you?*

His skull pounded as before, but his vision was less fuzzy. He rose from the bed, leaving behind a faint secular Shroud of Turin in dried blood and sweat on its sheets. Since his own clothes were too grungy to put back on, he found some fresh, ill-fitting pants and a dress shirt in the closet. No idea whose they were. Nor did he know who owned the woman's blouses and other clothing that hung beside the man's stuff. He downed more painkillers from the medicine cabinet and searched the other upstairs rooms.

Two girls, it seemed, shared an adjacent bedroom. One was older and, telling from the leather pants, paint-splattered cordovan clogs, and heavy-metal T-shirts, more a city than a country girl. He studied framed photos on the bureau but the smiling family in different settings left him feeling hopeless. None of what he saw was recognizable though the father seemed oddly familiar. In a fit of pique, he snatched up one of the pictures to throw against a wall, but caught himself midgesture and pitifully put it back. Until he knew what was what, it was important to leave behind as little evidence of his presence as possible, wasn't it? Meant he'd have to wash his dirty clothes and the stained sheets, make it look like a hungry burglar broke in, not a bleeding, maddened, confused, vengeful fugitive, though of course he was all these.

Downstairs again, he glanced at the kitchen wall clock and saw it was almost noon. Not that it meant much to him, what time it was. He absentmindedly ate some butter cookies in the pantry then made his way down a hall that led to the printing studio he'd noticed earlier. Its door was locked, so, using a butter knife from the kitchen and some innate knowledge about how to pry a latch from the outside, he handily picked it. How the hell did he do that, he wondered, staring for a moment at his proficient fingers and the knife they grasped.

Once inside the studio, the man was struck by a bolt of comprehension, the first he'd felt since his rebirth in the woods. The stately squat Vandercook printing press, the lovely Jacques board shear, the shelves of ravishing books along the wall—all these were known to him. The delicious scent of ink, tidy reams of heavy paper, stacked cases of type. Each was personally meaningful, even as he failed yet to remember his own name or how he'd arrived at this sketchy present. Unsteady on his feet, he leaned against the Vandercook, a workaday cylinder press of black and silver metal with its ink drum roller, flat bed, glossy red handle. This leviathan—used for fabricating letterpress proofs of pamphlets, broadsides, books—was one of the world's great inventions. The man was so moved by its presence that he began to convulse with tears until he startled himself by angrily shouting, "Shut the fuck up!"

He ground the heels of his hands in his eyes, thinking he must surely have gone mad. No other explanation for these memory failures, his wild disorientation, the jagged sine wave of emotional crests and chasms. And now he was getting jazzed over some inert heap of metal used to print words on pieces of paper? He may not have known his own name but he knew he was no weepy sentimentalist. He also knew that he must have gotten himself tangled up in some truly monstrous trouble to wind up like this, an amnesiac in grievous pain, a busted whirligig too paranoid to call an ambulance for fear there were other more serious problems that awaited him in the wider world.

In time it all would come clear. For better or, more likely, worse. As things stood, his viable choices were few. He might reasonably kill himself with a chef's knife in a warm bath, finish the job others had failed to do. Or press ahead, blindman's-bluffing his way toward lucidity and whatever revelations lay ahead. He wiped away his repellent tears and reminded himself he was still traumatized from burial in the woods and whatever violence preceded it. He drew in a deep breath, let it out. In, out. The puzzle pieces of his identity could well be right here in this farmhouse. All he needed was to summon the discipline and wits to sort through them, cobble together a picture of his life.

He browsed the wall of books for clues that might jog some useful memory. Most of the volumes were about typography, calligraphy, the history of printing. Also, shelves of literature. Ann Radcliffe's *The Mysteries of Udolpho*, William M. Timlin's *The Ship that Sailed to Mars*, Toni Morrison's *Beloved*. Library of an eclectic reader. Yet many of the titles were old friends that he himself had encountered, if not read. He felt drawn to them, and when he reached out to touch their spines—Poe's *Tales*, Christie's *The Murder of Roger Ackroyd*, Sara Coleridge's *Phantasmion*—it was a gesture that seemed second nature, gave him a strange sense of comfort amid the chaos.

An array of Henry James titles included some less valuable firsts, like an old British edition of *In the Cage* with its gray cloth spine stamped in plain black letters. Odd novel about a woman telegraphist who works in a London office where she is literally fenced off, imprisoned in her workspace by wire mesh—the titular "cage"—as she types telegrams and transmits them but also decodes private messages between, among others, a pair of illicit lovers. A tale of voyeurism, as he recalled, and class separation, haves and have-nots, the perils of love. With perplexing ease he could form a clear image of the much handsomer American edition, issued by Herbert Stone in Chicago, with its elaborate interlacing pattern in gilt against a green cloth spine.

But how in the world did he know all this? Arcane tidbits of use to nobody but bibliophiles who dawdled in dusty libraries and pawed through musty tomes in quayside bookstalls. More baffling yet, how did he distinguish that this fairly obscure James novel, one of the earliest published under the imprint of Gerald Duckworth, was the correct first edition based solely on the book's bland spine? Or know, before he'd even checked the copyright page for its publication date, that it came out in 1898, the same year as H. G. Wells's *The War of the Worlds*, another book bound in gray cloth?

Above all, and totally inexplicable to him when he did at last pull *In the Cage* down from the shelf, was that he saw its flyleaf bore an inscription in dark sepia ink, *To dearest Alice from her adoring brother, the Author*, and immediately suspected that neither Henry James nor his radiant if sickly diarist sister, Alice, ever touched this book, let alone wrote or read these uncharacteristically effusive words in it. In fact, wasn't it the case that Alice James had died and been laid to rest half a dozen years before *In the Cage* ever saw the light of day? But he knew the inscription seemed genuine in every other way. It matched the novelist's elegant, flowing hand. Wording was persuasive. Nib was right. Ink color right. Flourishes spot-on. There was even a smudge, an imperfection only the most sophisticated forger would risk adding.

He stood, swaying in place, nearly as dizzy as when he'd first emerged from the pit, and wondered who would bother to forge such an obvious anachronism. The more he studied it the more he admired the script, so confident in its unevenly inked pen strokes, its peculiar backward commas, its baselines trailing downward at the end of each line. Truly, it was indistinguishable from a genuine James inscription. Textual problems aside, there wasn't a handwriting expert in the world who would hesitate to authenticate this. Christ, he'd sign off on it himself, though he didn't have a clue what would qualify him to make such a judgment.

And yet, and yet—what about that name, Henry James?

Common enough man's name derived from *Henri* out of Old French, combined with classic Anglo-Saxon, *James*. More arcane factlets that were in his possession for no reason he could comprehend. Be that as it may, there was nothing arcane about knowing who Henry James was. "The Master," his literary acolytes called him once upon a time, author of magisterial novels—*The Portrait of a Lady*, *The Golden Bowl*—built of sublime amaranthine sentences that employed words like *sublime* and *amaranthine* with abandon. But something struck him about the name as even more familiar than *In the Cage* and its publishing history and its author's sister who'd died before that skillfully forged inscription to her was added to the novel's front endpaper. What the devil was it? he wondered, as his knees began to buckle and the books lined up so neatly on the shelves began to swirl and bend and scrunch.

When he came to, he found himself collapsed on the floor, the book still clutched tight as a bindery vise in one hand, a faded oriental rug bunched up beneath his head. His temples pounded, mouth was caked dry, lips were chapped and bleeding where he'd been chewing on them. The murky light suggested several hours had passed. Furious that he continued to faint without warning, he climbed to his feet and limped toward the kitchen, reeling as he made his way down the billowy hallway, grasping with his free hand at wainscots, doorknobs, the empty air.

He swallowed more painkillers from the bottle he'd brought downstairs and gnawed on a mostly thawed bagel he'd earlier pulled from the freezer. Sitting at the table with a glass of juice, revived again, he tried to focus his eyes and read the first page of the Henry James before him, hearing his scratchy voice utter aloud the words, "It had occurred to her early that in her position—that of a young person spending, in framed and wired confinement, the life of a guinea-pig or . . . or a magpie—she should know a great many persons without their recognising the acquaintance."

He wasn't young like this protagonist, but he had surely experienced confinement. The hole, the slammer, the jug, yes, he had indeed been in prison once, and there had read medical texts. What was more, hadn't he been compared to a magpie by fellow inmates who learned he was a literary counterfeiter? Staring at the book as if it were a pier glass or private speculum, he recalled how magpies were known for their trickery and thievery. Adepts at deception, they trafficked in dark magic and illusion and opportunism—the insight came to him not as some metaphoric bolt of lightning, but rose into consciousness like déjà vu. He too was adept at deception, was he not? A creator of illusions. Who but a skilled opportunist could so deftly unlock that studio door?

An abject mist of loneliness greeted him when he started in his chair, having yet again lost consciousness. What, had he become some goddamn narcoleptic? Okay, he had suffered a concussion, needed rest. But these unwanted fainting spells gave him no rest. They instead left him shakier than before, not to mention as vulnerable as a newborn. Which in some way he was. But what if he hit his head again? It would crack open like a ripe melon, and that would be the end of it.

He looked down. Saw he was white-knuckle clutching a book as if for dear life. *In the Cage*, as before. Of course, of course. His eyes followed the simple, almost childlike design on its cover, black telegraph wires running from one pole to another, reminding him of the game of cat's cradle that he used to play with his sister—whoever she'd been, wherever they had been raised. His head snapped up, eyes darted around the room, which seemed ever more familiar than before, then back to the novel in his lap.

Eureka, he thought. How could something so trifling and inadvertent suddenly seem so monumental? He shared this writer's name. Henry James, with its surname that could be a first name, and its first name that could be a last.

"James Henry, Harry James, Jim Henrick?" He rattled off different combinations of names in the voice of a child stricken with laryngitis.

Wasn't his own name Henry, or maybe James?

"James," he tried, but that wasn't right. Like the novelist who wrote this tale steeped in deceptions and secrets, the man's name—his name—seemed to be, had to be, Henry.

"Henry," in crisp articulation, sensing this was what must have drawn him to the book in the first place. Not only had he no doubts about the matter, it felt like settled law. And having remembered such a fundamental thing, Henry also grasped that on what was left of his journey ahead, he was bound to live up to the legacy of whoever had borne the name before. He'd somehow recover and remember, would shake off his somnolent confusion and make whoever did this to Henry Slader—for that was his full name, he knew without further thought—regret they had murdered him. Or, not-quite-murdered him. For now, he needed to save himself, get away from this haven, which was no longer safe, had never really been safe.

Morning sun chivvied across his blistered face when he woke up, this time after having purposely gone to bed in search of real sleep. He peered down at his martyr's body sprawled on the sheets. He'd been holed up here for how long? Three nights now, four? His first coherent thoughts were the same as his last. His name was Henry Slader and he couldn't stay here any longer. He needed to disappear, no matter how much he wished he could sleep for another week, a month of weeks. He touched fingertips to his face and head, winced. A band of blue jays outside the window, raucous as any magpies, were scolding one another. Or possibly him. In the bathroom, he washed himself, avoiding the mirror after catching an abhorrent glimpse of his glazed eyes and inflamed chin, cheeks, forehead. Peeking again, he saw that his pupils were wildly mismatched, one a pinhole, the other dilated toward the edges of his iris.

Moving with a kind of underwater dreaminess, he rinsed the tub, cleaned the sink, and nicked the pain meds he'd need on the road. While he washed his clothes along with the soiled towels and bed linens in the laundry room downstairs, he wiped every porcelain, glass, and metal surface he might have touched in both bedrooms and bath above, using a rag he found in the hamper. The load dry, he put on his old clothes. He then made the queen bed as best he could and hung the borrowed trousers and shirt in the closet. All the while something was plaguing him, viscerally, like the onset of a flu. As he set himself to the desultory task of erasing his presence in the kitchen, Slader couldn't help but feel a dawning conviction that he wasn't the only bad actor here. Yeah, sure, he must have screwed up in some epic brazen way to have provoked such hostility in the woods. But given his assailants had gone full medieval on him, weren't they as much the transgressors, the criminals, as he?

Change of plan. Fuck this maid routine. Dizzy still but determined, he strode to the printing studio, this time in search of its owner's identity. Whoever ran this press surely had a drawer full of invoices or correspondence with a name on them. He dug up a sheaf of receipts made out to a Stone Circle Editions, but nothing more specific. Next he pulled down type books and manuals, eyes smarting despite having put on a pair of women's horn-rimmed sunglasses he'd found in a kitchen drawer, and checked to see if whoever ran this so-called Stone Circle Editions might have signed his name or affixed a bookplate inside. No such luck. It wasn't until he glimpsed a certificate of authority for the business, framed behind glass and hung askew on the wall, that he discovered what he was looking for. Typed clearly on the document was the name of the proprietor with his neat, nondescript signature on the line above.

Will. As in willful. Or will-o'-the-wisp, as he could swear he'd mocked this man in the past. Will—a name he now remembered.

When he read it aloud, as if to assay whether or not he was hallucinating, some of the history behind the name began to fall from oblivion into place. He recalled having been in this house before, uninvited and unwelcome, in this very studio, then as now a pariah loathed by those who called it home. This confirmed his earlier notion that he was an adversary here. How could he have thought otherwise, having fought his way out of a grave where he'd been dumped and left for dead? Those voices he'd heard before in the garage—one of them was Will's. And the other?

He opened James's *In the Cage*, which had become a talisman of sorts, and reread the endpaper inscription, curious why Will would keep such a botched forgery. Flipping through, he discovered the book's title page bore a second inscription. Written in royal blue ink were the words *With happy birthday love to Daddy from N*, in what seemed to be a perfect replica of Alice James's handwriting.

Brilliant, Slader marveled. What Henry James giveth, Alice James hath taken away.

The work of a virtuoso, this sly little inscribed tome. Made by someone who wielded the power to create and destroy a forgery in one fell swoop, with enviable nonchalance and all

within the covers of a single book. More than admirable, this
was real genius.

A smile crept onto his face. It all became so clear. Nicole was
her name. And this bit of Mozartian flair, this Banksy bravado,
was her handiwork, something fabricated as a present for her
father when she was still young enough to call him *Daddy*. Like
Nicole, her father was a forger. And like Will, so was he, Henry
Slader, himself. Surely she was the one he'd heard in the garage,
she who had bludgeoned him on the back of his head, she who
had helped her father entomb him in that hastily dug hole.

Eyes blinking, throat rattling like a tray full of tumbled
stones, Slader knew he needed to get a move on. He ripped the
backing off the frame and removed the printed certificate, which
he folded and pocketed. In the kitchen he wrapped a dish towel
around one hand, not unlike the boxer who tapes his fist before a
bout, and proceeded to subvert, in a brief and fumbling rampage,
all the tidying he'd done earlier. He punched out the leaded glass
on an old breakfront near the fridge, then hacked away at the
curios displayed within, souvenirs from family adventures. He
opened kitchen cabinet doors, flung stacked Depression glass
plates and pretty painted cups across the room. The small explo-
sions of broken crockery were excruciating to his sensitive ears
but necessary. Vision wavering, he pulled a carton of eggs from
the refrigerator and threw them one by one against the walls,
the unbroken windows, the clock. Without pausing, he pitched
jelly jars and bottles of decoratively labeled olive oils, dry sherry,
balsamic vinegars haphazardly in every direction. A half-gallon
jug of syrup from one Nebzydoski's Maple Farm he poured on
the table, chairs, and floor, like some awful abstract expressionist,
though what he expressed by this juvenile vandalism—he knew
he was behaving like a surly child—was anything but abstract.

Tired, he swept a nest of vintage yellowware bowls off the
granite counter and watched them clatter across the floor in

pieces. An heirloom china tureen soon joined them, hurled with both sore hands over his head using far more force than was needed to demolish the thing. Heaving forward then back, he lost his balance as the kitchen became a carousel swirling around him before he tripped over one dining-room chair and toppled onto another. The room was abruptly quiet again but for the clock that ticked beneath its runny lacquer of egg yolk. He eyed the hanging rack of copper pots and pans over the counter and considered using one of them to silence the clock, but enough was enough.

Slader pulled himself up, stood tottering amid the wreckage, and surveyed the mess he'd made. Too worn out to continue, he wasn't so exhausted that the scene failed to give him grim pleasure. Sure, he could've just torched the house, burned it to its foundation. But that would have meant the fire department, police, arson investigators swarming the scene, and his arrest. As it was, he figured his attackers would be sorely put out but not enough to bring in the authorities. Slader spat on the floor in vulgar triumph, reeled toward the back porch door, and in one final gesture of retribution kicked the leg out from under a mahogany plant stand whose vined pothos, potted devil's ivy, came crashing down in a riot of mottled greens and yellows. Tucking the Henry James under his arm—how did he manage to still have it with him?—he lurched out the door looking like a truant schoolboy or else Lucifer's own bookish vicar wandering forth into his parish.

Henry Slader did not want to revisit the woods and his newly opened grave. But he needed to return to the site of his premature burial to find his missing shoe and whatever other stuff of his was left there. Furthermore, if he meant to disappear, to give himself a chance to invent a new life, to confuse his unwitting hosts about who their vandal had been, he'd have to restore the plot to its original appearance as closely as he could. Make an earthworks forgery of his own unmarked grave so it looked like he was still buried there. This way, when Will returned to the scene, as inevitably he would, he could marvel at the demise of his old rival, feel gratifying relief—tinged perhaps by a shadow of guilt—that Slader had left this earthly plane and could cause him grief no more.

He would nod his head, and he would be very wrong.

The music in O'Donnabhain's on Henry Street was classic Irish trad—think bodhrán and fiddle, guitar and concertina—and the players were high-spirited because it was Christmas, with Saint Stephen's Day soon to follow, the day of wren-boys and mummering. An exuberant scrum of locals sang along with the group. Most were drinking like mackerel, high as hawks, cheek by jowl in the crowded pub. My mother and Maisie and I found ourselves caught up in the festivities too, though way more sober than the rest, seated at a small round wood table in one corner of the room. Along with my father, we'd traveled to the village of Kenmare, nestled in the south of County Kerry, to celebrate our first Christmas together in Ireland where, twenty years ago, I was conceived.

Pints of stout were set on the table before me and my mom Meghan, with steamy hot cider and a cinnamon stick in Maisie's cup. We were trying our best to join in the singing, guessing at lyrics as we bayed and warbled, thankfully unnoticed in the din. The tavern glowed a coppery gold. It smelled of whiskey

and warm bodies. Festooned on the walls were framed post-
ers of rock royalty Rory Gallagher with his worse-for-wear
Stratocaster, of Shamrock Rovers football stars, and even the
Kenmare Kestrels Quidditch team flying through the air in
robes of emerald green and with back-to-back yellow Ks on
their uniform breasts. It was a chill damp night outside, and
we three would've been perfectly content to eat a simple lamb
pie or bangers and colcannon for our Christmas dinner right
here at the pub. But my father had a fancier meal in mind at a
restaurant at the top of the street where we would join him in
an hour, after he'd finished meeting up with his printer friend
and mentor from years ago, Brion Eccles, under whose keen
eye he had apprenticed at Eccles & Sons print shop and fallen
in love with letterpress printing.

Meghan and I shared the last of my Guinness after she polished off her own. While she settled the tab and we gathered
our things to head out, the band struck up the nation's unofficial
anthem, "The Fields of Athenry," and the tipsy, earnest crowd
sang along with such full-throated poignancy that the moment
bordered on the heroic. The tune was hopeful and melancholy
at the same time—not unlike myself—it occurred to me as we
stood up and listened, rapt as if we were hearing some great
Bach cantata. Soon a server cleared the table and others quickly
took our place, regulars in heavy wool sweaters and cable scarves,
their rosy faces radiating an enviable, settled ease.

Outside on the stone sidewalk we could still hear the lyrics, "For you stole Trevelyan's corn, so the young might see the
morn" as we made our way up the lane. I fell behind, since there
wasn't enough room for the three of us to stroll side by side, and
besides, I wanted to be alone with my thoughts for a little. The
singing faded and as it did I marveled at how like a fairy tale this
provincial village was with its cheery shop windows and lovely
facades, its cobblestone streets and hand-painted signs. The twilight settling over Kenmare only made Henry Street seem more

dreamy, more ethereal. No doubt, the Guinness contributed to
my modest flight of fancy as I glanced down to be sure of my
footing on the walkway. For a moment, I felt something akin to
settled ease myself.

And why not? Kenmare was, after all, uniquely significant
in my personal history. The place where I traded nothingness
for being. And while I don't remember nothingness any more
than anybody else does, I very much relish being, no matter how
much I've been cursed in recent times.

Context. Before I was born, my parents had lived through
my father Will's arrest as a literary forger and the disgraceful
punishments he suffered over the fabrications he had so artfully
created—faux inscriptions by famous writers in rare books, along
with magnificent, if counterfeit, letters and manuscripts by those
same writers. Had he produced them for his own pleasure, no
legal line would've been crossed. But he wanted to share them
with the world, gauge their quality under the harsh bright light
of expert opinions. To do this, he had to represent and sell them
as originals, and when money changed hands, as it had to do in
order to truly put his art to the test, the whole gambit became
criminal.

But there's crime, and then there's crime. This curious kind
of trickery can bring real happiness to someone who believes
they own, say, a copy of *Sense and Sensibility* inscribed by Jane
to her sister, Cassandra. However, the virtues of such pleasure
were useless as an exculpatory argument.

Will went, briefly, to jail. Paid his dues to our spotless society.
Mended his evil ways. When I was old enough and my parents
told me this story, I couldn't help but think that punishing a
forger who fostered joy in people's lives was like punishing a
fantasy writer because the sprites, dragons, gremlins, ghosts, and
frog princes they depict don't in fact exist. Say what you will,
my father's forger sins, and mine too on certain rare, needful
occasions, were more venial than mortal. And nowhere near as

spiteful as the messy array of misdemeanors we found in our kitchen those months ago.

I'm biased; sue me.

To his credit, my father disavowed forgery, banned it from his life. All our lives. But Henry Slader surfaced, even when he had every reason to stay away. His manic rivalry with my father when each was at the pinnacle of his game, world-class masters who fooled the foremost experts in the field, first came to a violent head right here in Kenmare two decades ago when he attacked Will in the same marriage bed where Meghan had gotten pregnant with me. Slader cleaved off several of Will's fingers in a mad assault that landed the man behind bars for a good long stretch, and put his victim through months of painful recovery. Whether he'd intended to murder Will outright or just disable his adversary's gifted writing hand the authorities were unable to determine, because the bastard never confessed his intent. Either way, his attempt to terminate Will's days as a forger failed spectacularly in that he injured the wrong hand—my father's a lefty. Joke was on Slader, though nobody laughed.

Then, this past summer, Slader was back with a literal vengeance. Prison time served, rehabilitated not in the least, he returned to our Hudson Valley farmhouse with a proposition. Turned out, he had a series of photographs that would prove my father guilty of a crime far more serious than forgery or mere assault with a deadly weapon. Damning pictures of Will in Montauk the morning of my uncle's murder, he claimed. Took them himself. He was willing to burn them if Will came out of retirement to perform one last high-wire act.

On the surface it was simple. Cooperating with a bookseller friend, Slader'd stolen a copy of Edgar Allan Poe's all but unobtainable first book, *Tamerlane and Other Poems.* They needed my father to make an impeccable forgery of the thing. Long story short, Will didn't want to do it but neither could he risk testing Slader's patience. The man was a year-round March hare, a bat in his own belfry, a dangerous player. So Will chose to go ahead and make the facsimile—perfectly spurious, spuriously perfect.

This was a house of cards that should've fallen apart at any point in its construction. But destitute Slader was going to make a much-needed commission when it went on the block. The rare-book dealer behind the conspiracy was going to profit. Will would be freed from any further threat of extortion and benefit financially as well. After a wretched and bewildering couple of months, our lives would return to normal. Angels would sing, roses bloom, risks and rewards would arrive in perfect balance, and no one would be the wiser.

Wrong; seven ways from Sunday wrong.

Here I ought to confess that I helped with the forgery. I should also admit it was beautiful work, though naturally I would never be able to tell anyone about it. And likewise, what happened at the impromptu meeting between my father and Slader in the woods behind our farmhouse, a meeting Slader called to get a cash advance ahead of the auction, was the worst moment in my life.

Midafternoon, sundown still a couple hours away. The last Monday in September, eleven days before *Tamerlane* was to go under the hammer. Classic upstate autumn with a robin's-egg blue sky above—the ravishing color landscape painters try to imitate by mixing phthalo blue with cadmium yellow to make a deep cyan, adding a dab of zinc white diluted with linseed oil to finish. A wispy scarf of clouds floating above the red and gold mountains out west of the Hudson River, while our resident murder of shiny black crows patrolled the downslope field, cawing and clacking like a bunch of O'Donnabhain's drunks.

Will had told me to stay at the house. But after he'd walked down the hill and disappeared into the forest where smoke wafted from what turned out to be Slader's campfire, too much time passed and my own patience ran out. I couldn't just hang around knowing what this troubled man was capable of, this bad actor who would demand more than the thousands Will had already brought to hush him up, money from a deal my father never wanted any part of in the first place. So after grabbing a shovel from the garage, I sneaked down, quiet as a falling leaf, unseen by the two men who were too busy arguing to notice me. My neck was pulsing and eyes smarting from woodsmoke when I saw Slader flash a butcher knife—one from our kitchen that I had used many times when helping to make dinner—then leap up from his simian crouch and lunge at my father. It was as if the shovel lifted itself in my hands, and somebody else ran those few yards from where I'd been hiding and dealt Henry Slader a quick hard blow to the back of his head. But where Slader'd surely had every intention of killing my father, I only meant to stun the man, knock him down, stop him in his dangerous tracks.

In shock, certain he was dead, we buried him. I must have been crying. It was all done in a haze. Any guilt, my father assured me, any blame for this lay at Slader's feet, not ours. An open-and-shut case of brought-it-on-himself, Will went on, saying that Slader orchestrated his own fate, as we all do. God, how I wanted to believe that. We tried without success to drown our guilt with a bottle of champagne and drove to the city the next morning to rejoin my mom and sister.

Some might condemn this as self-serving, myself among them. Skirting the law, dodging a manslaughter charge. They might even think I ought to have acted more high-mindedly toward this monster who had only ever tried to ruin the lives of every last member of my family. But I'm not sure, looking back, that my father or I could have done anything differently. Either way, I now had, as they say, *a past.*

My life before that horrific encounter had been that of a New Yorker, a city girl whose second home was the Met, an art geek who lived and breathed oil paint and mineral spirits. I had always been an outsider by nature. Not so much shy but happy to live in the penumbras. Classic loner, I guess. My tattoos were sparse compared to those my few friends sported, with an elaborate depiction of my favorite bird, a kingfisher, inked on my upper arm. I was viewed as an eccentric by those who didn't know me. I lost, or rather offered up, my virginity to a young wife and husband one confusing night my first year in college and was after that drawn to neither sex in particular, though if I was forced to choose, I'd lean away from Dionysus in favor of Sappho, who was at least an actual person. A novice Buddhist who tried never to harm a gnat, I was regardless devoted to the most vicious passages of Edgar Allan Poe. Above all, I was lucky enough to have parents who'd been supportive of my penchant to make art all the way back to childhood. One of my earliest memories—Christmas then too—I was sitting side by side with my calligrapher father, drawing concentric circles on sheets of heavy paper. Snow fell outside our East Village window. I remember the smell of hot cocoa and of the ink that flowed from the tip of the pen. I was five at the time, half a dozen years younger than Maisie is now.

Unlike my sister, I'd been abroad before this trip to Kenmare. I had made shoestring-budget pilgrimages to Rome, Florence, Berlin, Paris, and London, where I tried to see every last painting and sculpture in the Uffizi, the Pergamonmuseum, the Jeu de Paume, the Tate, and reveled in them all whether soaring masterpieces or just standard period fare. I'd made copies of a hundred different old master drawings, testing different pigments from blacks to maroons. Studied color theory in my head as I moved from salon to salon. And inevitably, whenever I emerged from a day in the galleries, I saw the world with hypersensitive eyes. Rekindled eyes.

Christmas eve in Kenmare was no different. While O'Donnabhain's was no Louvre, the world was changed and charged once we were back outdoors. There was something ineffable about the evening light here that transcended my grasp of art and language. Maybe it was the soft bay air or silvery mist

rising off the river. Maybe because I had only seen these build-
ings online before, or in books, and now they were present, vivid,
tangible. Whatever the reason, each pinpoint of color shimmered
brighter than normal, and the sky was a swirl of early stars not
as theatrical or mystical as Van Gogh's, but just as intoxicating.

Still straggling behind the familiar figures ahead of me, I
glanced across the street and was puzzled to see somebody I
recognized. Or thought I did. An older man. Ash-and-coal hair,
dressed in a midthigh-length parka, dark blue or black—it was
hard to be sure, as he was lit by holiday lights strung across the
way. Shoulders held in what looked like a permanent shrug, he
appeared to be paralleling me on the far side of Henry Street.
Without giving it a thought, I halted and stared at him, trying
to place where I'd seen the man before. In turn, he stopped,
returned my quizzical gaze as he thrust his hands in his pockets
and pulled out a cigarette and lighter. Never dropping his eyes,
he lit his smoke and slid the lighter back in one pocket. Me
being me, I was tempted to walk over and ask what he wanted.
But he turned away to peruse some holiday display in a shop
window and before I could make any move—what could I have
said anyway?—he set off in the opposite direction at a leisurely,
indifferent pace. I waited in vain for him to glance back over his
shoulder as he neared the triangle where Henry Street converges
with Main and the Square, down by Holy Cross Church, where
we'd made a sightseeing call earlier that day. He slipped like a
mirage, though, into the fog.

That settled ease I'd felt earlier had faded now. As I rejoined
the others, who hadn't noticed any of this, the word *pareidolia*
came to mind. It was a Greek term I'd picked up from my
father back when he tutored me in the thorny issue of perception versus reality, one of many arcane subjects around fact and
fallacy that were dear to his heart—mine too, over the years.
Pareidolia's at play when craters and valleys on the surface of
the moon merge into the face of a man. A face once seen you

can't unsee. Or when wallpaper with repeated patterns of leaves and flowers becomes a queue of dragons. Or a wisp of moonlight looks for all the world like a ghost. A skewed perception, in other words, when the eye tricks itself into believing what it sees is something altogether other.

"It's the artist's best friend, pareidolia. When perception trumps reality," Will memorably told me years ago. "Or, I should say, so-called reality."

Spoken like a true counterfeiter, I thought even then, in youthful awe of my father, who more than once shared with me his belief that reality ain't all it's cracked up to be.

As Meg, Maze, and I neared the restaurant, I decided the man across the street was a case of mistaken identity. A pareidolia image, a stranger who bore an unnerving resemblance to a different man, someone from my past I couldn't place. Or a man I had invented out of whole cloth, enhanced maybe by my pint. Either way, pareidolia and paranoia came together to work their tricks on me, which later, in turn, opened me up to all those memories I'd rather not have revisited but that refused to be suppressed.

In bed that night at the lodge where we were staying, the vision of the man and the song from the pub intertwined in my head, while the River Sheen below my window splashed and stuttered and a nearby fox let out a sharp bark. The lyrics of "Athenry" had morphed into gibberish, but their feeling of loss and hope, of being an outlaw on a mission of good, kept me awake most of the night as I thought about what had brought my own family to grief. And what misdeeds—call them that—I now had to commit to bring us peace. Nor did it help that the mirage I'd seen across Henry Street had now raised real fears in me of having been followed by the very troubles we'd come here to escape.

As I tossed and turned in bed in the wee morning hours of Saint Stephen's Day, trying not to wake Maisie, I remembered how my mind whirligigged when I stared with my family at the wrecked kitchen of our upstate sanctuary upon our return the following Saturday. It felt like we were standing in the kitchen of an antique doll's house that some raging child had shaken hard and slammed on the nursery floor. The vandalism was breathtaking. How long we stood there in numbed silence, I couldn't say.

When Meghan, cheeks flushed, finally pulled out her phone to call the police, my father, every bit as stunned as the rest of us, tried to maintain an appearance of calm.

"I don't think it's necessary to bring in the cops, Meg," he told her.

"But, Will—"

"Bad as it is," he said, raising his hands, palms forward, "I doubt any of our local Lestrades has got time to investigate one broken window and a bit of a mess on the floor."

This was the best he could manage? If he had hoped his lame attempt at levity might slow things a beat, give him time to gather his thoughts, he was mistaken.

"Lestrade?" Maisie asked, her forehead wrinkled.

"'Bit of a mess?'" echoed my exasperated mother.

"He's the inspector at Scotland Yard who Sherlock Holmes—" he started to explain.

But before he could finish, she calmly interrupted, "I know who Lestrade is, Dad. But I thought he tried to solve murders, not—whatever this is."

While our house had been broken into before—by none other than Slader—it had never been vandalized. As weekenders who also came up during summers and holidays, we were aware that an opportunistic trespasser might see the solitary place as an easy mark. We'd been lucky in the past—as had my grandparents, who used to come here part-time back in the day when nobody bothered to lock doors or bolt windows. But besides books, which most self-respecting thieves would beeline past on their way to our seldom-used flat-screen, antiquated audio gear, or other outdated electronic gadgets, we kept nothing of routine resale value around. And though the vintage printing press that Will and I used—not just for the Poe forgery but chapbooks and prints—was worth decent money in an esoteric niche market, at some three thousand unwieldy pounds it wasn't your everyday burglary fodder.

Books were what we most cared about. Books, music, art, and yes, one another. In both this nineteenth-century Hudson Valley retreat and our apartment in downtown Manhattan, the only actual factual valuables we owned were the used books, rare volumes, and autograph manuscripts that stocked my mother's East Village bookshop, along with Will's collection, a few of which were remnants from his lawyer father's library of high spots. And as for my own paintings, they hadn't yet found a market beyond a couple of group shows in Chelsea and a solo exhibit at my best friend Renee's gallery in Red Hook, Brooklyn. The former was like sailing my small boat in a large regatta, in the fray but hard to spot. The latter was an act of kindness, I supposed, although Renee—a handful of years older than me, an almost lover but never quite, independently well-off though the price of her wherewithal was her parents' deaths in an auto accident—was never into blind favoritism. She simply believed in me, was my most ardent critic—unafraid to tell me when a canvas wasn't working, unafraid to let me know her thoughts about most anything—and, thereby, my most trusted champion.

We searched the rest of the house for other damage or theft. But nothing else had been touched. That is, nothing my father and I, who didn't want to alarm the others, were willing to reveal. Judging from the broken eggs, maple syrup, and spilled milk on the walls and floor, which were still sticky to the touch, the vandal seemed to have recently left the scene.

"My opinion? This looks far worse than it really is," said Will when we reconvened in the kitchen. His voice sounded steadier to me, if less forthright.

"You've got to be kidding."

I didn't like to hear his forced laugh, but he forced a laugh.

"Meg. It's not what we wanted to come home to. It's not great. But it doesn't feel like the work of some master criminal who needs to be run to ground, handcuffed, and led off to lockup. More like a homeless person desperate for food."

Wishful thinking. Hungry people don't tend to throw food on walls and the floor. But when he looked toward me for support, I closed my eyes while nodding in agreement. The aching remorse, the nauseating private guilt that I'd been nursing since I was last here with my father, had been churned up by our discovery, and it took everything I had to keep it hidden from the other women in my family.

"But what if it's him?" Meg pressed. "What if Slader did this?"

"Impossible," said my father.

"Why? Seems exactly like something he'd do."

"Because he's gone. He's been taken care of and he's gone now."

"How do you know?"

He tilted his head over toward me and Maisie as if to say, *Not in front of the kids.* "I just do, Meg. He's been properly paid for his services—"

"Paid off, you mean."

"—and has left, never to return," said Will, dancing in a field of double entendres.

Me, I continued to stay mum.

"So with Slader out of the equation, I still think nothing positive will come from calling 911. It'll just mean boots tramping through the house, interviews, reports, follow-ups. And what'll happen is some poor vagabond will find himself in serious trouble."

"I'm not looking to get anybody in trouble," my mother said as she stared at, or out, the broken window. I often thought that she was the gentlest of our clan and perhaps a little willfully naive. "But what if they need help? What if they're hurt and need medical attention? Could be somebody with dementia or maybe Alzheimer's who's wandered off from home."

"What's Alzheimer's?" asked Maisie.

No further mention was made of Henry Slader as Meg explained how Alzheimer's sometimes turned its victims into disoriented, even belligerent, wanderers, while my father and I exchanged a brief glance because Slader was our greatest worry, impossible as that seemed. Dead and buried extortionists don't break dishes and throw food and furniture around a room.

Though we couldn't fairly argue her point about bringing in the police to investigate what happened here, Meg was aware of her husband's profound, even pathological aversion to the police. Cops, detectives, any custodians of the law outside the safe and treasured pages of Poe, Doyle, Christie, and company were anathema to him. He loathed the men in blue to such a degree that I often felt, as his biological daughter, I had inherited his antiauthoritarian genes, given my own sporadic outlier leanings. Will's antipathy toward—and fear of?—law enforcement was well known to my mother, so she must have been wildly distressed even to bring it up.

Meaninglessly, I proposed to no one in particular, "Live and let live, is how I see it. And let's hope they'll get whatever help they need."

Empty words spoken into the void.

"Look there," Meg interrupted her conversation with Maisie, pointing at a kitchen window facing the green-gilt field that extended to the woods at the bottom of our yard. "Blood, that's dried blood on the outside of that unbroken pane, where they must've been peeking in."

"Mud, more likely," said my father. He negotiated a winding path through china shards and flung cutlery over to the sink, where he wetted a sponge before making his way outside onto the back porch.

"He's right, you know," I tried, my voice low and unconvincing. "Not like this is a crime scene."

"It is, though," my sharp little sister countered.

"Not one that would interest Lestrade or, for that matter, the Chevalier Dupin," I said, adding Poe and his inspector into the mix even as I obfuscated like so much fog on the Ring of Kerry coast.

Face framed in the broken window, my father interrupted. "No damage to the trim or hardware. Easy repair, looks like. I hate to say it, but the real damage here may be more to our sense of safety than anything."

My mother hunched her shoulders a hint, dropped them, and said, "I don't know."

"But I do," Will gently insisted. "Let's fix what's fixable and the rest will take care of itself. There's not enough damage here to even make a claim with insurance."

We began cleaning up. As I gathered potentially salvageable objects from the floor, I mulled how this felt like Slader's handiwork. Had he not in fact been dead when we buried him? It would've been feasible in one of Poe's tales, as he was a writer who buried his characters alive with impressive regularity. Hard to forget that Roderick Usher interred his darling Madeline while she was yet living for reasons I could never quite fathom. Or that Fortunato was buried alive by his friend Montresor in "The Cask of Amontillado." Or Berenice, who was not only interred alive but afterward exhumed, still alive, by her obsessed fiancé Egaeus—Egregious, I nicknamed him—who stole her thirty-two perfect teeth while she screamed in vain until he buried her again. Not to mention "The Premature Burial," Poe's crowning achievement on this subject.

But that was fiction and this was real. Henry Slader was no Fortunato, no Usher. He was dead when we laid him to rest in the woods. At least, he wasn't showing any signs of life, though admittedly we'd been moving fast and the light was fading.

No, no, I assured myself. However ghostly Slader often looked, with his bony head and wraith-pale complexion, he couldn't have transformed into some nightwalker arisen from the mists of lifelessness. This had to be the work of somebody else. But who? We knew only a handful of people upstate, so it stood to reason we had few, if any, local enemies.

After collecting the broken fragments into trash bags, we swept and mopped the floor, washed the walls, and covered the empty window with binder's board, then gradually settled into our normal rhythms, or tried to. We kept reminding ourselves that this, on its surface, could hardly be seen as a catastrophe. But not everything lay on the surface, as I and my unusually rattled father knew. Like it or not, we would need to pay a secret visit down in the woods to put any questions to rest.

Here in Kenmare, finally growing drowsy, breathing deep into my tangled sheets as that fox on the far bank of the River Sheen yipped again, I wondered, would anybody in the world even have noticed Slader's absence? Missed him? Been concerned for his welfare? He had, from what my father had told me, wrecked every relationship he'd ever made, including the treacherous one he shared—forged, really—with Will himself. Slader always seemed the archetypal man without a country. The big bad lone wolf, loyal to none. He didn't appear to have had a childhood, no spouse or lover, though questions lingered about the nature of his long-ago bond with my mother's brother, Adam. Uncle Adam, whom I never knew because he died before I was born. Died, or rather was slaughtered and disfigured, some believed at the hands of Slader himself or even my father, though nothing was ever proven. Either way, it was as if Slader had crept onto the scene fully formed, a cyborg forger with no life beyond the wizardry—my dad openly avowed he was a master—of his fakes.

I rolled over in bed yet again to face the windows overlooking the star-bright water. Seeing that the man in the moon had settled into the fog, I dreamily asked myself, why was it a man in the moon instead of a woman? Made no sense. Artemis, Esther, Luna, Diana were all moon goddesses. So why not the veiled shadow face up there too? Meantime, the fox had either caught her prey and taken it back to her kits, or else given up and gone to her den hungry. Sheen River voices had faded to sighs while a distant cuckoo persisted in singing its name over and over and over. And I, embracing my pillow like a life raft, finally fell asleep.

B y some miracle almost as unexpected as surviving a premature burial, Slader stirred to life miles from the farmhouse, lying in a patch of stinging nettles at the end of a rural cul-de-sac. A quintet of indistinct days and nights had passed since he awoke underground. His head and limbs still smoldered with pain, yet he seemed incrementally on the mend, thanks in part to the painkillers he continued to palm down like so many shelled sunflower seeds. The bicycle he had stolen from Will's garage, after he'd restored his gravesite as best he could and added a small personal touch, lay mangled in the prickly brush beside him.

Predawn birds whistled in the treetops. Close by, a brook rustled. He kept his head low, looked around. No cars, no other bikes. Not a soul was near. Nor were there any houses or other structures in the vicinity beyond an abandoned foundation for a house they never got around to framing out and finishing. For all the randomness of his clumsy nocturnal journey, this place seemed weirdly familiar, much as the woods below the farmhouse had, but he couldn't recall having ever been here. His

memories, other than those of rare books, were still a mélange
of ambiguities, and part of him wondered if it wasn't better that
way. Fewer memories, fewer woes.

He was wearing a navy peacoat jacket that he vaguely
remembered nicking from a porch along the way. His grimy
day pack, retrieved from the grave, he shrugged off his shoulders.
Rubbing his hands together, he blew on them even though the
early breeze was warm and clear skies promised a temperate
day. For all that, he wished he had a pair of gloves and a hot cup
of Ethiopian, black, three sugars, to chase away the chill that
likely was a symptom of his injuries. He frowned at his shoes,
one still polished, the other sullied from where he'd found it
buried in the loose dirt of his open grave.

Main thing was, he was safe for the time being. It wasn't like
Will was going to risk compromising himself by siccing the cops
on him, not with the auction coming up in which they both had
a stake. Or at least were supposed to, though now he was sure
Will had always intended to cut him out of their deal.

He probably shouldn't have knocked together that spur-of-
the-moment installation at the grave site. Should have left well
enough alone, simply smoothed over the shallow burial pit and
covered it with leaves, as he'd planned when setting out from
the house to the woods the night before. But when he unearthed
his pack, there was the photo from Montauk, right where he'd
hidden it in the lining. Proof that Will was guilty of murder.
He'd had every intention of revealing this sample picture from
the damning stash he possessed—which at the last minute he'd
decided not to bring along, as he didn't trust the bastard—but
all hell had broken loose during their meeting, and he never got
the chance. So, tired as he was, the sunset's light nearly spent, he
left it there as a warning to his adversary in the hope it might
neutralize him, at least for a time.

Nor should he have given in to the urge to steal the Schwinn
Black Bomber, all but identical to the one he himself used to

ride up and down the hills of Fall River back in a childhood
mostly forgotten or ignored into oblivion. But it made for a
faster escape than walking. What a clownish, pathetic figure he
must have made during his exodus, handlebars decorated with
pink tinsel wobbling in his clenched fists, soles slipping like fish
off the worn pedals, guessing his way forward by moonlight—
a waning gibbous moon, stingy but enough to see by—as he
struggled through fields and woods and then a hamlet of scattered homes. At a fork in the road, he'd veered to the right,
where the houses and occasional double-wide were fewer and
fewer until there were none.

Along that final length of lonely asphalt, Slader had felt a
visceral if unwarranted terror of being followed—who would
bother trailing him in the middle of the night?—before he'd run
out of road and crashed into the rusted guardrail at its terminus.
Damned lame of him. And avoidable if he hadn't kept looking
over his shoulder in what would have been a classic nightmare
chase scene had he been dreaming or, for that matter, chased.

At least he had crashed far enough away from Will's place
to give himself time to figure out his next moves. He gnawed
on a piece of turkey jerky he'd boosted from the farmhouse
kitchen and chuckled when he recalled the damage he had
wrought there. At the same time, he couldn't avoid wishing he
had made better decisions before he was knocked unconscious
in that meeting gone terribly wrong.

Getting in touch with Will last month, unannounced after
so many years of silence, had been part of a plan dreamed up
not by him but their mutual friend Atticus Moore, a rare-book
dealer who had done business with them both. Slader, who
trusted few, trusted him. The precious forgeries Slader and, to
be sure, Will had provided Atticus in years past had brought
top dollar from clients around the world, storied institutional
repositories among them. And it wasn't as if Slader had to be
coaxed into taking part in Atticus's latest lucrative scheme to

produce an exact copy of Poe's *Tamerlane*, of which previously there had been just a dozen known copies. Published by an obscure Boston printer in 1827, it was known as American literature's Black Tulip, rarest of the rarest, a bibliophile's dream possession. One of the dealer's blue-blood clients owned an unrecorded copy, an heirloom that had sat in her New England library for generations. Hidden inside a small solander box, her *Tamerlane* would count as the thirteenth known example had it ever been included in any census. But who knew if she herself even remembered inheriting the thing when she came into her large estate? Not like it was a beautiful piece of bookmaking, as her Kelmscotts and Golden Cockerel Press books were. Nor was it as pretty as her leather-bound sets of classic authors. Atticus had only noticed it himself when appraising a Benjamin Franklin collection intended to be donated to the Houghton in Cambridge. It had been misshelved upside down among some various later editions of *Poor Richard's Almanack*.

When Abigail Fletcher was summering in France, Atticus engaged Slader to "borrow" her copy and deliver it to Will, who would, on his letterpress, execute a perfect facsimile using period paper that Slader himself was able to provide, and handcrafted ink, meticulously wrought plates, and misleading defects to give it casual authenticity. Will's forgery would then be surreptitiously returned to her collection, while the original, enhanced with a fake authorial signature that would make it unique, was put up for auction where it would surely command a seven-figure result.

Elegant, clean, quick. Proceeds would be divided, end of gambit.

Could have said no, and in retrospect, sitting here in a tangle of thorned weeds, should have. Mistake one.

Mistake two was, after having taken the job, seen it through, and with the auction coming up in a matter of days, his refusal to accept the eight-grand advance on his share that Will had

offered him. Could have bided his time in relative comfort while
waiting for the rest of what was owed. But distrust, irritability,
greed had overtaken Slader. What had he done but strike out at
Will with a knife, drunk on adrenaline, hate, and an impromptu
bottle of single malt scotch, and end up buried for his efforts.

Among the many lessons he had learned over his decade-
plus in prison, doing time for a similar if more brutal attack on
the same man, were sobriety and patience. He'd not practiced
either and thus blown it.

Bygones, he told himself. Any regrets he harbored over recent
actions were a waste of time. What he needed to do was drag his
sorry carcass to a local hospital, get himself looked at. Problem
was, he was leery of checking into the system, any system. Once
signed in, it's impossible to sign out. Hospitals admitted the sick
and injured, but eventually they needed intel on who they were
treating, and right now Slader embraced his anonymity more
than his health. He sensed he was guilty of acts far worse than
mere assault, trashing a kitchen, and being part of an elegant
conspiracy of literary forgers and respectable fences.

After steadying himself on a guard post and climbing to
his feet, he limped through a forest of thigh-high ferns, past
pokeweed and chokeberry bushes to a trickling creek. Beneath
the low-slung bows of an old hemlock, he knelt on hands and
knees and drank from the crisp cold water. Afterward, he washed
his face and hands as gingerly as a rabid raccoon before leaning
against the rough-barked trunk of the pine.

Selective memory or not, he knew he needed to contact
Atticus. Needed to phone a friend nicknamed Cricket, even
though he couldn't say who Cricket was or how to reach him.
Needed to move around the Hudson Valley unnoticed until he
could leave it behind. How he wished he could hide at Atticus's
house in Providence—where he was unwelcome—or his sister's
home half an hour away from there, over in Fall River—where
he was even more unwelcome. Black sheep, bad blood, a long

domestic novel's worth of childhood trauma too common and boring to dwell upon.

What he needed now, above all, was to find his car. Chevy, was it? Some such make. Unsightly jalopy. He was pretty sure he had parked it out of sight near Will's farmhouse. Powder blue with pitted silver trim, he could picture it as he lay back on the cushion of needles and listened to the mesmerizing brook.

After nodding off in the warm midmorning embrace of playful breezes, he opened his eyes and saw, on the opposite bank, a lanky girl staring at him. Nine, ten years old, her head was tilted, with a concerned frown set on her pale oval face framed by straight blonde hair parted down the middle. Her eyes were as gray as local slate.

"You okay, mister?"

Instinctively, Slader hunched himself back up against the tree. Too startled to respond, he simply stared back at her.

"You need help?"

She looked like an apparition in her faded pink shirt and worn skinny jeans. Slader blinked hard, then stared down at a dying wasp traversing the rough jungle of underbrush between his feet. Its sheer determination in the face of the death these changing seasons promised, its summer of treacherous splendor over, antennae twitching as it wrestled its way along, provoked his admiration. When he glanced up, she was still there.

"I can go get help if you want," she said, taking a couple of tentative steps closer. "Looks like you could use some, you know, help of some kind."

Slader's first instinct was to run across the creek and silence this interloper, though she meant no harm. Instead, he managed to say, "I'm fine, little girl," sounding like some dotty geriatric.

She half turned to go, plainly apprehensive of the look that had clouded his face, a face that was covered with yellow and reddish-brown scabbing from his burns.

"Okay then—" she said, breathless.

"No, wait. Hang on," Slader called out as he climbed to his feet. His voice, hardly used since his unceremonious burial, was unrecognizable to him. Sounded like a dull rasp drawn across pumice.

"My bad," she said. "Looks like you're okay after all."

"Yes, I'm—I was just enjoying sitting here in the sun," he said from deep in the shade of the tree. "I'm not trespassing, am I?"

The girl had already fled, arms flailing at her sides as she vanished into the wetland meadow. While he watched, standing with one hand impotently outstretched, he wondered if she hadn't been an apparition in fact.

His car. Had to get to where he had stashed it, hidden from the road in a thicket of foliage. He'd stuck its key beneath a stone near where he had parked, rather than stowed it under a floor mat or, worse yet, left it in his pocket. Prophetic move as it turned out—paranoia has its occasional merits—since it might have gotten lost underground. He stumbled back to the Black Bomber, where he straightened the handlebars, wrestled the chain back on, jiggered some bent spokes until the attached ends snapped off. Who knew how far it would travel before giving out, but as long as the thing got him to the warren of houses where he could ditch it and find another to expropriate, Maisie's bike—he remembered her name now—would have served its purpose.

Absurd, he thought as he pedaled away, unsteady and swerving about. Having fled Will's farmhouse, he now found himself forced to return. His mind wasn't right. Should've remembered the car and gone straight there the night before. He was scurrying to and fro like a mouse in a cage. He felt rare embarrassment—self-derision was, in times past, a character trait he preferred to encourage in others—at how startled he had been by that encounter at the brook. He hoped the girl hadn't raced home to her mother, or, if she had, that the woman had blamed the whole thing on an overactive imagination. Or better yet, on hearing that the gentleman hadn't accosted her daughter but merely sat in peace beside the waters, that she'd scolded her for talking to strangers.

Slader smiled at his fantasy. A chap-lipped, crooked smile. As he wobbled along, his head clearer than it had been since his resurrection, he found himself thinking about Nicole, she of the leather pants and paint-spattered clogs. In many ways, she was more dangerous to him than her father. More dangerous and potentially more useful. She'd proven herself, he remembered, as such a prodigy with her work on *Tamerlane*, not to mention her distinguished Henry James forgery with its deliberate anachronisms, that it was possible one day she'd surpass Will and even Slader himself. If she decided—or was coerced—to put her full skills to work, there would be no end to her ability to fabricate the past, remake history with ink on paper.

What was more, despite himself, he admired her for crowning him with that shovel when he'd gone after her father. He hadn't seen her do it, of course, but knew it couldn't have been anybody else. His head still hurt like hell, but she'd meant for it to hurt. Would that he had a daughter with such spirit, he thought without irony.

Pondering this uncharacteristic sentiment, Slader emerged from the woods at the edge of a neighborhood of modest capes and clapboard two-stories. He squeezed the brakes, reeled to a halt, and hid the bicycle behind a dense flank of bushes. In the near distance, he heard the whine of an unseen lawn mower. Otherwise, all was blessedly quiet as he made his way along, keeping to wooded backyards, hunching behind fences and hedges, careful not to be seen. Soon he spotted what he was looking for. Another bike, lying on its side, prime for plucking. He walked it between two houses whose curtains were drawn, and rode off, awkwardly trying to seem casual while sensing he looked anything but. Once he came to an intersection where he saw a familiar white-steepled church, shuttered tavern, and gas station, he was surer of his bearings.

He wheeled across the main road back onto the lane girdled by trees that would lead to the farmhouse and, beyond it, his hidden car. Given how dangerous it'd be to pedal past Will's, he jettisoned the new bike in a gully and trudged through a thicket of woods out of sight, ducking whenever a car passed along the road. Took all day, but eventually he located his ride—blue Chevy, he'd remembered correctly, a good sign—and groveled around the clearing in search of its key stowed under one of many lichened stones.

Just when he was about to give up, he recalled his clue, his simple mnemonic. *Leaves of three, let it be.* On sore hands and knees, he looked skywards and there it was. Festooned in dangerous foliage gone from green to yellow-brown, an enormous poison ivy vine wound its way like a serpent up a nearby ash tree. Thick and hairy, it circled its way to the crown, where nimble birds fed on its white berries. At its base was the flat stone where Slader had tucked the key on its ring, together with another to a safe-deposit box somewhere. He had no clue why he possessed the safe-deposit key, but figured it would come to him as his memory returned. Assuming it ever fully did. After unlocking the car door, he retrieved his cell phone from under a floor mat. To his relief, it still had battery and a decent signal.

"Can't lose 'em all," he muttered with a grim smile, in the same grating voice that, along with his battered looks, had scared the poor girl earlier.

After powering down his phone, he looked at himself in the rearview mirror and saw that his pupils were now almost the same size. Not a week out of the grave, and life was slowly starting to feel within reach. Sure, his head continued to pound despite all the overdosing on ibuprofen. Sure, he was famished and parched, and his gut was queasy from the questionable

water in that stream. And, sure, of course he harbored a sear-
ing rage over what they'd done to him in the nearby woods at
Will's place. But he did feel stronger than he had in days. A
good meal and some serious antibiotics and he'd be good to go,
he thought as he settled down in the warm safety of the back
seat of his car, where he lay undisturbed, off the grid, into and
through the night.

He woke up disoriented and stiff. *What was that stench?* he
wondered until he realized it was his own. Pulling himself up,
he surveyed the clearing walled by maples and beech and pines.
No cops tapping their flashlights on the hood, no curious kids
cupping their filthy hands on the car windows to peek in at
him. Just a gray squirrel foraging for its winter store, infinitely
indifferent to his predicament. As he came around little by little
and his amnesiac fog began to lift, the landscape of his life that
emerged was nothing as tranquil as this natural world around
his car. Instead, it was littered with reasons for the distress he
found himself struggling with.

A few truths. Even before his resurrection, hadn't life
amounted to little more than a wasteland of mistakes? He
couldn't deny, at least not to himself, that his long-ago cleaver
attack on Will and Meghan in Ireland was merely among the
first of sundry maniacal moves that culminated in his recent
burial. Own worst enemy and all that crap, he thought. Other
memories, real or imagined, tortured him too. Hadn't he argued
with his childhood friend, good old Cricket, about percentages
and proceeds from the ill-starred Poe scheme? An argument
that ended in a fight, which ended in an accidental strangula-
tion as he tried to hold the squirming man down long enough
to reason with him. The familiar road where he had crashed
young Maisie's Schwinn the other night? Wasn't it the same iso-
lated stretch where he'd dumped Cricket's body? But no, that
was wrong because surely he would never have hurt Cricket.
And yet he could see the man's pleading, shocked, struggling,

reddened face as he looked up into his assailant's eyes, Slader's own eyes.

More memories flooded back, unbidden and nightmarish. The cold-hearted way he had lured Will back into making a forgery of *Tamerlane* and how it had led him to that lonely road where Meghan sometimes went to be by herself, listen to Clara Schumann's first piano concerto on the car radio, step out of her life for a time. She had been there when he dropped Cricket's body. Had seen his blue car though perhaps not its driver. After he'd backed away and fled the scene, he even wondered whether the authorities, fools by trade, might blame the murder on her.

Even so, as he lay back down in that very car now, hands over his eyes to block the sunlight, he was swarmed with regret for both Cricket and himself. And when he did recall Cricket's real name, he felt sick with something akin to guilt. John Mallory of Fall River, Mass. Mallory whom he'd known since youth, and who in later years would provide him with vintage virgin paper that only a fifth-generation papermaker would have access to in his company's rich archives. Paper from most every decade through the nineteenth and twentieth centuries, period sheets that had never been used but were still wrapped up, stacked on the topmost shelves of the time machine that was Mallory Paperworks and Printing. John Mallory, whose murder the authorities were likely still investigating unless, with luck, they'd arrested someone who was innocent of the crime and the cogs of injustice were grinding away behind the scenes.

He knew what had to be done to regain control of his life. With a sudden sense of urgency, he got out of the car, took a deep breath of sharp air, and turned on his cell phone. For reasons he couldn't decipher just then, her mobile number was stored in memory.

She didn't pick up right away. Impatient, he was about to hang up when she finally answered, "Nicole." How young her voice sounded. Young but self-possessed, far older than her years. Wary too.

Slader hesitated, paced the clearing. Ideas of what to say flitted in and out of mind, most of them unformed, many not even presenting themselves in sentences, accusatory or otherwise. He questioned his first impulse, wondering if he ought to disconnect from both the call and, while he was at it, his entire previous mess of a life.

But wasn't this his world too, every bit as much as it was hers or her father's? And wasn't he ultimately fated to triumph in it? He needed money to survive, under the radar or not. Maybe he could confine his connection, for the time being, strictly to Nicole, whom he felt might be savvy enough to keep his confidence. Or else sufficiently afraid to know better than to betray him. As he was about to speak, a white butterfly flew in jerks and starts across the scape, like an albino flame shuddering through the air. Winter would arrive soon enough, he thought, and take this fragile doomed creature with it. Shouldn't he take heart in its struggle to lurch its way through the fall breeze? If a failing butterfly could show such courage, why not he?

In the wake of having discovered the vandalism at our farmhouse, Meg and Maisie drove up to the town of Hudson to scout vintage stores for dishes and other kitchen things to replace what was broken, and shop at the market for groceries to replenish our cupboards and fridge. This left Will and me alone to meet in the printing studio where we could talk in confidence.

"You don't need to come," he said, anticipating my question when I walked into the room.

"I do, actually."

With his left hand he rubbed and then clasped the back of his neck so that his elbow dangled over his chest, and he tucked his right fist under it for support. Rodin sculpted a man in this posture, it occurred to me, though I couldn't place where in his Paris museum I'd seen it. Portrait of a troubled soul.

What struck me most about the pose had nothing to do with Rodin, though. Noticing my father's mutilated right hand reminded me yet again of the brutish attack Slader had made on him long ago. If clobbering Slader on the back of his head had brought an end to his grotesque siege against Will, it was probably worth it, I reasoned, trying to find some way to forgive myself for what I'd done. But, no. I knew there was more wisdom in a thrown stone than solace in such a lame idea.

Breaking the silence, I added, "I don't see how it could've been anybody but him."

No need to say his name. Will knew whom I meant.

"Yes, no, maybe," he said softly, as if to himself. Crossing his arms now, he snapped out of his brief reverie. "One of my shirts upstairs? It's exactly where I hung it in the closet, but it's wrinkled as if I'd slept in it for a week, and stained with what I swear is dried blood on the collar. And that shovel you hosed down after the incident—"

"Hardly an incident."

"—disaster in the woods last week? After you cleaned it up, you put it back in the garage with the other spades and rakes against that back wall, right?"

I nodded as my heart skipped.

"Well, I found it lying in the grass near the broken window when I was washing blood off the glass."

"So it wasn't just mud," I said.

"Wasn't mud, period. He—or somebody—cut themselves breaking in. Both the handle and window, not to mention the doorknob, were smeared with blood."

The intruder's identity was nothing a forensics lab couldn't easily resolve, I thought, but I listened with increasing distress to Will's further disclosures. Some files here in our printing studio had been messed with. The Stone Circle Editions business certificate—he pointed behind me—was missing. Strangest of all was that a Henry James forgery I myself had made in my preteens, much to Meghan's dismay and my father's mixed chagrin and pride, had also vanished.

"We can order a new certificate, but why would anybody want the James?" I asked. "Not like your everyday thief would have the slightest interest in stealing that book."

"Certainly not Slader, who'd know in half a heartbeat that it was wrong."

The two of us returned to the kitchen, where we put on windbreakers and field boots and, without a further word, stepped outside. While I went to the garage to fetch that same shovel, my father waded into the unmowed stretch of grass between the back porch and the forest below. Partway down the hill, I noticed that the vegetable garden gate, a wobbly sculpture of chicken wire and wood, was unlatched and hanging open. Veering off to shut it, I saw that someone had been rummaging around inside, feasting on the vine-rotted squash and tomatoes, though leaving the bitter Swiss chard untouched. Human footprints ruled out a hungry animal. I noticed that the intruders were both wearing shoes and barefooted. Maybe kids, I tried to persuade myself. Surely not the ubiquitous, pestiferous *him*.

My father had paced ahead, arms swinging at his sides, and was past the thorny hedge of barberry and into the woods, beyond a stand of paper birches. The birds were unusually quiet; the air was becalmed. What I saw when I caught up with him took my breath away.

Looming like an unholy crucifix over Slader's grave was a crude stick figure fashioned of three dead tree branches tied together with what seemed to be a shoelace. Rickety, stuck in the ground at an angle, clearly built in haste, the effigy stood as tall as a living person. At the ends of its outstretched arms were clawlike twig fingers that reminded me of Max Schreck's in *Nosferatu*, elongated pincers that came to sharp tips. One of Will's rarely worn silk neckties, a bright scarlet, hung from the stick man's neck, done up with a haphazard triangular knot. That it was surrounded by such pastoral beauty, by Edenic autumn leaves in an otherwise virginal forest, only made the thing more surreal, more macabre.

"What the actual fuck," Will grumbled and staggered back a couple of steps.

No words came out of my mouth. I was literally struck dumb. Glancing over to make sure my father hadn't fallen, my eyes quickly darted back to the primitive figure. Just above the necktie, wedged between a couple of fishhook twigs along the upright, was a blown-up black-and-white photograph of a man standing on a promontory next to a row of cliffside cottages. He was semicrouching and looked as furtive as a cornered alley cat. Grainy and shot from a distance, possibly with a telephoto lens, the glossy photo appeared to have been taken either just before dawn or after dusk, and a skein of mist blurred the edges of both subject and background, giving it a dreamlike feel. As I peered more closely, I could just make out that the man was glaring toward the camera, his image distorted but eyes and mouth wide open, as if he'd seen a ghost.

The look on my father's face when I turned in his direction wasn't unlike what was captured there in the photograph. I cast my own eyes around the nearby woods, searching for other anomalies that might help explain what we'd encountered here. But nothing else seemed out of the ordinary. Countless early fall leaves had been brought down by winds and now blanketed the forest floor with burgundies and siennas and russets, so the clearing looked much as it had when we'd buried Slader and camouflaged the scene. Just as fresh-fallen snow softens the details of any landscape, here the patchwork of colorful leaves made his grave look immaculate, undefiled by human activities. Even Slader's firepit looked aeons old, an artifact from when the Lenape lived in this valley, and now of interest only to an archaeologist or ethnographer of indigenous peoples. One would never suspect anything indecent had happened here but for the bizarre figure that stood sentinel over the clearing.

"Any idea what's going on?" I asked, stepping over to Will.

"No, none."

His voice sounded light-years away.

"You know who that is in the photo?"

Will turned toward me and asked meaninglessly, absurdly, "We're sure this is the right spot?"

"No question." I pointed toward the ring of stones where Slader had tripped headlong into his guttering fire. "You were right there when he jumped at you with that knife. And that's where I came from behind and stopped him."

Before I'd finished saying these words, he abruptly strode over to the stick man, yanked off its knotted tie, and shoved it into his jacket pocket. Then, in a blink, he snatched down the photograph and began tearing it in half, and again in half, and again until it was reduced to jagged squares.

"Stop—what're you doing?" I shouted, bewildered by his ferocity.

"Not going to get away with this," or something to that effect, he half muttered as the sun disappeared and reemerged from behind the clouds.

Before I could gather my senses, he'd started pulling apart the stick man's dry limbs, cracking them over his knee, and heaving them into the woods in different directions. I couldn't remember ever seeing my father in such a fury. Dazed by the craziness of his behavior, I quietly picked up the black shoe-string that had fallen on the ground, trying to recall what Slader had been wearing on his feet the evening of the incident, now wondering if the shoe prints I saw in the garden weren't too large to be those of children. If the shoestring was Slader's, how did it get here? Had Will pulled it out of one of his shoes with the intention of tying his hands? Those frenzied minutes grew murkier the more I thought about them.

"Somebody's having a nice laugh at our expense," said my father, out of breath.

"What was that photograph?" I asked, trying to mask my frustration at his impetuous rage and my growing horror at what I suspected. Its fragments lay at our feet like black-and-white petals amid the earthy tones underfoot.

"No idea."

"If you didn't know what it was, wouldn't it have been better not to—"

"This isn't Slader's handiwork," he interrupted.

Ribbons of light ran across the carpeted ground as soft running air stirred the forest canopy. Was he so bent on Slader's being dead that a deep distorted impulse to gaslight both of us had overtaken reason?

"I don't see who else's it could be."

He paced a few steps away, put his hands in his pockets, turned to face me. "Before we came down here," he said, his mood curiously mellowing, "I'll admit I thought it was possible that Slader had somehow dug himself out of his grave and broken into the house. Somehow wreaked havoc in our kitchen as a kind of calling card, a big *up yours*. But now, seeing this—seeing nothing beyond this juvenile prank—I'm suddenly supposed to believe he somehow did all those things, somehow managed to make his grave look like nothing happened, somehow made Mr. Stickman, then somehow disappeared in a puff of smoke? That's way too many somehows."

While it occurred to me that defying such odds and redecorating reality were just what master forgers did, I didn't bother to argue his point. If the worst evil I ever committed in my life was hidden here by nature, I was in no position to complain and, in fact, destroying that stick man was for the best. On the other hand, if Slader had escaped, defying that swarm of somehows, it meant I wasn't guilty of murder.

I knelt and began gathering the torn pieces of the photograph as my father went on talking, his voice gaining confidence even as his will to proceed with the ghastly work we'd come here to do seemed to wane. "You know, rather than dig around and make a mess," he said, "I'm starting to think we might better leave well enough alone. This way we don't flag the spot for anybody out looking for a missing person—dead or not."

"I don't know that I agree," I said, not sure I didn't.

"Trust me on this," he said, squatting to pick up a couple of scraps of photo paper at his feet. "Slader looked sickly when we saw him. Acted even more mental than usual. After you intervened, he was out cold, wasn't breathing. The man was gone. Best leave him be."

Live and let live, I had said the day before. It seemed Will had settled into a die-and-leave-dead philosophy.

"So how do you explain the chaos at the house?"

"Must've been random, somebody else's joyride, since Slader clearly didn't rise like Lazarus from the dead."

At first I stayed mum. Something was not right here. Then, echoing his words from before, I said, "Yes, no, maybe."

"No maybes about it," he shot back. "We're tilting at windmills." Looking away from me, he said, with firm finality, "We should get out of here and never come back."

"What? You love these woods."

"I used to love these woods."

Taken aback by his remark, I stood, stuffed the fragments of the photograph in my pocket. I leaned my shovel against a tree and regarded my father, trying to hide my distress behind a puzzled frown. It was obvious all this had aged the man. If the weight of the world is love, as the poet wrote, it is, by the same token, hate. Not to mention deceit. His shoulders were rounded and head lowered as if he were bearing an imperceptible boulder on his back. I sensed a rift, a slight but awful fissure, had opened between us. A chasm I'd never dreamed was possible, so close he and I had been over my lifetime. Was it possible he so cherished the idea that Henry Slader was dead he'd forgotten it would mean his daughter was a killer?

"Nicole," he said, after a moment, looking at me with a warm, somewhat forced smile. "Let me continue to thank you for saving my life, because that's what happened here. I know what you must be thinking, but for us to confess, volunteer what took place, even to the most understanding judge and jury, would end our lives as we know them. Would end Meghan's, end Maisie's. It's not worth it. Not for Henry Slader it's not. Given the life he led before you put him out of his misery, he might even be grateful."

I knew what he was trying to do by saying this, but it didn't make me feel less guilty. "I doubt he'd agree that death was better than misery."

He gazed up into the thinning foliage. "I'm convinced that exhuming his body and asking if he's really most sincerely dead might be the worse thing we could do," he said, adding, "There's nothing more to see here."

Branches before us and behind were liberally dropping crisp parchment leaves that seesawed to the ground, landing with a gentle shush. Way far off, I could hear a pileated woodpecker hammering a drum-hollow tree.

I shrugged, holding back a stirring urge to cry or scream or both. Instead, catching my breath, I said, "You're right. We should just go back to the house."

Will and I hadn't allowed ourselves any self-defensive clichés in the immediate aftermath of the raw violence that had gone down earlier that week. Hadn't allowed ourselves the luxury of spoonful-of-sugaring what happened. And though what he said was strictly true about judges and juries, it still felt morally soft at best. If Slader was under the ground there, then I did what I did, ended a man's life. How does one move on from that?

"Mind giving me those pieces of the photo?" he asked, his palm held out before him. "I'll get rid of them."

Reluctant, I handed them over, and without another word we left the woods, circling away from that star-crossed clearing as if it had become the lair of a beast that, lifeless or not, was reasonably left in peace. Yet reason, I thought as I hung my jacket by the back door where the plant stand with its once-cheerful pothos used to be, never outmatches curiosity. Especially when curiosity is driven by guilt.

That night after dinner I told my family I needed to do some painting for a project I was trying to finish. Whenever the weather was mild and I wanted to stay up late working, I would crash in the guest bedroom above the separate garage, where I'd set up a studio with an oak upright easel on casters at the far end of the room, along with a couple of smaller triangular traveling ones adjacent. Stretched canvases in various states of completion waited there in the company of a worktable arrayed with tubes of paint, jars filled with brushes, palette knives, linseed oil, gesso. I adored this haven. Since we rarely had guests who spent the night, I thought of it as my personal room of one's own.

It also gave me and Maisie, who shared an upstairs bedroom in the farmhouse, the chance to have a little privacy now and then. Given the decade age difference between us, some might think we would prefer sleeping apart. But I was already a teenager when six-year-old Maisie's mom, a single mother who was my own mother's best buddy and bookshop partner, succumbed to cancer. When our family adopted Maze, I became her big sister, protector, sounding board, mentor, pal, whatever she needed me to be. Rather than cramping each other's freedoms, we fitted together like mortise and tenon.

My unassuming garret was where I retreated to shake off that dubious afternoon visit to the woods. Harmless as my father's words were intended to be, "Nothing more to see here" troubled me the moment he uttered them. They looped in my head during dinner, weaving themselves in with Poe's monotonous raven—nothing more, *nevermore*, nevermore, *nothing more*. Just because Will wanted to leave untouched the place that hid our terrible secret, it didn't mean the grave didn't bear literal looking into.

Now, some people doodle to focus their thoughts. Me, I draw spooks and grotesques. I did my best to exorcise Will's words at my worktable, sketching oak leaves with furious goblin faces that resembled those of Arthur Rackham, one of my favorite childhood illustrators. As my pencil scratched the paper—imagine the feathery sounds of a mouse scurrying along a wainscot—I realized that if my assault on Slader had left me morbidly distracted during the week after my father and I'd returned to the city, then revisiting the woods today recentered me. Leaving the grave unexcavated resolved nothing. There *was* more to see. Every bent bough down in the swimming darkness of the woods formed a question mark, pointed an accusatory finger. If Henry Slader was dead, I needed to see it with my own eyes.

After doing a little painting, then lying down to nap, I woke from a shallow sleep at two in the morning, paradigmatic witching hour. Unsnarling myself from my tangled blanket cocoon, I got out of bed, reached for my black leather jacket draped over a department-store dummy scavenged from a Sixth Avenue flea market, and pulled on my Doc Martens. I shoved my cell phone in my pocket and felt my way downstairs without a sound.

Outside, the world was hushed, licorice black. Under the stars and crescent moon, I set off toward the woods. Damp long grasses lapped at my legs. When I glanced back at the house, it hovered on the rise behind me like a cutout silhouette.

My feet knew the way. The sky gave off just enough light that leaves and twigs glowed and shimmered as I picked my path to the glade. I cupped my free hand to protect my eyes as if I were shading them at noon. Dew had dampened the leaves underfoot, dulling every footfall. As I neared the clearing, an Emily Dickinson line that Maisie and I were fond of and sometimes bantered with—"I am out with lanterns, looking for

myself"—occurred to me. Was that what I was really doing out
here? Looking for myself? And if not, then what?

My shovel was just where I'd left it on purpose that afternoon. Tapping the phone on, I positioned it against the side
of a fallen tree, carefully angled so its light shined away from
the general direction of the house and toward the spot where
we'd buried Slader. If his corpse was still there, it would be in
the early phases of decomposition, and a semisweet stench of
decaying flesh would accompany maggots crawling in and out
of its exposed membranes—eyes, lips, mouth, nostrils. If one
reads as many gothics as I have—and has seen the movies their
tales inspired—one has some notion of what to expect. While I
scraped away leaves with the side of my boot, I wondered what
would be worse—a classic cadaver or gaunt Slader looking much
as he had alive.

I dug as methodically as possible, careful to deposit dirt
beside the hole and prod gently so as not to hit the body with
the tip of my blade. Excavation went faster than I had imagined
because the soil was loose. Goes without saying I was careful to
make as little noise as possible, pausing every so often to step
over to the phone, tap the light off, and make sure I hadn't
awakened anybody at the house. But all remained quiet. Even
the owls and coyotes were asleep. And when I thought I heard
a distant pulsing creek, I realized it was just blood coursing in
my ears.

In no time, I stood on the edge of an empty trench, directing
the phone's unreal LED brightness along its base and over its
surfaces. I saw countless white broken root tips and bands of
pale cinnamon and coffee-colored clay and sharp stone noses
along its sides but found, to my relief and dismay, no trace of a
body. To make sure, I scooped the edges of the pit along one side
and another until the hole was wider than we'd originally dug. I
did uncover the printer's plates my father and I'd used to make
our forgery of Poe's book, which we had buried much earlier

in this same spot—the discarded evidence of a counterfeiter's work—and I decided to leave them where they were.

Nothing else. Not only did I not locate Slader, but the few possessions he'd brought with him—a knapsack, his wallet, a used bus ticket stub—were missing, along with the empty mailer that he'd falsely claimed held photographic evidence of Will's guilt in the violent death of my uncle. Unless the snake had crawled from this pit to give up the ghost elsewhere, Henry Slader was as alive as I was. Which meant a lethal threat to me and my father was somewhere out there skulking around in the world, no doubt plotting retribution. Meant an undead Slader was behind the pretty mess at the house. Meant those damning photos might still be hidden somewhere, assuming he hadn't lied about their existence, an assumption—after what we found that afternoon—it was no longer safe to make.

It also meant—and this was of existential importance—that I was no murderer. Not first, second, third, or any other degree.

As I shoved dirt back into the infernal pit, strewed leaves and branches for a second time over it, I understood, if reluctantly, my father's declaration that these woods were tainted now. My life had always been about seeing. And the forest— now haunted with every kind of transgressive wickedness—had been pure and rich with things to see. Since my days as a kid in ill-fitting tomboy overalls and scuffed Jack Purcells, I had ventured here to draw woodland flowers, a shy mink spotted at dusk, a sleeping fawn. It was a ritual I'd lived for, one I continued to this day. Now any such sense of tranquility had been snuffed.

Shovel on my shoulder like a sexton returning from the cemetery shift, I tramped back up the hill. After replacing it in its corner, I silently climbed the stairs to the studio bedroom. Removed and scrubbed my silver rings, washed my hands and face, shed my soiled clothes, and slipped into bed, where, despite my roiling thoughts, I fell asleep.

Creamy sun pushed through the plain beige curtains next morning. Sunday, the last day of September. Our family's original plan for the weekend had been to come up on Saturday, pick a basket of local orchard apples and make cider with our hardwood press today, go back to the city early Monday. It was an annual family ritual more important than any Easter or Fourth of July. A farewell-to-summer observance. When I joined the others in the kitchen, I thought the apple pick would be called off because of what had happened, and was happy to find that everyone had decided not to let the vandal hold sway.

Migliorelli and Cedar Heights were among the orchards we'd visited in times past, but Maisie liked Kelder's Farm because it had an animal-petting pen, a corn maze, was a little more down-home. So we drove across the river toward Kerhonkson, where we picked Galas, Cortlands, some Jonamacs. My sister and I climbed the hay mountain, because how could we not, and walked the labyrinth whose cornstalks reached high above our heads.

All the while I felt we were trying too hard to have fun. Our smiles went on a bit longer than they naturally would have. Maisie's laughter seemed more shrill than normal. As for me, was it paranoid exhaustion after so little sleep that caused me to notice a man who seemed to follow us around? While I took cell-phone shots of Maisie posing with a pair of slot-eyed goats and a stubborn peacock, this man—maybe late middle-aged with hunched-up shoulders, salt-and-pepper hair, and cheeks creased like one of my fan brushes—hovered at the edge of the frame. One moment he watched me watch him, the next he was nowhere in sight.

My curious hide-and-seek with him came to an abrupt end when Will got stung by some of the bees that swarmed his apple basket. We settled up hastily and headed back over the Kingston–Rhinecliff Bridge toward home, not having further laid eyes on the man. At the house, after dressing Will's stings with calamine lotion—old-fashioned iron and zinc oxide pink—we all pitched in turning the crank of the apple press. Six quarts or seven. We ate roasted apples with chops for dinner. Every activity that was part of the ritual was tended to, and it was, by and large, a good day that helped mitigate some of the distress we'd all been feeling since we arrived.

After dinner, I stepped outside, saying I needed to check on my project in the studio. Upstairs at my table, I laid out the remnants of the photo I'd retrieved from my father's jacket the night before, having surreptitiously replaced them with a fistful of tightly torn fragments of a black-and-white still of my own. One forger falsifying another forger's document ruined by yet a third forger. It wouldn't be too hard, I figured, to reassemble the original, confirm both why it was posted on the stick figure and why my father felt compelled to destroy it. As with a jigsaw puzzle, I started on the white border, but before I was very far along I was jolted by a knock on the door. Quickly, I covered up the puzzle pieces on my table with a rag, certain it was my father who'd come to say he'd been awakened by my nocturnal excursion with cell light and spade, had figured out what I'd been doing in the woods, and wanted to know if Slader's corpse was there or not.

The relief I felt when Maisie, not Will, entered the room and wandered over to stand in front of the canvas was palpable. In that moment, I realized my dad and I had parted paths in some meaningful way, and I had no intention of volunteering what I had or hadn't found in the clearing. If he was content to leave me a murderer, that was his choice. Maisie and I turned off the studio lights and returned to the main house, where, soon enough, we said good night to our parents and went to bed.

Early next morning, my parents and I drank coffee from newly replaced mugs in the antiseptic-smelling kitchen, dawn's light partly obscured by the boarded-up window. Maisie was upstairs getting ready for the ride down to school in the city.

Mom was dressed for her day at the bookshop, and Will for his at the auction house, where the *Tamerlane* sale was coming up on Friday. Meg looked pointedly at my bare feet and my mismatched dark blue Super Mario pajama bottoms and the faded alizarin hoodie I'd slept in.

"What's your story?" she said.

"I'm thinking you guys should just go ahead. I'll call the hardware and let them in to fix the window. As it is, anybody could break in again."

My mother set her cup in the porcelain sink where it smacked like a full stop. "No way you're staying here alone."

"No worries. Fridge is full. I'm set."

"That's not what I'm talking about, as you know. Besides, you have class."

I had to suppress a smile. Much as I loved my mother, I was way beyond mothering.

"Why use their studio when I'm nicely set up to work right here?" I countered, meaning every word of it. My head was two-thirds gone from college anyway. "Once things are squared, I'll take the train down."

"Sometimes I wish we kept a gun here," Meghan told Will, who appeared not to be listening.

Trying to leaven her mood, I said, "No need for firearms. I've got my asymmetric buzz cut and these"—holding up my fingers and thumbs adorned with their array of heavy rings, a double-skull signet, an oxidized moonstone, a twisted serpent. "Anyway, it's not like I haven't stayed here by myself many times."

"Not like we've been broken into before—"

Will interrupted to say he would take the day off too, help get things straightened out. Said he might check with nearby neighbors—people we barely knew and whose houses couldn't be characterized as nearby—ask if they'd seen unusual activity on the road. Because of the Poe sale, he couldn't linger beyond that, but at least we two could tie things up. Meg agreed and within a quarter hour led Maisie out to the car.

Hubbard's out of Red Hook was able to send a man over that afternoon to replace the window and install a new lock on the door to my studio. Will drove our crummy upstate tin-can second car to visit some distant neighbors along our road, while I set myself to work on a recent painting that matched my mood. If it was, like other new panels of mine, derivative of Cecily Brown and Francis Bacon—rough as roadkill (latter); figurative where it's most abstract, vigorously abstract where it tends toward figuration (former); bleak but not dreary (latter); playful but serious (former)—that was a criticism I was happy to embrace. I had gone through many phases to arrive here, some of them improbable—Diebenkorn and Kandinsky, Dorothea Tanning and a bouquet of German expressionists—but each feeding a part of me. When painting, I became detached from my surroundings. No music. No media. No visitors. No food. No wine or weed. No nothing. Just my mistakes, retakes, and getting it right now and again. It was bliss even when I painted badly.

With only a few hours alone in this sensual autumn light, I took advantage of my ability to shut out the rest of the world and focus strictly on color and line. Slader was as far from my mind as I could drive him. I was texturing a variety of whites into the foreground of a tableau commandeered by three elongated figures with bird's-nest-like crowns when my cell phone rang. Maybe Will had discovered information about our intruder or Meghan was calling from the shop. Instead, the display was lit with a number I didn't recognize. Any other day, in any other place, I'd have let it go to voicemail.

Today, however, after half a dozen rings, I answered, "Nicole."

Prolonged silence at the other end, perhaps in response to my own drawn-out delay. Rather than cutting the connection, I bided my time, staring at a flaw in my painting. If the caller was who I imagined, I wasn't willing to give him the satisfaction of a second greeting. But neither was I going to hide.

"It's me," he said at last.

His voice was raspy, guttural, and not a little startling. My stomach seized up, in spite of my efforts to stay cool.

"As you can tell, I'm not where you and your father left me."

Wasn't like he'd asked a question, so I gave him not one word. Until he laid out why he'd called, other than to confirm he was alive, all Slader was getting from me was crickets.

"I hope you'll agree it's a very good thing I'm not."

I slowed my breathing, tried to be calm, and, while still firmly pressing the phone against my ear, angled it up and away from my mouth so he couldn't hear me inhale and exhale. It was, of course, far more than a very good thing he wasn't dead at my hands.

"Are you alone?"

I sensed a rising impatience and an edge of pain in his tone.

"Here's what," he said, raising his voice now, hoarse but clear. "And who knows, you might be pleasantly surprised by my requests. Or call them requirements. First, I want you to leave me dead. You murdered me, so leave me murdered. Second, I need money."

Despite myself, the words came out of my mouth as if of their own audacious accord.

"Why does a dead man need money?"

"Funny lady. That slays me," he said, with no hint of humor.

Ignoring this, I told him, "I don't have any money to give you, Mr. Slader."

"Mr. Slader," he mulled. "What a polite young person—oh, wait, my mistake. You're the bitch who tried to kill me."

"You mean tried to stop you from killing—"

"Christ Jesus, please shut up and listen," he cut me off. "Dead or not, I need money."

My turn to mull. I repeated the truth to him, that I didn't have any.

"Your criminal father does," he rebutted.

"You turned him down when he offered it. None of this had to happen."

"My mistake, again. Upon mature reflection I've changed my mind."

"That's his money, not mine."

"Well, in point of fact it's mine."

After a moment, I said, "I'm curious. Why did you steal that copy of *In the Cage?*"

"I also need clothes," he added, ignoring me. "Your father used to be my size, more or less, before he settled down as a family man. He's a collector, which means he's a squirreler, so rummage around in the back of his closet and bring me a couple nice shirts and pants from his earlier days. Fresh socks and a sports jacket. Whatever he won't notice's missing."

"You're actually willing to wear his clothes?"

"Beggars not choosers dilemma, so yeah, sure. You two ruined my humble wardrobe, so I figure that's the least you can do."

"I'll see what I can find," I said.

"Don't see. Just do."

"All right, I will," I said. "But tell me. I'm curious. Why did you steal the Henry James when you know the forgery inside is as wrong as two left shoes?"

"I'm dead" was his response. "This call never happened. Get some money together, that original eight thousand for starters. Get me those clothes. I'll be in touch."

"Answer me why."

He hesitated before saying, "Because it is very beautiful."

D ying is a difficult business. So thought Slader as he tossed the pit of a stolen peach into the nearby tangle of sumac whose autumn leaves shone as bright as fire. Difficult, dangerous, unmerciful. The dead can no longer explain themselves, make excuses, offer apologies, dismiss criticisms. Silenced, they lose control of the narrative. Rumors become realities. Accusations ossify into facts. For the dead, deprived of breath with which to argue or explain, all bets are off. The dead may only observe and long and regret.

Slader squinted at his fingertips sticky with peach juice and, licking them one by one, pondered how best to go about being dead. He had always excelled at staying under the radar. But dead was next level. First, it would be useful to alter these fin-gerprints. Couldn't go about being heedful at every moment of what he did and didn't touch. So yes, he would need some sort of emulsion, maybe a poultice of naphtha used by bookbinders to clean up gold on leather bindings. Or, less expensive because free, he could quickly singe his fingers on a hot skillet and, after they blistered over, singe them again. Aside from being painful, this method would be too slow. Sanding them down with a coarse nail file and applying Japanese-paper-thin rubber strips to each finger pad was another possibility. Hydrochloric acid? Problem was, finger pads have a habit of growing back, their telltale ridges reforming with impressive obstinacy. He decided he'd ask Nicole if she happened to have naphtha in her studio and a sheet of fine-grit sandpaper.

As he sat back in his car—which, unfortunately, would also have to be ditched and switched—he perused the spoils of a recent scavenger mission to a house down the road from Will's, where he'd conducted a nimble theft of food. Back-of-the-larder stuff. Half a dozen slices of bread from an already opened loaf, couple of hard-boiled eggs, fruit from a wooden bowl, cold cuts. Wished he had some salt and pepper, he thought, as he slowly peeled an egg and resumed cataloging next moves.

As important as fingerprints was his identity. He needed a new driver's license, for one, simple enough for him to fabricate, just a matter of altering his own. Again, access to Nicole's studio—her scanner, photo paper, X-Acto knife, adhesives—was essential. Too, a forged passport, though that was more dicey. Either way, both meant a new name. Had he ever so embraced being Henry Slader—Henry Wordsworth Slader in full—that to assume another name would be all that traumatic? He had not.

But still, Wordsworth, for godsakes. His mother's idea. A high-school English teacher devoted to the Romantics, Charlotte had her son's middle name legally changed from Samuel—the name of his worthless father, Sam Slader, who had abandoned his family when Henry had just turned five—to Wordsworth, her favorite poet. Having remarried a retired surgeon with a large Victorian house in the once-fancy Corky Row neighborhood of Fall River, Charlotte immersed Henry in literature from his earliest days, partly to spite her estranged

husband, who'd never read a book in his life, and partly because
Henry's sister showed no interest.

The boy took to reading like a glutton does to sweets. Poetry,
novels, fairy tales—the classics were the shared joys between the
two of them. While Henry and his stepfather never had much to
say to each other, his mother remained devoted to her son even
as he started getting himself into trouble—fights, petty thefts,
absences from class. She was, he believed, the only person who'd
ever loved him, aside possibly from Adam, also motherless, also
a literature lover. Nor did he blame her for shunning him after
he was convicted of assaulting a man in Ireland with a deadly
weapon—a very non-Wordsworthian meat cleaver—and sent
to prison for his crime. Even then he honored her in his own
admittedly odd way by refusing ever to forge William Wordsworth's signature, though he was once sorely tempted to create
the world's most desirable association copy of *Lyrical Ballads*,
when one came into his possession, by inscribing it to Coleridge
from Wordsworth. For all he knew, such a copy already existed
in the British Library, not that it would've stopped him from
foisting it off on some greedy noob bookslinger as unique. But
he kept this promise, he who kept few of them.

I wandered lonely as a cloud, he thought. Wordsworth's line
described the arc of his life quite well.

Prints, identity, appearance.

Inarguably, he was bald. And bald is bald. But the idea
of a wig revolted him. So he would adopt a watch cap or
slouchy beanie. He would also grow his stubble and dye it
chestnut, a convivial shade. He resolved to ditch his longtime
habit of wearing urban black from head to toe. He'd have to
don whatever Nicole was able to extract from the depths of
Will's closet until he had funds to outfit himself, but when he
did, he'd maybe go full-on conventional with a pair of chinos,
white shirt, navy blazer—but without one of those fakenstein
bullion crests, thank you. He could also add to his inventory

several pairs of different-colored contact lenses so he could change with the seasons. Some nonprescription glasses. A musky cologne might complete the overall aura, with hints of oakmoss and patchouli.

He needed to blend. To be an Everyman. And, as such, a nobody.

The rest of what he had to accomplish—the shape of his future was molding itself in his mind with every passing hour—was a matter of stealth and cash money. Stealth because he had recently veered outside the law in more than a few different ways. Money because he needed resources to settle more than one score, and afterward situate himself in some remote cottage far off the beaten path. Maybe there, he could write the truth about his life. *Memoirs of a Dead Soul.* A bit of Gogol, a dash of Dostoyevsky, a touch of wise Oscar Wilde, who famously proposed, "The truth is rarely pure and never simple."

The sun set over the mountains as he stepped outside and lay down on the front hood of the car, his back against its windshield, fingers knitted behind his head. Framed by the surround of trees whose leaves were combed by gentle air, he watched the stars come out. Jupiter began to gleam brightest in the blue-black twilight, a pseudo-star among a pavane of real ones. For a transient moment, he felt no pain. Even felt an unusual stirring of hope. After all, he had escaped death. Any future he planned would surely be a cakewalk after that. And what he proposed to do had been done by others before him, of course. Many times in many centuries. Confidence men, double agents, runaways had all changed identities as simply as these trees switched their colors and feigned death before budding and blooming again.

"Sometimes what you think is an end is only a beginning," Agatha Christie wrote, he now recalled. Even Christie, a usually reserved and well-mannered Burkean conservative to the marrow, had managed once to vanish for eleven long days. This was after her handsome war-hero husband had told her their marriage was over and that he planned on spending Christmas, December 1926, with his mistress, one Nancy Neele. Heartbroken and shaken to her core—abandoned, confused, humiliated, but maintaining an air of calm—Agatha left their daughter, Rosalind, in the care of the housekeeper, and drove away from Styles, their house in Sunningdale, Berkshire. To this day, the exact circumstances surrounding her disappearance were the stuff of speculation.

The faint fast thread of a meteorite fell across the sky as Slader imagined her, this woman in her middle-late thirties, fashionably dressed, checking into the grandest of hotel spas in Yorkshire, in the North Country of England. She was fortunate to get a room that time of year without having made reservations. What curious pleasure she must have felt in telling the desk clerk that she'd decided to take an impromptu rest cure and simply hadn't planned ahead. Christmas was coming in a matter of three short weeks and one liked to be refreshed for the holidays. Slader whispered the words *refreshed for the holidays, you see* softly to himself, picturing the scene as he'd done in the past, her disappearance having always been a source of fascination for him given he considered it the ultimate forgery—a person forging none other than themselves.

A chilly evening. The slender, pale, redheaded lady who wore her hair stylishly shingled wasn't dressed properly for the weather. She arrived at the hotel with no luggage beyond her black handbag and attaché case. With early stars outside glittering then as they did here right now, she ought to have been wearing a warm fur coat rather than a cardigan. Her trunks would arrive soon, she misinformed the manager, saying she had only recently arrived from Cape Town, South Africa, and giving her name as Teresa Neele, adopting her faithless husband's girlfriend's surname.

Mrs. Neele would prove to be a gracious guest at the Harrogate Hydropathic, one who kept to herself but did love to shop at the apothecaries and antique stores of the village. She would often be seen reading in the dining room or working a crossword puzzle, and at night listened to the live band in the ballroom, even rising to dance a Charleston when the spirit moved. Given that Harrogate was a community wedded to discretion, no one pressed her with questions about her life.

Nor did they engage her with gossip about the front-page news in all the papers, the story about the mystery writer who had herself become a real-life mystery. It was all anyone could talk about. The missing woman who ostensibly attempted to take her life by running her car off the road near Newlands Corner in Albury, then abandoning it in the bushes by a chalk pit in Guildford, Surrey. As police and hordes of volunteers searched the surrounding countryside, it seemed she had vanished, was possibly dead of hypothermia in a ditch somewhere, or by suicide as a result of the imminent breakup of her marriage.

The masquerade came to an end when a musician in the hotel band recognized and reported her presence in Harrogate, hiding in plain sight. When the police brought in a mortified Archie to verify Agatha's identity, the couple tried to save face by claiming she had suffered a nervous breakdown, had mislaid her memory in a fugue state, and such. Though the Christies returned home under a lightning storm of flashbulbs, Archie wasn't sufficiently shamed into keeping his family together. He soon enough divorced his wife and, free of her, married his mistress.

A grimace then a smile broke across Slader's face, as he shook his head with disgust toward Archie and admiration for Agatha. His story was base, boring, par for the golf course where he'd met his lover. Hers was a plot worthy of her most intricate mysteries and, since parts of those eleven missing days still mystified her biographers, it remained one of the trickiest plots she ever devised.

Unlike Agatha Christie, however, nobody was really search-ing for Slader. At least nobody he happened to be aware of. This was a good thing. Still, he waited until it was fully dark before deeming it safe to move. Thank God he'd had enough forethought to gas up his car—no fancy Morris Cowley like the one Agatha had abandoned—before going to the woods to confront Will.

Headlights on, he pulled out of his hiding place and drove east toward Millbrook. He couldn't recall ever having been there before, and that was what drew him. Though few cars were out, he drove well within the speed limits, keen on not drawing attention to himself.

Somewhere between Rhinebeck and Millbrook, he parked in the darkest corner of a lot behind a gas station convenience store, where he slipped into the unlocked outside men's toi-let that faintly stank of urine and Lysol but fortunately had a pocked mirror over a low sink. Slot-lock in place, he studied his lacerations and bruises in the flickering light. Several flies wheeled about in the close room, bumping against its graffitied walls and frosted wire-mesh glass. He pumped soap from the dispenser, gingerly washed his face and head, which still smarted but was nicely crusting with scabs. Using the makeup he'd taken from Meghan's medicine cabinet, he made himself presentable enough to go inside the store and buy a bucket hat to hide the welts on his skull, although the only one in his size was embroidered with trout in repeated patterns. He purchased a bottle of soda and a cheap pair of sunglasses. The kid behind the counter, distracted by whatever music was streaming through his earbuds, handed Slader his change, never noticing that his customer liberated a few chocolate bars on the way out.

"We need to meet," he told Nicole the next morning on her cell. "My want list has grown."

Revived after an undisturbed night parked behind a hedge-row that bounded a horse barn with rows of empty stalls, he'd weighed whether to drive to Providence or Fall River, where he could ask for money, even though it would betray to Atticus or his sister Bethany that he was alive. Or else he could lie low in upstate New York until he shook down Will's daughter. Or, a third possibility tempted him—he might go to the city, sit in the back of the salesroom during the auction, and leap to his feet when the lot was hammered down, shouting at the top of his lungs that the Poe was stolen, the signature fake, and the literature expert at the auction house was party to the conspiracy. At least this way he and Will would together go off a cliff, like Holmes and Moriarty at Reichenbach Falls.

Unlike the last time they spoke, Nicole didn't hesitate. "I have the clothes for you. Your want list worries me, though."

"Nothing to worry about," Slader said, and told her what he needed in order to forge himself a new license, passport, and fingerprints. "And, of course, what about money?"

"I've given some thought to your demand," she said, relieved his other needs weren't all that hard for her to help him with.

"And—"

"I think we can work something out."

That came as a surprise, which he concealed with the words "I think you haven't much choice."

"But," she said, firm and clear, ignoring his tough-guy cliché, "I have no way of knowing if the photos you claim you have that implicate my father are real or fantasy, or whether—"

Slader cut in, "Oh, they exist all right."

"So you keep saying. But the folder you were waving around in the woods that day was empty. No photos, no photocopies, no proof, nothing."

Hadn't she seen the keepsake he'd left in the forest? God only knew the effort it took him, as lousy as he felt, to construct that stick statue of her father holding one of the very

photographs he'd taken the morning of the murder. Granted, it
was one of the images of Will emerging from Adam's Montauk
bungalow after he'd butchered the man. But he was discernible,
even peppered with blood on one of his cheeks.

"If you bother to visit my grave, like most murderers who
are compelled to return to the scene of their crime tend to do,
you'll find—"

Her turn to interrupt. "Your sculpture was very impressive.
Nice touch, that Windsor knot on my father's tie. But the photo
proved nothing. That man on the bluff could've been anybody."

"I know how to tie a lot of different knots," he said obscurely.
"But to the point, I have far clearer images, unmistakable cap-
tures of your father where he shouldn't have been, all date- and
time-stamped. Made no sense for me to subject my best pics to
the elements, or, worse, to your dad."

"My point still stands."

"As does mine," he said. "Look, I have no reason to lie to you
about the evidence. It'll even be a strange pleasure to show them
all to you, so you can see what your beloved dad was capable
of back in the day."

"Why didn't you have them with you before?"

"Because I didn't trust him," Slader said. "You have to agree
I wasn't wrong."

"We're going in circles."

"You'll get your photos. And you'll wish you'd never brought
it up. Meantime, I need what I'm asking for."

"And I need time," she responded.

"Time's one thing I don't have, my dear Nicole—"

Now came a lapse, which Slader attributed to his having
called her by name. And done so with nonchalance, familiarity.
He noticed two ravishing chestnut stallions galloping side by side
in a field, then breaking off in different directions, not quite but
almost free in their white rail-fenced paddocks. He was tempted
to stride over to the stable, open the gates, and release them.

"—I wish I did, but I don't. Look, I really don't want to go into a police station and confess everything, report your father and you, report your mother. Leave your sister in the care of the state."

"I can get you a couple hundred and the supplies you need for your fake documents," she said, ignoring his threat. "Otherwise, you should be talking with my father."

"He had his chance and blew it."

The horses, having noticed a stranger leaning against their enclosure, made their way over toward him, nodding their great heads as if in agreement with his notion about setting them free.

"Another idea," he continued. "Why don't you take some of those nice first editions in your studio library and make them nicer? For all I know, you're the best fabricator of the three of us."

"Best artist, okay. Best forger, no. Besides, not willing."

"Unwillingness doesn't figure in here," said Slader. "I'd do the work myself, but for some reason my hands and fingers are messed up. That happens when they're burned and then buried."

Taken aback by the hard truth of his words, she said, "Go on."

"So I shall. And so shall you," said Slader evenly. "With your talent, it ought to be as easy as riding a bike. It'll give them more panache and, of course, market value."

"Speaking of bikes, where is Maisie's?"

"Oh, that," he said. "Sad story. Tell you what, though. I'll let you know after you agree to this first step. When I have some money, I'll be happy to reimburse her for repairs."

Such a lengthy, galling silence ensued that Slader had to check his screen to be sure they were still connected. The stallions stood near enough that he could hear their breathing and see the eyelashes on their impressive globular brown-black eyes.

"All right," she finally said. "A few of those books are mine, gifts from my father. Poe's *The Conchologist's First Book*. It's not *Tamerlane*, but still."

Slader didn't hesitate. "Inscribe it to his teenage wife, Virginia. Sepia iron gall ink, medium nib, double-check me on that, 1838, '39, right? And make it contrite, have him ask forgiveness for having put her and her mother through those starving first weeks in Philadelphia," he proposed, feeling his memory returning to him in richer detail than at any other point since he had exhumed himself. "That I can convert into money."

"I'm not sure Poe would be begging forgiveness in a book about shells," she said, wondering if he hadn't come up with the idea because he himself had reason to be contrite.

"Point taken," said Slader without missing a beat. "Just write, *Virginia from the author.* There were a lot of Virginias in Virginia back then, so I can say that I was told it was Edgar's wife and let the chips fall where they may. What else?"

"For my sixteenth birthday, my father gave me a gift his father'd given him."

"Being?"

"Arthur Conan Doyle's fountain pen from—"

"That could be tricky," he sniffed. "What's the provenance?"

"Oh, it's real enough. I have all the auction paperwork."

"Regift it to Henry Edgar Wadsworth in the paperwork then," tweaking Wordsworth by a couple of letters and adopting Poe's first name without a moment's thought.

"Who's Henry Edgar Wadsworth?"

"By the way," Slader persisted, "didn't I see a first of *Dubliners* on the shelves there? Spine darkened, looked like."

Nicole felt like she was dodging knives tossed at her from different directions. "Even as is, it's worth a lot of money."

"Four, five grand at best? That's not good money. Just have Joyce sign and date it close to when it came out. Make sure the baseline runs up from left to right a smidge. Then it'll have some real value."

"That one's not mine."

"You're right, it's not. Can you have them finished by tomorrow?"

"Don't be ridiculous. You know about these inks, the aging, plus I couldn't say off the top of my head what's the pub date of *Dubliners*. Need to research it."

"Ever heard of Google?" Slader gibed, absently reaching his free hand out toward the nearest horse, wishing he had some sugar cubes. "Don't even bother. Came out in June 1914, somewhere in there. Date it a hundred and four years ago today, how's that? Think he was in Zurich, not Paris or Trieste, so add that. I'll need these by end of day tomorrow and I don't care how you get it done. Use a hair dryer if you have to. Setting on warm, not hot. You have access to a car?"

"I'll figure it out."

"On Bulls Head Road due east of you there's a Quaker meeting house. Look for a small white sign that says 'All Welcome.' Pull in the lot there. Six o'clock. I'll be waiting."

"How do I know you're not going to hurt me?" Nicole asked, more than a little shaken by the premeditated specificity of this drop-off place, the rapidity with which Slader made his demands, the depth of his bibliographic and technical expertise, the detailed knowledge he possessed about her family and their property. By everything.

"Not in my best interests," said Slader, feeling sorry for her though he knew he shouldn't. "You and I have far better ways to straighten out our problems. Hurting you would be counterproductive, though I must admit I admire the impudence of your fearing *me* hurting *you*, of all people—"

"How do you know I'm not going to show up with the police?"

"Same reasoning. Not in your best interests," he said.

"None of this is in my best interests, so far as I can tell."

"You're failing to see the bigger picture, Nicole. I'm being helpful in the extreme here and have to believe you'll come around to realizing it. See you tomorrow."

And with that, Slader's mind wandered back to the grassy paddock before him where, mesmerized, he found himself staring at the great oblivious stallions. He pocketed his cell phone and reached both hands and arms over the post-and-rail, gesturing them to come closer to where he stood, hoping they'd let him stroke their forelocks. But after looking his way, they soon lost interest in his gesturing and wandered away into their green fenced world.

The drive from Kenmare to Dingle would take over an hour on any given day. But this was Wren Day, the Mummers Festival, and many lanes and thoroughfares across Ireland would be filled with celebrants, as Wren Day was a Celtic tradition in honor of Saint Stephen, the first Christian martyr. The morning after Christmas promised to bring out throngs from the very youngest to elders on canes who'd observed this revelry since long before men walked on the moon, well before the aviators Alcock and Brown made the first nonstop transatlantic flight and crashed their biplane in the Derrigimlagh Bog at another Atlantic spur due north from here.

"Get up already," Maisie enthused, rousing me from sleep as was her habit whenever she was excited about the day ahead. She knew her sister well, so brought me up a pot of hot coffee from the breakfast room. "Don't forget, going to see the Murmurs was your idea in the first place."

She was right. After we'd decided to come to Ireland for the holidays, I read a lot about Wren Day, or *Lá an Dreoilín* as it's

called—"law on droh-leen"—and wanted to make sketches of
its celebrants, work up abstracts for new canvases.

"Ugh," I groaned, yawning. "If I were on my feet, I'd be dead
on my feet."

She laughed, then flattened her chin against her neck, inton-
ing like some Victorian barrister, "So how do you plead? Bad
night's sleep?"

"Guilty as charged," I said as I sipped the strong black coffee, keeping to myself the rotten memories that had kept me
up until dawn's first light. "And it's Mummers, not Murmurs."

"Ah, crikey, you can't still be jet-lagged," she insisted, showing
off her new word as she flopped down on the large bed and sat
crisscross applesauce. "We've been here a whole week."

"Maybe life-lagged?"

"How very dramatic," she trolled, draping the back of her
wrist against her forehead and dropping sideways on the bed,
feigning a swoon. Then, popping back up again, she said, "Come
on, I want to get there early so we can save all the wrens."

"They don't kill real wrens anymore, Maze. Now it's just
symbolic."

Her forehead crinkled. "Why'd they want to kill them in
the first place?"

"Because of Saint Stephen," I said, pouring a top-off.

"So, and?"

"So, and—a few decades after Christ was crucified, when
Christianity was considered a dangerous cult—still is, if you ask
me—he hid in some holly because these guys were after him—"

"Wait. They had holly bushes in Jerusalem?"

"More like trees, I think. But anyway, Stephen was safe in his
holly-whatever until a little wren perched on one of its branches
and started singing. He tried to hush it up but the gang found
him and stoned him to death. That's how he became a martyr
and a saint."

"I don't like that story," Maisie said, stretching her arms over her head, fingers intertwined, a frown on her face.

"Don't stone the messenger," I said, adding, "So over the centuries people celebrated Saint Stephen by hunting for a wren to kill and string to the top of a pole where it'd be paraded around the village while they'd beg for money to bury it."

"Cray-cray, if you ask me."

"That's organized religion for you," I agreed. "Still want to go?"

"If you're going, I'm going."

Inspired anew by the odd mix of personal tragedy and public merrymaking that defined the occasion, the weirdness of the tradition, and the prospect of making art, I threw on a patchwork outfit, gathered my pencils and sketchbook, and walked with Maisie downstairs to join the others.

Dingle was even more crowded than we'd anticipated. Having no sense of where the parade began or ended, we wove our way toward the town center. Onlookers jammed the sidewalks while paraders in the street strutted and danced. Dressed in whimsical clothes and oat-straw suits that made them look like prancing haystacks, they held colorful poles aloft with fake wrens nailed to the tops, asking for coins to "bury the wran." They played whistles and accordions; some banged drums and chanted,

> *The wren, the wren,*
> *The king of all birds,*
> *Saint Stephen's Day*
> *Was caught in the furze.*

For all her earlier frowning distaste, Maisie soon started humming and singing along. Even Meg got swept up in the spirit of the thing as she tried to make out the words and join in, much as we had the evening before in O'Donnabhain's. Reaching into her jacket pocket, she gave my sister some harp-faced coins to drop in the hats held out along the boisterous route. Irish euros that would later turn up in the cash drawers of pubs, I thought with a smirk, as the song continued,

> *Up with the kettle*
> *And down with the pan,*
> *And give us a penny*
> *To bury the wran.*

Seeing that my sister needed no encouragement to throw herself into the doings, I told Meg, "I think I'm going to sit here for a while and sketch." She asked that I try not to stray far from the stone bumper where I'd perched, then meandered off with the others to take in the festivities.

I was used to sketching still lifes, of course, but also limning things in motion, which I did by using my eyes like a shutter and impressing the images in memory, much as a cartoonist drawing panels might do. But there was motion and then there was this, a full-tilt show of life's hues and shapes, accentuated by the rhythm of songs and tripping the daylight fantastic. Spurred along by the crowd's energy and my sense that what I was seeing here wouldn't last long enough for me to rework anything on the spot, I roughed out patterns without looking at the paper. Then, using colored pencils—clay, crimson, peach, brown, tamely monochromatic in the face of this riot of color—I sketched in the faces and figures of onlookers across the way. I don't think I'd ever worked so spontaneously, without casting a critical eye on what I had accomplished before flipping over the large page of the pad on my lap, tucking it under, and starting a fast fresh composition.

My back was cramping a bit, but I pressed on until, there—there he was again. The man from last night. Staring at me from the far side of the marching mummers, a ways farther up the street. Unmistakably him, with the raised shoulders and a parka over a rumpled suit that looked to be corduroy.

Unsettled, I kept drawing the portrait of him I'd begun before that stab of recognition had shot through me. I drew his face and shoulders and clothing, and started shaping out parade watchers who were standing next to him, so I could get a sense of his comparative height. But when I glanced down and back up, he'd melded with the crowd. I stood, spilling the box of pencils balanced on my lap. The celebrants—their staffs swaying up and down, their chanting keen and loud—blocked my view as I searched the street. Only when there was a brief break in the flow did I see that he'd moved directly across from me. He tilted his head like some curious crow and raised his right hand, palm up, fingers beckoning me to join him.

No way, I thought. You want to talk, you can come over here. Which made no sense, of course, since I was the one with questions. The one who wanted to know who he was and what he wanted.

With the help of a couple of eager kids, I gathered my pencils, offering them one each as a reward. They grabbed their gifts, in pure wren-boy style, and scattered.

"Excuse me, but aren't you Nicole Diehl?"

I turned on my heel and there he stood. He seemed younger close-up, his crow's-feet more impish than hoary. Though he'd asked a question whose answer he plainly already knew, he did so with such an unsettling, thoughtful smile and warm gray-blue eyes, it was disarming. He didn't give off an air of dodginess or aloofness or bad intention. Hands clasped before him, that delicate tilt to his head, the man appeared to be benign, even kindly. All the more reason to be on my toes.

He was speaking again. "I didn't mean to startle you. My apologies. Too much time spent in the company of me, myself, and I"—trying to elicit a laugh, I guessed, maybe break the ice with charming self-deprecation.

But I wasn't in the mood to laugh, and with the parade carrying on noisily, it was hard to hear him.

"My name is Pollock," he continued. "And I'd love to ask you—"

"I'm sorry, Mr. Pollock," I cut him off. "Do we know each other?"

"We don't."

"But I've seen you before. Weren't you in Kenmare last night following me?"

"There's a tea shop just here. Could I offer you a coffee or tea inside, so we can hear each other? Very deafening, this mummer business. Here," and he gently reached out to touch my elbow, an old-fashioned, gentlemanly gesture indicating he'd escort me inside.

Instinctively, I withdrew my arm. "If I say no, are you just going to keep shadowing me?"

He shrugged his already half-shrugged shoulders. I looked around to see if my family was anywhere nearby, but the crowds were at their peak. Peering through the bow windows of the pretty tea shop, I saw customers inside nibbling Jaffa Cakes and drinking their Assam tea. Innocuous, respectable, on the up-and-up. If I wanted to find out how he knew my name—I had gone by my mother's maiden name, Diehl, from earliest youth, my parents' idea so as to avoid any inherited fallout from my father's legal troubles back then—this seemed the easiest way to do it. Not like he'd attack me in a tearoom with so many witnesses around. And not like I couldn't stab him with one of my Faber-Castells if he tried, though admittedly nothing about his manner suggested any such necessity.

"Can't you just tell me what you want right here?" I asked.

"Really, Nicole. Best discussed off the street," he told me, with the easy manner of one who seemed practiced in the art of patience. "Cake and cha's on me."

I figured I'd be able to see my family outside the window when they came back looking for me, so I led him into the shop and we sat at a table near the door. He ordered a selection of crumpets and a pot of India tea. I asked for an espresso, then turned to him and said, "All right."

"All right. So you still haven't answered my first question. I'm going to assume it's yes, since you're sitting here with me."

"The real question is, why should you care, Mr. Pollock?" I said, trying not to show the awkward defiance I felt at being in this uncomfortable situation.

"My first name is Bernard, Nicole," he said. "But Bern will do."

"And what is it you want from me, Bern-will-do?"

He acknowledged my sophomoric jibe with a forbearing thin smile and said, his voice dropping into a lower register, "As you've been aware for most of your life, and I'm sorry to bring this up on a Saint's Day surrounded by so much merriment, your uncle Adam met his end under mysterious circumstances—"

Thrown by his directness, even though I'd asked for it, I retorted, "Saint Stephen was violently murdered, so today's as good as any to talk about such things. By the way, I don't think 'met his end under mysterious circumstances' really cuts it if we're talking about what happened to my uncle."

"A savage unsolved mutilation-murder. And a cold-case homicide at that. I agree, words don't quite wrap themselves around such brutal acts."

"So you've come to confess you did it?" I asked, hearing again that juvenile stridency in my voice and wondering where it was coming from. Sure, I had as sharp a tongue as the next person, but facetiousness was not in my everyday nature. "You want forgiveness before you turn yourself in?"

"Ah, Nicole," he said calmly. "I'd like to think that if I had attacked and killed your uncle in such a vicious manner, my

conscience would have long since gotten the better of me, and
I'd have confessed right then and there."

His words seemed earnest. I kept my mouth shut and waited.

"How I wish whoever committed such evil had spoken up
long ago," he went on. "That they didn't and still haven't is a
frustration we each share in our different ways. I was assigned
to that case more than two decades ago now. February '96. All
over the tabloids, where they trade on the grisly and freakish
until the next grisly, freakish act comes along, and the next.
Did you know your uncle survived ten days in the ICU before
he passed?"

"Maybe," I said, trying to remember if I'd ever heard that.

"He knew his assailant, I'm sure of it. Even tried to speak
to us—"

"Hold on," I interrupted, a shudder running through me.
"Shouldn't you be showing me a badge or something?"

"Sure," he said, reaching into his jacket pocket. "But I don't
have my badge anymore. I retired a few years ago."

His identification card confirmed that the man sitting across
from me in this quaint shop that smelled of fresh soda bread,
a man whom I'd never heard about from either of my parents,
was indeed one Bernard Pollock, Detective First Grade, retired.
Naturally, I couldn't help but wonder if it wasn't a forged document. But why would this seemingly sane, gentle-mannered man
bother to carry a counterfeit ID on him?

Putting his wallet away, he added, "Other than averting a
speeding ticket or maybe getting me one last round on the house,
the card's worthless. Says what I did, not what I do. Besides, I
quit drinking when my wife died, so one for the road isn't the
medicine I need."

"I'm sorry," I said, quieted by this.

He glanced away for a minute, reading the list of specials
fancifully chalked within a pretty frame of flowers on a black-
board over the counter, apparently weighing what to say next.

For my part, unwilling to add to what I'd just said, I looked at the crowd outside and was floored by what I witnessed. I could swear my father was out there staring at me and Pollock through the shop windows, a look of distress clouding his face. My eyes shot over to the detective, to see if he noticed Will out there too, standing in place as the crowd hustled around him, but the man returned his gaze to me, as if to reset the conversation.

"I attended Adam Diehl's funeral," he resumed. "Stood at a distance, anyway. Out of respect, to be sure, but also I wanted to see who was there, observe how people behaved, not an unusual practice. I went out of my way to be thorough when I was working the case. I don't know whether or not you're aware I even brought your dad in for questioning once."

Numbed by both my weird sighting and this revelation, I lied, "So he told me."

"Actually, more than once."

"Right," I muttered, looking again to see that Will had meanwhile disappeared into the throngs, or else I'd seen a doppelgänger, a daytime ghost out there.

Had Pollock noticed my disconcertment, my hesitation? It seemed he hadn't, as he continued, "Well, that's a good sign, his being honest with you. Can't have been easy for you to hear that your father'd been a person of interest in your uncle's murder."

"I trust my father," I told him, hoping my face portrayed the very image of honesty and resolve, though I was churning inside.

"We questioned a lot of people, potential witnesses, folks out jogging on the beach in Montauk—pretty darned hard-core, if you ask me, running on a winter morning along the Atlantic. Interrogated the mailman who found your uncle and called the ambulance. Spoke with Diehl's closest friend, man named Henry Slader, whose alibi was strong though he was my number one suspect. Person of interest with a criminal record, assault—"

"Assault on my dad, I know. Right here in Ireland." I wondered why he was telling me all this, sensing he wasn't letting on all that he knew.

In point of fact, I believed that Bern here might've been trying to trip me up.

"I was so absurdly confident I'd catch whoever did it that months slipped by, then years, and whoever the perpetrator was managed to melt away. Enough time has passed that, for all I know, the murderer may be dead too, though I doubt it. Either way, the lack of DNA evidence always made me think it was a premeditated homicide."

"How's that?" I asked, despite myself. I hadn't touched my cup, hadn't eaten any of the pastries he'd ordered.

Pollock brightened a little at my show of interest. "You got to plan ahead, and I mean deliberately, intelligently, not to leave evidence behind. Particularly on such a—such a murder."

"You mean bloody, gory, grisly?"

"I do, I'm sorry," he said. "I'm even sorrier that the case went cold and stayed cold, our every effort to find the killer stymied."

My espresso was room temp when I finally lifted it to take a sip. "Makes sense," I said, holding the cup in front of my lower lip and absentmindedly blowing on it.

"Adam Diehl was not the only cold case left on my docket when I was wrapping up for retirement, but it was the one that I couldn't quite walk away from. So I decided to revisit persons of interest, those still alive, including people who'd been out running on the beach that morning—jogging, it turns out, has no real connection to longevity—and see if anyone had let their guard down. See if I could turn up anything different from what we saw during the active investigation. Long shot, and very unofficial."

"And no luck."

"Hints, whispers, guesses. But no luck."

My mood changed. "So what you want from me is to know if my father confessed, or if I happen to have some dirt on him for you?"

"Not in so many words, but I wonder if you have any personal insights into who might have had a motive and means."

"This is where I stop talking with you," I said, rising from my chair and taking up my pad and pencils.

"Then you do know something."

"Wrong," I prevaricated—that is, bald-faced lied again. "But if you think you can fucking follow me across the ocean, buy me some sweets like I'm five years old, and basically trick me into getting in your car, you're seriously mistaken."

"That's a very unfair representation," he said. His face suggested that he was less offended by my quip than disappointed in me, a disappointment I shared.

"Maybe, probably," I managed, knowing I was in an ethical free fall. "I'm sorry but, believe it or not, I've got nothing to offer. And if I did, I'm not sure I'd tell you."

"What do you know about Henry Slader?" he asked, his tone of voice abruptly darker, looking at the plate of crumpets rather than up at me.

Which was just as well, since I felt my face flush at the question.

"What about him?" I asked, trying to sound calm.

"You tell me. You're the one who's still in touch with the man."

I sat back down.

"Another espresso?" he asked.

This was unexpected, dangerous terrain. Here I had believed I was on the cusp of settling debts with Slader, fabricating something that would erase the sins of the past, or at least pave our way free of them—mine, my father's, Slader's own; all of us bound together in a cat's cradle of miscalculations—and this Pollock emerges from the past with queries and feelers and insinuations.

"Who are you again? I mean, I know who you are. But what's your purpose, asking me all these things? I wasn't even alive when it happened. I never even met my uncle."

He sadly smiled, as if he felt sorry for me. "That's just part of the tragedy. I'm sure you would like to have known him."

"Don't patronize me," I said, surprised once more by my petulance. "Answer the question."

Ignoring my outburst, he responded with an unruffled soliloquy of sorts. "Taking another person's life on purpose is a sublimely complex act. Anger, vengeance, jealousy, we all know the standard motives. But people who murder violently—and your uncle's was a notably violent murder—are often lacking a firm grasp of what's real and what isn't. The emotions involved before, during, and after are all interconnected but at the same time highly distinct. Unless the homicide is the work of a psychopath, somebody who skirts any normal sense of compunction or guilt or regret or even reality, verity. Somebody who doesn't share the feelings most of us would experience. A murderer's conscience is a mess of crazy conflicting emotions."

"What does this have to—"

"Hear me out."

My second espresso arrived, and I burned my tongue on it.

"Long story short, it takes an impressively skewed sense of self-preservation to compartmentalize and lock away a murder you've committed, and then go ahead with living your life as if it had been something best forgotten for your and everybody else's sake." And with this he took up a scone and bit off an edge. "These are really good. You should try one."

I picked out a pastry and set it on my plate.

"I'm asking about Henry Slader because he seems to me to bear some characteristics of a psychopath. Somebody who could've killed and moved on without compunction, could pass any lie detector test, breeze any questioning with no more effort than it takes for him to breathe."

"So why didn't you arrest him? Why don't you?" I said, hoping to distract our talk away from me, as my lip and tongue stung.

"Witnesses, in a word."

"Maybe he hired somebody to do it."

"No motive, in a couple more words."

"So why ask me about him? I hardly know the guy."

He took another bite, chewed, swallowed. "Because I wonder why you met with him in secret last October in the parking lot of a church."

That threw me. Quaker meetinghouse, I wanted to correct him to buy time, but instead said, "So you've been following me. I thought I saw you at Kelder's Farm when we were picking apples. Think I even have a photo of you on my phone when I was taking a picture of my sister and father."

"In my dotage, I've been following a few people, Nicole," he explained. "Let's just say I'm cursed with my own mental issues. Being obsessive-compulsive served me well in my chosen career, but in retirement it's become a bona fide nuisance."

"I see," not a little amazed by his frankness but growing impatient with his method, if that's what this was.

"And being a completist, when I start something it's got to be finished. I used to do jigsaw puzzles, the harder the better. Getting that spinning sky in Van Gogh's *Starry Night* to fit together on the kitchen table? Pure joy for me. Drove my wife nuts."

"So no ethics, no outrage in needing to solve my uncle's case? Just that you can't stand leaving the puzzle unsolved?"

"Please," he said, with justifiable annoyance. "I hate that a psychopath is strutting around, free as a bird, knowing he eluded me and everybody else. Over time it's become personal as well. From my distant vantage I've watched you grow up, watched your mother lose her best friend on top of losing her brother, seen her adopt Maisie. I've grown fond of the women in your family."

"This is way too creepy," I announced, standing again.

"I imagine it does sound off, hearing it in so many words. But there's nothing sinister about it. If anything, I'd like to see your father exonerated once and for all, so you can have a good life together. But creepy wishes, as you put it, don't always match up with unsentimental instincts."

"Don't get this wrong," I said. "I'd actually like to help you. But I can't."

He pulled a card from his day pack, a smooth practiced gesture. "I understand where you're coming from, Nicole. I really do. But if you happen to remember anything that either Henry Slader or even your father might have said in an offhand moment, even the slightest detail you overheard, I'd appreciate a call, an anonymous tip if you prefer. Just—here," and handed me the card.

Jolted by his bringing up my father again, by the formality of his demeanor, by the entire freaking encounter, I slipped his card into my pencil pouch and left in a daze.

The crowds had thinned. I returned to the spot where I'd been drawing, sat again, and tried to calm myself, deliberately refusing to look back and see if he'd followed me out. My sketching was done for the day. Any joy I might have experienced watching and listening to the paraders was gone. Instead, I found myself thinking about the words *aiding and abetting,* and imagined they must have meant kind and positive actions some long time ago. Aiding somebody—where was the harm in that? To aid was to help, to encourage. And didn't *abet* mean the same thing, once upon a time? To lend a hand?

"Where you been, Picasso?"

Maisie's words startled me from my reverie. Anyway, there wasn't any etymological dictionary that could whitewash the clear meaning of aiding and abetting, something I'd known I was guilty of for a while now, but which I'd ignored out of love for Will. And though Pollock's words were meant for my uncle's murderer, and I didn't fit his profile of a psychopath, my own sense of what was real and what wasn't had become more fuzzy over these past months, I had to admit. I'd nearly killed a person myself. Had been able somehow to live with it for the better part of a week. It was a relief that Slader survived. But what if he hadn't? What if I'd dug up his grave that night a few months ago and discovered his decomposing body interred there? Would I have decided as my father had that Slader was better off dead, and dismissed the whole thing as a forged check of an experience?

"Hello, Nicky, anybody home?" my sister pressed, placing her hands on my shoulders and gently shaking me.

"I'm sorry," I said, seeing Meg and Will standing behind her. "I got sidetracked."

"No worries," my mother said. "We thought we'd lost you there for a minute."

They had, but not in the way she meant. I explained that I'd simply trailed behind a particularly awesome group of wren-boys whose traditional outfits I wanted to sketch. "Time to head back to Kenmare?"

"Let's," my mother said, with Maisie chiming in, "Come on, already."

My father was noticeably quiet.

After dinner at the lodge, still sitting at the table, Maisie asked to see my drawings of the "awesome wren-boys," and when I showed her my sketchbook I was too distracted by the events of the afternoon to engage in our usual sisterly bantering as we turned the pages.

"You okay?" she asked, knowing something was amiss.

"Tired is all," I explained with a forced smile.

"You need to eat more" was Maisie's response. "You're starting to get too thin."

When she went upstairs to our room accompanied by Meg, I sat in the small hotel lounge with Will for a nightcap.

"Your mind's been elsewhere these last couple of days," I said, playing with my coaster on the dark oak bar. We had ordered a couple of Jamesons neat, his a double.

"Really?" he asked, seemingly surprised by my comment.

"Just making sure you're having a good time. Clearing your head after the insanity of last summer, like we're supposed to be doing."

He nodded, swirled the golden liquor in its cut-glass crystal tumbler. "I'm all right."

"Good," I said, and sipped, savoring the whiskey, feeling it glow through my chest.

"Why do you ask?"

"I have something I want to show you," pulling out my cell phone and scrolling through photographs until I found the series of shots I'd taken in September with the mysterious Pollock in the background. "Any idea who this is?" I held the screen out toward him.

"What am I seeing here?"

"Remember our apple pick?"

He took the phone and brought it close to his face.

"I see Maisie and myself at what looks like Kelder's Farm," he said, squinting against the bright light. "Ulster County, sure, a few months back."

"Right," I said. "But see that other person standing a little behind you? He's the one I'm curious about."

"Pretty blurry. Why?"

Was it possible Will didn't recognize Pollock? I could fathom how, after so many years, the detective might look unfamiliar to him. And yes, his face was a bit out of focus and a little obscured by Maisie. But he was there, clearly Pollock.

"You're sure you don't recognize him?"

"I'm sure I'm supposed to, right?"

He took a drink and I followed suit. If my father was withholding, dissembling, that meant things were even worse than I'd imagined. And what I imagined was bad enough.

"Maybe not," I said. "You may have met him too long ago to remember. Or else he looks a lot different now."

"Gravity's no friend to our faces over the years," he said, faintly smiling.

"Truer words," I told him, watching his mouth turn from a smile to a frown, as if to prove his point about gravity's downward pull.

"So let's fast-forward. You're telling me that this is the same man I saw you with in Dingle today?"

I swallowed. "Yes, I'm pretty sure."

"So who is he? Wait—I don't think I want to know."

"Really, you don't? His name is Pollock."

"Don't know anyone by that name, I'm relieved to say," he coolly responded. "My question for you is, what are you doing having tea with this stranger?"

Rather than play along, I excused myself and went to the bathroom. This was new and weird terrain for me to negotiate with my dad. I'd always thought, perhaps naively, we'd been straight with each other. Though I had to admit, as I washed my face with cold water, in recent months I'd not been holding up my side of that unspoken pact. Now I had to wonder if he too had been failing to be straight with me.

Back at the bar, I said, "The man in Dingle was Pollock and I'm sure you've met him before, since he certainly knows who you are, who Uncle Adam was, and like that. But you're telling me you don't know him?"

"No," he said, looking at me with such firm conviction that I had to conclude his decades-ago encounter with the detective was either long forgotten—scrubbed away by either the passage of time or the alchemy of denial—or that my father was lying straight to my face. Lying in a way that bore the very characteristics of a psychopath that Pollock had described. "No," he repeated. "But I think you'd be wise not to hang out with strangers like that. And God knows, not with gaslighters like this Pallack."

"Pollock."

"Pallack, Pollock, whatever his name is. Or's supposed to be."

He signed for the drinks, kissed me unexpectedly on the cheek, and left, saying he'd had it for the day. As for me, I lingered another quarter hour before heading upstairs to bed as well, my mind a roiling mess.

It had taken some convincing, a fair bit of truth bending, but Nicole's parents finally agreed to let her remain at the farmhouse, having been assured that their daughter's art-gallery friend Renee would come up from Brooklyn to join her. No such plans existed, they hadn't even texted in a few days, but Will, hard-pressed to focus on his upcoming auction, saw no reason to doubt his daughter, and took the train to Penn Station that Tuesday. Left to her own devices, Nicole worked into the night on her forgeries of Poe and Joyce. Not that she would've minded a visit from Renee, very much the opposite. Just that she couldn't afford to pause and consider her outspoken friend's opinions about what she was up to here, whether negative or, just as likely given Renee's unpredictability, enthusiastic. Plus which, unlike her parents, she wasn't worried about her own safety.

No, she needed to stay focused to the point of purblindness, she thought. One of her art instructors had used that term, *purblind*, to encourage students to concentrate on the work before them. To be blind to everything peripheral when painting.

One's canvas was the whole damn world. Any distracted glancing away, any gazing out the window, would poison the vision
inherent in the painting. Studios should never have windows
other than a skylight, her teacher had said. And preferably a
filthy dirty skylight.

A personal favorite, the Poe conchology book was one Nicole
knew intimately, even though she had no particular interest in
seashells or, for that matter, this or any system of testaceous
malacology alluded to in the volume's subtitle. The first edition,
which she reluctantly took down from its place of honor on the
shelf, was bound in its original dirty-pink lithographed boards,
which depicted a macabre scene of snakelike fronds dangling
above a pile of shells. A quick collation verified that all twelve
beautiful lithograph plates featuring many dozens of shells, from
the toothed *Pteroceras* and urn-like *Strombus* to the butterfly-
wing *Argonauta* and cornucopia *Carinaria*, were present. Following to the letter the instructions she'd been given, her forgery
came along nicely after she'd practiced Poe's cursive on vintage
paper, found in a flat-file drawer, that was similar in finish and
porousness to the text stock used in the 1839 original. As for
the inscription itself, though Poe was capable of fun honeyed
flourishes when signing his name, Nicole, his amanuensis of sorts,
decided to limit the language to the spare and simple wording
Slader had proposed, skipping Poe's autograph altogether. Fewer
words, fewer pen strokes, fewer chances of making mistakes.

The first edition of Joyce's *Dubliners* was perched on a high
shelf that required her to stand on a chair to reach it. Dark red
cloth, color of dried blood, stamped on the front cover and spine
in gilt. For such a revolutionary work, such a dingy, forgettable
format. One that with its rare original green dust jacket avowing
its Irish subjects, missing from this copy as with most, was never
intended to draw attention to itself in bookshops where censors
lurked in the stacks. While she had always been an admirer of
Joyce's stories—"The Dead" was the one she loved best, with its

wizardly last paragraph—forging *James Joyce Zürich 3.X.1914* didn't carry the same emotional resonance, the uneasy feeling over altering the historical record of the author, as it had with the Poe, the earliest of her literary loves.

First, to expunge any provenance, she used a Staedtler vinyl eraser to remove penciled notes of secondhand booksellers or owners who'd handled the book in times past. A price in British pounds, cost codes, an annotation that this was one of 746 copies. She then used a dark sepia iron gall ink to insert the author's slanted signature on the front endpaper before carefully putting away the calligraphic pens, ink mixtures, the magnifying glass used to check hue and feathering in her practice runs. Afterward, she rearranged books on the shelves to hide her thievery, or at least forestall its being noticed by Will.

Nor did it escape her that because she stood one day to inherit her father's library, this was in truth a theft from her own legacy.

As it happened, working on such a tight deadline improved rather than hindered her performance. Satisfied with the two forgeries, insofar as she would ever be satisfied by the act of counterfeiting inscriptions, she tissue-wrapped and neatly placed them in bags together with the clothing she'd found among her father's unused shirts and trousers. She then drove out into the dusky evening past Saw Kill Creek, through the tiny hamlet of Milan, got briefly on the Taconic toward the turnoff onto Bulls Head Road. Her face, her fingers, her heart were numb as she watched the painted lines on the roads fly past. Was it possible that another car was following her at a distance, headlights off, although legally they ought to have been on given it was just past sunset?

Slader was waiting, as promised. The unpaved parking lot, flanked by mature Norway pines with the modest meetinghouse set at the far end, was otherwise empty. The car that had seemed to trail her continued along Bulls Head and disappeared around a bend, its driver oblivious to her, neither craning his neck to look back nor checking his rearview mirror. Her anxiety over being shadowed appeared, at least at the time, to be the product of rattled nerves, nothing more.

Parking parallel to the road so that her license plates weren't visible, she walked over to where the man was leaning against the trunk of his Chevy, arms crossed, looking more than a little freakish in his floppy fisherman's hat, coal-colored jeans, torn sable T-shirt, and mismatched black Oxfords. Reed thin, he didn't come off as dangerous, but Nicole kept her distance when handing Henry Slader—Henry Wadsworth was *not* a name she was going to be able to get used to, and she refused to think of him as Edgar—the cache of things he'd demanded.

"This is right on the road," she said, looking around. "I imagined somewhere more off the beaten track."

"Quakers are pacifists, Nicole. Simple compassionate spiritual folks. They see no need for preachers or priests. They respect people's eccentricities. They value silence, which fits perfectly with our needs. And right now all of them, except for us, are home washing dishes and communing with their fictitious god."

"Except for us?"

"Just for our few precious minutes together, I want you to think of us as a couple of kindly Quakers who took that 'All Welcome' sign over there seriously. What better place than this for friends to get together?"

"We're hardly friends," she scoffed.

Ignoring that, Slader asked, "So how did it go?" as he opened the canvas bag to examine the books.

"You tell me." She took a couple of steps back, even though she sensed she could push the man over with a feather, so frail he seemed.

The work was beyond professional—"inspired"—Slader soon affirmed, examining her holograph from several angles in the fading light, rotating and holding it out away from him so he could study the ink's reflective qualities across the flat plane of the page.

"You know, some people think Poe mostly plagiarized other people's scholarship when he wrote this thing?" he said, not lifting his eyes from the volume. "Much of it's lifted straight out of Thomas Brown's *Conchologist's Text-Book*, which came out in Glasgow half a dozen years earlier. Even the plates are lifted from the Glasgow edition if I'm not mistaken."

"I don't think Poe would agree, but maybe so."

"Oh, definitely so," he said, glancing up at her with a squint. "Kind of makes your inscription a fake inside a fraud, doesn't it."

Wanting to change the subject, Nicole said, "Speaking of the plates, I read that for an extra charge you could buy copies at the time with the plates specially hand-colored. So I took the liberty of watercolor tinting some of them."

"So you did," he said, flipping to an example and studying her handiwork at a far more leisurely pace than the situation might have warranted.

"Figured it couldn't hurt the resale value," she added, thinking, *Get on with it already*, as she looked to see if the Quakers had installed any security cameras, wondering if such devices might be against their beliefs.

"All things equal, you should've done all of the plates or none. But I know how to get around discrepancies. Half my life's been about turning sow's ears into purses—"

Or the other way around, Nicole mused.

"Still, it's a much better copy than I'd expected," he went on, as if talking to himself, "though it will be the harder of the two to sell because it'll draw closer scrutiny." He then gazed directly into her eyes with what resembled a genuine smile. "But that's my problem, not yours."

Slader next removed the tissue from *Dubliners*, examined it like a gemologist does a diamond. He nodded in approval.

"Yes?"

"Frabjous work."

"Are we done here then?"

"Sweet baby Jesus and all his scruffy saints. Are we done here, you're asking? Surely you realize we've barely begun."

Nicole let out a brief incomprehensible expletive.

"Listen, and hear me out," she said, her cheeks flushing. "How much would it take for you to leave me and my family alone once and for all? Give you a running start on living a life that didn't dwell on the past—your past or ours?"

"There's not enough money in the world that—"

"No, damn it," she interrupted, squaring off with him in a way that ruffled his earlier authority. "Give me a number, Slader. Or Wadsworth. Or whatever name you go by. Make it a sane number, if such a thing's possible for you. One where we can draw up some kind of contract, like serious people do, two copies, one for each of us to sign—do you actually have a signature of your own?—and destroy once the terms have been fulfilled."

"Utterly unenforceable, serious lady."

"So what, then? We do a pinkie swear?"

"The fact of it is—" Slader started, manifestly surprised by her demand and tough, firm, even cocky tone, staring at the menacing kingfisher tattoo on her arm, which lay bare, as she'd worn a sleeveless vest.

"Fact is what?"

"In another life, I think we might indeed have been friends," he remarked, in a very different tone of his own. "Maybe even family."

Nicole's turn to be surprised.

"This is this life," she said, refusing to waver.

"I'd like to say several million," he continued. "One for *Tamerlane*. One for burying me alive. And one just because. But I fancy your idea, Nicole, so let's do be serious people as you say, no haggling, no clumsy back-and-forthing," and with that he gave her a figure.

A million's worth of manuscripts. Work done by her and her alone, it went unsaid. Quality over quantity. No more book inscriptions, no more writers in the usual wheelhouse, which meant no Conan Doyle Sherlock Holmes, no Lake-Isle-of-Innisfree Yeats, none of H. G. Wells's men, be they invisible or on the moon. And absolutely no discussions or even the slightest hints about their agreement with Will or anybody else.

"While we're talking about sharing, I think this is yours," she said, handing him the black shoelace she'd retrieved at the grave site.

He took it, pocketed it, without saying a word.

"Let's not forget that you still need to give me those photos that supposedly prove my dad's guilty of—"

"What happened to the one I already left?" Slader inquired.

"He destroyed it," she told him. Not a lie, given she'd as yet been unable to piece the thing back together. "You need to give the rest of them to me, plus any negatives, any digital files, or all bets are off for me too."

"I'm not a digital files kind of fellow," Slader said with a smirk, glancing down at his laceless shoe on the hard-pack gravel surface of the lot.

"You know what I'm saying. I need every last bit of evidence that you claim proves Will had a hand in my uncle's death."

"I love *had a hand in* your uncle's death, given your father's the only one who came away in one piece. You do know, I'm assuming, that they never found his hands, Adam's? What kind of inhuman beast would do something like that? I've got my shortcomings and then some, but I don't have that level of crazy in me."

She stared past him, recalling Slader's savage acts against Will while he slept next to her mother in Kenmare. Her mother who happened to be pregnant with her at the time.

"But to your point," he went on, "those photos are yours. I never wanted them in the first place."

"Agreed," she said. "But I may need upward of a year to get everything ready for you, just so you know."

Slader's closed-lipped smile once again appeared genuine, if condescending.

"Listen here, love. You're the one with a roof over your head, food on your table," he said. "This," holding up the books and heirloom pen she'd given him, "will keep me going for a brief stretch. But I don't have anywhere near a year. Your birthday's in early February, if I'm not mistaken. That's the deadline, though sooner'd be better."

Considering the firm look in his bloodshot eyes and set of his bruised jaw, she said, "I'll do my best."

"Aquarius," he mumbled with a wince of sharp pain that now and then seemed to stab him out of the blue. "Unconventional, imaginative, creative. You'll do more than your best, I'm sure, Nicky."

"Let me work up a contract we can sign when I see the other photos," she said, antsy to move on. "And FYI, nobody except my family calls me Nicky."

He sucked his teeth, amused. Turning his back on her, Slader reached into his car, retrieved a book from the front seat.

"This bit of brilliance is yours, Nicole," and handed her the double-inscribed Henry James *In the Cage*.

She took the volume from him, surprised he was willing to give it back, and simply said, "You need to get some medical care, you know."

"In due course. Meantime, when Mary eloped to Paris with Percy Shelley, they somehow managed to lose a box of her earliest manuscripts. Never been found. So why don't we quote unquote find them?"

"You mean forge from scratch her juvenilia? No effing way. Impossible."

"All right. Fair enough. Then give me an important cache of undiscovered Mary Shelley letters to Percy, or her father, or, better yet, her mother, from a later period, and I'll take it under advisement."

"But she never knew her mother, as I'm sure you're well aware."

At this, Slader brightened. "Right you are. A heartbreaking and moving clutch of previously undiscovered letters written to Mary Wollstonecraft Godwin from her little girl turned adult who suffered from guilt, like anybody would whose mother died after giving birth to them. Wollstonecraft and William Godwin had made all kinds of creative plans, in vain of course, for how they were going to raise their boy—"

"Boy?"

"Mary was supposed to have been a boy, so even that dream died in childbirth. I have to think the father was disappointed in a thousand ways suddenly to have a daughter to raise by himself, even though she had the most beautiful hazel eyes. Not unlike your own."

She drew back. Despite her impulse to distrust the man— she'd later double-check him on the hazel eyes and find out he was correct—Nicole listened to Slader's intriguing idea. Maybe there was a way to do this that wouldn't haunt her for the rest of her life. Maybe it could be seen, in the right light, as a chance to paint a story with words. If she could think of the task as merely writing fiction, the whole thing might be more palatable. Yes, it could be fiction when it was in her hands, and only after she passed it to Slader would true fiction become fake fact.

"Once upon a time," she said, "my dad thought about doing an exchange of letters between Mary Shelley and her half sister Fanny. Would have been when the Shelleys were living in Bath, blissed-out lovebirds reading *Don Quixote* to each other while Fanny was alone and desperate and went to Swansea to kill herself. With laudanum, I think he told me."

"Fantastic scheme," exclaimed Slader. "World class. Why didn't he do it?"

"He didn't feel confident enough to pull it off."

Slader crossed his arms again as he leaned against the car and looked up at the sky that soon would be filled with fields of stars. "You'll forgive me if I find that hard to believe. Same guy that had the *testiculos* to forge all manner of Arthur Conan Doyle manuscripts?"

"He wasn't as well read in Mary Shelley's world as Doyle's," she explained.

"But you are, I strongly suspect."

For some reason, it occurred to her that her father didn't possess the same capacity as she—a bleak enough gift—to understand the guilt Mary Shelley harbored her whole life over her mother's childbirth death. A guilt that was redoubled when she and her beautiful poet husband, with whom Fanny was painfully in love, failed to take care of her fragile, older half sister. Despite Nicole's efforts to conceal her own deepening guilt about Slader's injuries, she nodded yes, as she more intently studied his still-fresh burns, scars, bruises, all of which must have been wildly painful.

"I'm serious about you seeing a doctor," she told Slader, shifting the subject in the hope of bringing their conversation to a close. She had never really before given thought about whether Will was incapable of guilt, and the prospect of it was upsetting.

"Look," Slader said, uncrossing his arms. "I appreciate your concern about my health. Appreciate the clothes, the dough, these gorgeous fabrications that'll make some poor rube out there very happy. But as far as doctors go, until I'm somebody else altogether, the system's off-limits. No sawbones, no insurance forms, no authorized next of kin, no nothing."

"I hope you know I'm sorry, I never meant to hit you so hard—" she began.

"Of course you did," he interrupted, his expression solemn, though his feelings toward the girl were undeniably sympathetic. Even fatherly, strange and irrational as it felt. "Please stop with the apologies. It's not a good look. Anyway, you don't need me to forgive you. I was no innocent angel that night myself. Far from it. The cold hard fact is, the person who ought to be begging for forgiveness is neither one of us."

She knew exactly what he meant. Had no response to offer him.

"And please, forget writing up a contract that would serve as evidence against us in a court of law. This is about trust. Something neither of us is used to," and without another word, Slader got in his car, backed up, and drove away into the gloaming.

My encounter with the not-quite-retired Pollock was, for all his polished manners and the festive distractions of the Mummers parade outside, a hard punch to the heart. Perspectives were suddenly shifting of their own accord inside me, a process that felt as agonizing as the growing pains that had kept me up nights with arm and leg aches when I was a girl. Pollock had revealed himself as the mysterious stranger, to borrow that old gothic trope, both at Kelder's and here in Kenmare. It had been Pollock who'd followed me, with only his daytime running lights on, when I supplied Slader with those first forgeries. Pollock had probably been in my sights, just as Will was surely in his crosshairs, more often over the years than I cared to imagine. And here I had always considered myself such a keen observer. Lame-ass hubris, I thought after we'd returned from Dingle and I had my chat in the bar lounge with my father, as a tranquil peat fire flickered on the hearth. How blind I'd been my whole life. Sharp as a marble.

Before the others were up next morning, I took a ramble
beside the River Sheen in predawn light, watching jackdaws
wing about as they chattered like lunatics in the mist. Sitting
on a rustic bench far from the lodge, I had a frank dialogue with
myself. I needed to face, once and for all—no backsliding, no
second-guessing, no wishful reconsidering—the heinous truth
that my father was a murderer. Devastatingly, Slader had not
been lying to me. Slader, whom I'd grown up believing was
some satanic madman, the unindicted perpetrator of my uncle's
death, may have been innocent of that particular brutality. His
photographs might in fact be all that Pollock would need to
arrest and charge Will. Indeed, the only reason Slader himself
resisted handing them over to the cops was to keep his own
house of cards from toppling down.

How could I be so sure? Because I had finally managed to
reassemble the print Will had torn into postage-stamp shards
when we'd encountered Slader's stick man, his scarecrow Gia-
cometti, in the woods. Some pieces were missing, left behind
in the clearing or else still crumpled in Will's pocket. Others I
may have arranged wrong. The better part of it was still there,
though, and after meeting Slader in the Quaker parking lot, I
was keen on seeing what had provoked my father to rip it up
before I could get more than a glimpse.

Once I had the whole image more or less reconstituted, I
took off my boots, climbed on top of the worktable, and photographed the photograph, straddling it from overhead like a far
less modish version of David Hemmings in Antonioni's *Blow-Up*.
Afterward, I photoshopped the jigsaw of the still image—my
world was composed of jigsaws, it seemed—digitally manipulating it the best I could to reveal the original.

Many details in the picture were tricky to interpret. A row of
trapezoidal shapes that repeated across the lower right portion
of the image—were they some kind of balustrade or series of

windows? Was it morning (guilty) or evening (innocent) light?
The male getting into a car, his three-quarter profile grainy from
having been photographed from below and afar and then resized,
did look a lot like Will. A younger Will, obviously. Thinner, skin
less wrinkled than in later years, hair darker. He looked fatigued
but also hyped up, with an expression on his face that in a lifetime
of watching my father I had never seen. One that fused wary
shock with grim emptiness. Shark eyed, I hate to admit, with his
mouth agape, as if gasping for air. Photos often freeze us mid-look,
though, I reminded myself, and make our plastic faces appear
grotesque or giddy or even psycho. This one suggested all these.

It also reeked of guilt. If Henry Slader were to give Pollock
clearer pictures than this, maybe time-stamped, maybe others
snapped after he'd scrambled up the Montauk beach cliff that
led to Uncle Adam's bungalow, shots of Will's car leaving the
scene, license plates that could yet be traced, Pollock's cold case
would turn broiler hot.

Yet I had to wonder if it was worth being Slader's pawn to
protect my uninnocent father, whether it might have been better
if I'd actually taken him out with that shovel. Questions only
a monster would ask. A woman lost as ever in her self-serving
fantasy of being on the right side of good and evil.

In times past I'd always deemed myself to be a decent person,
if quirky, imperfect but principled. Now, here, on an overcast
December morning, St. John the Apostle's Day, the sky streaked
with shades of mackerel gray, I was overcome by doubts. Guilty
of a violent assault, I was no longer an innocent even though few
would know it by just looking at me. Any casual observer would
see I was close to my family, particularly my adopted sister, who
was, of all of us, the most uncorrupted. It was Maisie, I realized,
who truly needed me—whether or not I was a monster—to follow through with what I'd been tasked by Slader. Maisie who
could least afford to lose her parents and sister to the chaos that

would befall us should I fail. More than Will or Meghan, it was Maisie who needed my protection.

How I wished Renee were here. I had nobody to blame but myself that she wasn't, as I knew she would've happily accepted an invitation to join us. She would without a doubt have been able to laser right through all this dense psychic fog around me if only I'd let her in on my troubles. I so easily pictured her standing by the Sheen, looking at me with her pure green cat's eyes, the morning light illuminating her disheveled French bob, her classic body with its Renaissance belly and small breasts often draped in the colorful silk clothes she designed herself—"True fashion is wearable art," she liked to say, echoing Emilio Pucci or Leonard Paris, the fashion artists she most admired. Renee with whom I supposed I was as close to being in love as my diffidence, or whatever it was, would allow.

Fact was, I had avoided her ever since I thought I'd killed Slader with that shovel down in the woods. The last thing Renee needed was for me to drag her into my worst nightmare. I knew she'd be furious with me for not sharing such a mind-blowing act as that, especially in light of my drunken confession earlier that fall about participating in the *Tamerlane* fake, which she considered an admirable shenanigan, a trippy anti-capitalist countercultural performance art piece. If anybody could have helped put my attack on Slader into perspective, it would have been Renee Severn, whose surname always seemed preposterous to me, as my friend was the least severe person I'd ever known.

So yes, I now began to doubt, even chide myself about my decision to keep Renee in the dark. She would have opinions about Slader, Atticus, Pollock, Adam, my father. The whole lot. We were birds of a feather, as she liked to say. She even had a quetzal tattooed on her upper arm on the same day and by the same ink artist who'd done my kingfisher several years earlier.

With that thought I began to cry. Just gave myself over to the grief of avowal. Of acknowledgment, admission. Hadn't I known all along? Hadn't Will, in his way, already confessed? I had never let myself give in to the raw, brutal truth of what he had done—one of the reasons I'd continued to keep this sick family skeleton away from Renee. Nor did I have any insight into why he would have committed such an atrocity. I rubbed my eyes and knew I still loved him, would always love my father. But I didn't understand the man anymore. All these years at his side, and I never knew who was sitting next to me, teaching me to draw when I was just a grasshopper of a girl, helping me learn about the arts, literature, life itself.

That being said, I was sure Will would never abandon me if I myself had done some grievous wrong beyond my temporary dabbling as a forger. He'd already proven as much, I remembered, having made me promise to let him take the blame and consequences if we were caught. So, while I was no St. John, I was honor bound to protect him, move ahead with fulfilling my side of the deal with Slader. The sooner the better. And if Pollock was able to carve out a path on his own to prove Will's guilt, or Slader's, then it wasn't within my power to stop him. It was an existential decision that might trouble me for the rest of my years, but I made that pact with myself as day overtook dawn and the jackdaws took wing when I meandered back to the lodge, promising myself that I would call Renee later that same day to to propose that she join me in London.

My parents and sister were downstairs in the grand breakfast room, which teemed with guests. I ordered coffee and grapefruit juice, then joined Maisie at the buffet, set out with an extravagant array of fresh bread and black pudding, smoked salmon and trout with sliced Meyer lemons, boxty and grilled tomatoes and eggs in fancy rows of silver roll-top serving dishes. Coppery sunlight broke through the last of the morning brume over the river below and poured in through the long bank of windows.

"Where you been?" Maisie asked, skewering some bacon onto her plate. "Out with lanterns?"

Emily Dickinson, one of her favorite riffs, and in this case spot-on.

"As a matter of fact," I replied.

"Did you find yourself?"

"You know, sometimes you're too astute for a child your age," I deadpanned. "Makes me wonder if they got your birth date wrong."

"Don't call me that."

"What?"

"A child my age," she grumbled, with a theatrical pout.

"My apologies, Emily Masily," I teased, prompting her to laugh.

"You should take more marmalade for your toast, skinny person," she said, not altogether wrong, as I had lost some weight along with my appetite over the past months.

We joined our parents at their table, but I could tell she knew I was distracted and she couldn't understand why. From the very beginnings of our sisterhood—up until Slader came crashing into our lives—we had leveled with each other, told each other the straight dope. It had proven a sound approach, one that allowed Maisie to share private griefs and worries with the person closest to her in age and experience in her adoptive family.

I had intended to tell everyone at breakfast that I wasn't going to fly back to the States with them but head to London instead, where I'd hook up with Renee—no longer a lie like the one I'd told after the break-in upstate but, I hoped, the truth. We planned to hit the major Gustav Klimt and Egon Schiele retrospectives at the Royal Academy and the National Gallery's new Impressionist exhibition. Since we'd both travel on her frequent-flier miles—we often bartered, shared, gifted—it wouldn't be an impossibly expensive adventure. Given how hilariously cool, not to mention discreet, she'd been about my involvement in the Poe business, I'd resolved to take her into my confidence again. Get some much-needed moral, or at least amoral, support.

But instead of announcing my plan to the whole family at once, I decided to tell Maisie first, though I'd omit my need to go there to fabricate the Shelley forgery. This way we'd share a bonding secret before I let the others know. No matter what happened during my counterfeiting weeks ahead, I wanted Maisie and me to remain tight because, at the end of the day, she was the soul in my family I trusted most. Besides, wasn't it better not to share this with Will and Meg until the last possible moment? The less time they had to try to talk me out of sticking around in Europe—or, worse, insist on accompanying me to England—the better.

Later that morning, we drove into Kenmare village. While our parents wanted to say goodbye to their friends from when they lived here, I proposed to sketch The Shrubberies, a nearby Bronze Age stone circle after which our small press, Stone Circle Editions, had been named, with an eye toward possible other logos for our imprint. Maze came along with me and raced around the boulders that were stuck in the ground like Finn McCool the Giant's teeth. While we were there, ringed by fluffy fir trees, I told her a version of my plans.

Not unexpectedly, she wanted to come along.

"One day, we'll travel the world together, how's that? Right now, this is something I need to do on my own."

"That'll be awesomesauce," she said, to my relief, but then added, "Are you going to tell me what you're really going there for?"

"You're a little scary freaky, Maze," was all I could say.

"Meeting a lovey-dove I don't know?"

"A nosy scary freaker at that," I said. "I'm working on a project I can't talk about."

"Not even with me?"

"I'll tell you sometime down the line. Promise."

"Cross your heart," she said, then pointed at something behind me and asked "What's this?" before abruptly moving on.

As we walked to the burial boulder set atop several large stones at the center of the circle, I thought about what I'd withheld from Maisie. Primarily my mounting worry that several months had passed since I'd made my agreement with Slader, and I still owed him the sheaf of Mary Shelley letters and fragments. He and I had met two more times after our original rendezvous in the Quakers' parking lot—once, of all places, in a diner on Myrtle Avenue in Queens; once, later, in Hudson around Thanksgiving because he needed more money. In Queens, to my confusion and surprise, he returned the Conan Doyle fountain pen, saying it was rightfully mine and he couldn't bring himself to sell it. Grateful as I was he'd twice seen fit to return sentimental possessions, I was still obliged to extract more books from the studio library, embellish them, and hand them over. Going forward, I chose only thin volumes, ones that wouldn't leave telltale spaces on the shelves that Will might easily notice.

"I'll grant you, Paul Bowles's *Two Poems* is a rare book, rarely signed," Slader had said during that third meeting in upstate New York. "And a nice unfaded copy of *Before the Flowers of Friendship Faded Friendship Faded* inscribed by Stein to Bowles is a glorious thing."

"I wasn't sure if another copy she inscribed to Bowles was already out there," I'd admitted, ignoring his kudos, "but I couldn't find anything online."

"If another one exists, *that* one's the fake," said Slader with a straight face. "Or else the Sibyl of Montparnasse inscribed it to Bowles more than once by mistake. They were friends and collaborators, so, not impossible. But my problem is that at the molasses rate you're going, my dear Nicole, even with ten-, twenty-thousand-dollar books, it'll be years to square things. I'm impressed by your range—Stein's no breeze to replicate—but not your choices. I thought we settled on Shelley."

What could I say? He was well within his rights to be concerned, as I hadn't shown him a single leaf in Mary Shelley's holograph, and that was back in late October. I told him I was working on it, and I was, sort of—reading and rereading Mary's writings, and plotting an overall structure for the faux sheaf of letters. But now my birthday, and my deadline, were just over the horizon. I had to get on it, already. Done right, I'd come to believe, and with enough material to make it a major trove, I knew it was within reach. Time had come for due diligence and to extricate myself.

We paid a last visit to O'Donnabhain's before eating a farewell dinner at Mulcahy's on Main Street. I kept expecting to spot Pollock in a corner of the pub or hidden in shadows on the sidewalk or even at the restaurant, but he was nowhere to be seen. When Will received a text on his seldom-used cell phone and told Meghan to go ahead and drive us back to the lodge, explaining he needed to meet one last contact here and would take a taxi back to Sheen Falls afterward, I should've guessed what might be afoot.

But I didn't. Fooled by his calm demeanor, I thought nothing of his impromptu after-dinner appointment when the three of us returned to the lodge. Maisie and I got into our beds, read for a while—she, N. K. Jemisin; me, Mary Shelley's journals—then turned off the lights. My last reflections before falling asleep were about how prosaic, even dullish, were most of Mary's accounts of travels through France and Italy, how minor a writer she might have seemed to posterity if these diary pages were all we had to judge her by, rather than *The Last Man* or *Valperga* or, of course, *Frankenstein*.

Deep in the night, I half heard the door to our bedroom open and felt someone touch my shoulder and whisper, in Will's voice, "We need to talk. Meet me in that antler room," then leave, quiet as our feral cat, Ripley, back home upstate. Ripley, who was able to appear like a djinn and evanesce like a ghost.

My heart raced as I slipped out of the sheets and, careful not to disturb Maisie, pulled on some clothes.

The look on my father's face when I caught up with him in what was meant to be a sportsmen's hunting room was stern and ashen. He stood surrounded by leather club chairs and lamps with stag lampstands on mahogany side tables. A trophy Atlantic salmon was mounted over one mantelpiece and a badger pelt was framed over the fireplace opposite. Sika buck deer heads lined the dark green lacquered walls, making this chamber of taxidermied beasts—an eagle-owl on a side table near the windows was poised to take flight—unnerving, at the very least.

More so, however, was my father's glare. His face reminded me of a death mask I'd seen in a late-night Brooklyn bar that doubled as a wax museum, a weird mixologist's mecca atop City Point center that has on display the original Castan's Panopticum collection of anatomical wax faces and figures from nineteenth-century Berlin. But for a twitch in his jaw, my father looked as half alive, half dead as any of their paraffin masks.

His first words were "I'm going to ask you to tell me the truth," spoken in a low voice even though no one was about. The hotel staff had all vanished for the night. Even the front desk in the elegant lobby was unattended.

"I always try to," I said.

"You always try to. Then, Nicole, tell me what the hell is going on."

"What do you mean?" I asked.

"You talked with Pollock."

"But I already told you I did. He pulled me aside in Dingle as you saw for yourself. And you said you didn't remember him."

"Right, but what you didn't tell me was that you spoke with Pollock about Henry Slader."

I felt flummoxed, defensive. Crossed my arms, uncrossed them as I said, "That's not really true," wondering how he could've known this. Wondering at the same time if he was using the old roundabout maneuver of throwing out an idea to prompt a telling response.

Abruptly, without a word, my father walked away from me between burgundy morocco ottomans and deep-cushioned chairs. I could smell the whiskey on his breath and saw he was unsteady on his feet. Half a dozen paces toward the middle of the maybe-once-grand parlor, he turned and asked, exasperated, "Then what is really true?"

The irony of a master forger asking that question was not lost on me.

"I would never have brought Slader up of my own accord. You ought to know that. Pollock was the one with questions about him, and had even been stalking me upstate, if you want to know."

"Stalking you? Slader, you mean?"

"Pollock."

"And so Pollock saw you meeting with Slader?"

Now I grasped why I'd been summoned to this insane tête-à-tête. Having kept my business with Slader a secret, in itself a form of not telling the truth, I knew I was at a crossroads. Trying to save Will from exposure to punishment for what he'd done years ago meant being dishonest with him now? We were playing a variation of the prisoner's dilemma game.

"He saw nothing of the kind," I equivocated.

Will put his hands in his pockets, cocked his head. "Your stories diverge, Nicky."

"So do yours," I said. "Why should you believe some has-been detective over me?"

"Sometimes enemies have an easier time telling you the truth than the people you're closest with."

"Is that why he as much as told me he thinks you killed Uncle Adam?"

I watched Will's face darken and a muscle in his jaw twitch. To say he looked furious would be a vast understatement.

"This I highly doubt," he half whispered.

Having viscerally made my decision without giving the matter much if any thought, I pushed ahead and built on my mistruth. "Look, I don't know what Pollock's trying to do. Pull a divide-and-conquer with us, get us to answer questions better left unanswered. Either way, I know you must realize he's still trying to solve Mom's brother's murder."

"The murder Slader did," he tried, having forgotten he'd all but confessed the crime to me not so many months ago. He seemed nothing like himself tonight.

"If you say so" was all I could come up with.

"Say so I do. Say so Pollock will too once he knows all the facts."

Gently as I could, I asked, "You all right, Will?"

"No, yes. I'm all right. Just trying to understand what Slader and you are up to here. This trip was meant to be a respite from last summer, and so it was for the first days. Now it's like there are sharp teeth nibbling at the edges of my sanity."

My heart went out to him, I couldn't help myself. Why he left Pollock off his list of those he was trying to understand was curious. But rather than coming up with some fuzzy response to his undisguised cry for help, I strode over to the man, wrapped my arms around him—an unusual gesture, as I wasn't much of a hugger—and held my father close. I half expected him to push me away, given how weird he'd been acting, but he barely moved. I felt his palms patting me on the back, either from impatience or embarrassment, or as if mollifying a needy dog he'd rather not tend to. Sensing this embrace wasn't what he needed then, or wanted, I pulled away.

"Dad," I said. "How much trouble are we in?"

He sat in the nearest club chair and I lowered myself onto a settee across from him. We both noticed my use of the word *we*.

"Are you giving money to Slader?"

"No," I hedged.

"I hope that's the truth, because I'm sure he still wants money from the Poe sale and I know he'll be back looking for more from me, from us, and the best, only way to get him out of our lives is to ignore him. You give the man any hope and he'll be after you until the end of days looking for more. He's an endless maw. Like Saturn in that Goya painting. You have to promise me you'll give him no money."

"What money would I have to give him anyway?"

A wave of uneasy relief passed over me. Of course, I was splitting hairs, leaning on the little fibs of nuanced phrasing. But how many fibs, little to large, had Will been living with over the arc of my whole life in order to remain a free man? Borrowed time, like a cup of borrowed sugar, must eventually be paid back.

"Let me ask you a question," I ventured. "And this is just theoretical."

"I'm not fond of theoreticals, as you know."

Doesn't a forger's very being depend on the theoretical trumping the genuine? "Hear me out," I said. "What if I could make Slader and the rest just go away?"

His face relaxed for the first time since we'd begun our discussion. "If you could do that without murdering anybody, I'd say you were a miracle worker."

The ease with which he used the words *murdering anybody* was breathtaking.

"No more murders," I said, expecting him to push back, which he didn't. "I can't promise that Pollock won't keep pursuing his case, to be honest. But Slader's another story."

"So the truth comes out," he said, with an *aha* look on his face. "What's your deal with him? Does it have anything, just for instance, to do with some books missing from my shelves? Or with all this reading you've been doing about Mary Shelley?"

"Not only shouldn't I tell you, but I won't."

"Nicole, I'm your father. You absolutely can. What's mine is yours, but I need to understand what's going on. I've known this man way longer than you have."

No argument there. Still and all, I told him with as much authority and finality in my voice as I could gather, "But like I said, I won't."

The look in his eyes was easy to interpret. Slader would delude me. He would use and betray me. No matter what I thought or hoped to the contrary, before all was said and done, Slader would triumph over me. Nothing, Will plainly believed, would deter him. And if I refused to listen to reason, what happened next would be my fault and mine alone.

B efore Slader could convert Nicole's enviably persuasive forgeries of Joyce and Poe into legal tender, he needed to see how the auction turned out. If the *Tamerlane* went bust, any money Will owed him would go to less than zero fast and his leverage over Nicole would be compromised. Under such circumstances, he might as well exit from her life, everybody's lives. Cash out the books in hand, move to Belize, sleep on a beach there, work in a fish shack, swim with sea turtles as endangered as himself.

Fantasies aside, Friday the fifth of October was upon him. The auction date honored, in a mildly mercenary way, the anniversary of Poe's death, which wasn't, in any case, until that Sunday. Slader's prudent pessimism aside, *Tamerlane* was expected to break all previous records, making it the most valuable book in American literature, the Third Imperial Fabergé egg of American letters. Its plain-Jane *Mona Lisa*.

The auction room teemed with book people. Some had already staked out a seat in the array of chairs that faced the auctioneer's maple podium while others milled about before the sale began. Half a dozen representatives sat at tables on either side of the podium to handle remote bids, talking among themselves, studying their laptops, speaking to distant bidders on landline phones. Potential buyers who hadn't previewed the sale pressed around glass display cases that housed a miscellany of other lots. Prominent at the center of one case nearest the podium was the great treasure itself, the unpretentious pamphlet that would soon go under the hammer for the first time in almost a generation.

He knew better. Knew he shouldn't be anywhere near this place. But Slader himself loitered along a back wall, thumbing through the auction catalog, blending in with other bibliophiles in a new navy blazer, a white button-down dress shirt, and chinos. His hint of a goatee, dark gray herringbone newsboy cap, and round-rimmed glasses from a vintage store completed the new look.

Withal, a plausible disguise. Though he hadn't registered to bid and didn't speak with others, his manner when studying the Poe lots in the vitrine nearest him might have suggested he knew his way around rare books, had anyone noticed, which, as he'd hoped, nobody had. Cap worn indoors notwithstanding, Slader drew no attention to himself.

So why was he here? Wasn't there a risk he'd be caught on one of the security cams in this room, this building, the nearby streets and avenues? He was aware you couldn't walk from Harlem to the Battery without being caught on some video or another during the entire journey. And what if a rare-book dealer he had worked with in the past noticed him and asked what was with the Brooks Brothers getup? How had he come by the injuries he'd tried to hide with makeup, like a bad color match on a dust jacket repair?

He should have stayed way far away. But Slader had to see the full spectacle of his masterpiece of theft-forgery come to fruition. Sure, Atticus had come up with the notion to swap copies with his Boston collector—though the catalog ascribed provenance to an upstate book collector, now deceased, he'd never heard of, in whose library the *Tamerlane* was discovered by chance. And sure, Nicole and her father had done some printing and ink work. But it was he himself who had, like the conductor of a symphony orchestra, brought all the players together to this historic crescendo. This was, in fact, his *Tamerlane*. His triumph to observe. Even if unfair circumstances forced him to view the proceedings as a ghost in the machine of his own making, it was because of him that all these people had made their pilgrimage to this crowded room.

Will was working one of the phone lines when the proceedings got underway. For his part, Slader tucked into a seat in the next-to-last row, where he was able to get a good bead on his preoccupied accomplice, while biding his time as lot after lot went for prices well over the high estimate. He, Slader, did find it curious that the phone bidder Will represented was successful in nailing down half a dozen higher-priced lots. Made him wonder just who was on the other end of the line. Could it have been Atticus—blessedly absent here—buying for a client with deep pockets? Someone unknown to Slader, who fancied he knew all of Atticus's collectors? Dubai mogul, expat businessman in Singapore, the Library of Congress?

"Next up, lot forty."

The auctioneer, an aristocratic yet hip presence in his vivid three-piece suit, spoke in a deep, assured voice. Given his calm, even understated, delivery, it was clear he believed the lot would sell itself and his responsibility was mostly to stay out of its way.

"An historic lot indeed, and rare beyond hyperbole. Here we have the only recorded signed copy of Edgar Allan Poe's first book, *Tamerlane and Other Poems*, 'by a Bostonian' and published by Calvin F. S. Thomas, Printer, in 1827. Of the twelve

other extant copies, none of which Poe necessarily ever laid
eyes on, let alone autographed, this is one of three remaining
in private hands. It's being sold with a contemporary letter—"
and after finishing his summary said, "Considerable interest here.
We can begin with sixty, eighty, we're going to start this off at
ninety thousand. Ninety looking for a hundred. One hundred,
hundred ten against you. One hundred twenty, one thirty online
now," and as Slader watched the chin chucks and subtle nods,
raised hands and paddles, the range of tics bidders used in the
curious choreography that distinguishes an auction room, his
lot reached half a million within minutes.

Slader's attention shifted to Will once the lot achieved its
next milestone. The look on his face when *Tamerlane* achieved
a million was hard to read. Cautious bidding was scorched out
of the action which proceeded now in hundred-thousand-dollar
increments. Whoever Will's buyer was, so active before, had gone
quiet, although he still had them on the line. Whereas before
he'd been focused on making notes during the sale and glancing
up only at the auctioneer to confirm bids, Will now scanned the
room, looking relieved and distressed, satisfied and nervous, here
and far away. Whatever he was feeling, Slader mused, nobody
would have a clue he had a personal stake in the lot.

Longer stretches of deliberative time passed between bids
as the numbers climbed. The seasoned auctioneer adjusted the
tempo, reminding his room that this might be the only chance
to own the book in their lifetimes. Once the competition was
down to three and then two contenders on the phones, bidding
stood at one million six hundred thousand.

Then, to everyone's surprise—certainly Slader's—the client
working with Will rejoined the auction.

"Bid" was all he said, voice steady and clear as he nodded
toward the podium.

The auctioneer called out the new figure. "One million seven
hundred thousand on the phone. Looking for one million eight."

"Eight," his colleague countered, after whispering to confirm her customer's intent.

"Nine," said Will, without pausing.

How dearly Slader wanted to fulfill his fantasy of rising to his feet and shouting, *The book is stolen and the autograph is a fake. I know because I stole it myself from Mrs. Abigail Fletcher of Newton, Mass., and the copy I swapped it for in her library is a forgery made by that man right there.* Instead, he clutched the seat of his chair and held his tongue. When the lot was finally hammered down in excess of two million—not to Will's bidder—the room broke into applause. Slader, who may or may not have caught Will's eye before withdrawing, vaulted down the stairs rather than wait for an elevator. Nor did Will come racing after him, but stayed behind while the rest of the lots went off, rather anticlimactically, until the sale came to a close.

Back on the noisy street outside, Slader stepped slowly at first, head down, then at a brisk pace toward Grand Central, where he caught a Metro-North train up along the Hudson, past Dobbs Ferry and Croton-Harmon to Poughkeepsie. Leaning his head against the window, he stared at the broad gray river and occasional trackside stretches of foliage that flew past, and eventually nodded off. He was jolted awake when the train pulled into its last, northernmost stop.

Uneasy about leaving his car in the lot there, he had parked it on a residential street up the hill within walking distance. His thoughts were, as the lyric went, a crossfire hurricane. He felt gratified that once again he'd hoaxed the experts and defrauded some wealthy elite, which aside from illicit profiteering, in itself a thrill, was half the point of making forgeries. Yet he was torn over whether the look in Will's eyes was one of fear or disgust or menace, and whether it even mattered given the man was essentially dead to him. Besides, during his ride along the river he had decided Will was gaslighting the room with his late-entry bids, a risky gambit indeed, but one that had succeeded.

At the same time, despondency settled over Slader as he looked for and found his car. Like postcoital tristesse or postpartum depression. The accomplishment was made, he had cleared the highest possible hurdle in what was easily the greatest caper of his career, and now his involvement was over. Much to be celebrated, yet no one to celebrate with. The breeze that rose up from the Hudson behind him rattled stubborn leaves in the half-naked trees, presaging winter. He knew he should feel more than this. Pride, disdain, triumph. But it was like willing himself to fly, or for that matter, walk across the river. Much as he would have loved to experience any of these emotions, from the good to the bad, all he was able to summon was a terrible emptiness.

If it's a short walk from the hallelujah to the hoot, as Nabokov said, it's a long walk from the hoot to the hallelujah. For Slader, however, there were neither hallelujahs nor hoots. His Pyrrhic victory hadn't been so much as heralded with a tin trumpet and broken drum. He got into his car and drove back toward Millbrook, where he'd rented a rustic Airbnb under his assumed name.

For all his erstwhile swagger and confidence, Slader descended that evening into a loneliness that bordered on despair. He thought about calling Nicole, thought about reaching out to Atticus, but instead phoned a dealer in the Berkshires he'd worked with in the past to see if he could sell a couple of books Nicole had enhanced.

On hearing Slader was in the area and what he had to offer, the bookseller, whose South Egremont shop was closed on Saturdays, said he would love to make an exception. "Be good to see you after far too long," he said, likely recalling a cache of scarce *Narnia* titles he'd bought from Slader some years ago, each signed by C. S. Lewis, that he'd sold for a healthy markup to a private collector.

"Just a heads-up," said Slader, who would be going to this appointment as himself, having realized too late that he couldn't do otherwise, "I was in a car accident recently—"

"Sorry to hear it."

"—so a little banged up, as you'll see. Main reason I'm willing to sell these beauties, which I never intended to part with."

"Insurance these days."

"Thieves and scam artists, all of them," Slader agreed, grateful his unwitting fence invented the rest of his story for him.

The low mountains were wet from a morning of steady drizzle. Slader was cautious driving on the leaf-slick roads lest his white lie—a fabrication meant to cloak another fabrication—come true. Because he knew that Nicole was obliged to give him more of what he asked for, he decided not to press for a stratospheric price on his wares. Finding the right number, where your buyers felt they were getting one over on you, though not so much as to provoke pity or a sense they were thoroughly screwing you, while at the same time making a nice profit over your cost—in this case, zero—was a skill Slader had long since mastered.

If leery of the Poe association, Slader's fellow bookman was willing to pay far more for the signed *Dubliners* than expected—he had a customer for it and anticipated a quick sale—so they each felt well satisfied with the transaction.

Asked if he'd like to go for lunch at a nearby bistro, Slader politely begged off, saying he had to get back to Connecticut in time for dinner with friends that evening. "Friends of my wife, an annual get-together in her memory," he lied.

"I hadn't known she passed," the man told him. "Very sorry."

"Well, it's been several years now," Slader lamented. "I'm glad we had mutual friends who're still willing to get together to reminisce over old times." He placed his hand on the disputed

copy of *The Conchologist's First Book*, which lay on the table
between them, and said, "Did you hear what happened with
the *Tamerlane* sale yesterday?"

The dealer nodded, deep in thought as he glanced at the
drifting mists out the French windows of his shop. "A tick over
two mil, all in."

"Phenomenal, whoa," said Slader, feigning restraint and
excitement at the same time. "That bodes very well for my
Conchologist, I have to think, no matter whether this Virginia
was Poe's missus, mistress, or somebody else. We both know the
Poe market's always been strong. It'll definitely get a bump out
of the sale. How did the rest of the Poe sell?"

Ignoring or perhaps not having heard the question, the dealer
said, "I'll confess I'm hesitating on it because, in truth, the association seems just too good to be true. What was the provenance
on this?"

While Slader spun an imaginary chronicle of how he came
upon his copy, its flights of fancy camouflaged by the confidence
and expertise of a gifted prevaricator, his colleague picked up the
volume once more, admired its hand-colored plates, its overall
condition, and scrutinized the inscription with a magnifying glass.

"How much were you thinking on this again?"

"Actually, hearing about that *Tamerlane*, I'm not so sure I
want to part with it now."

"Oh, come on. You brought it here to sell, and for a good
reason."

His memory jogged about his insurance problems, Slader
said, "Well, can't argue that point. I was looking for seventy-five,
figuring you could more than double up at least."

"Fifty," the dealer said, setting it back on the table cluttered
with other books, all of which were dross by comparison. "Fifty.
No questions asked. Not returnable."

"You can ask any questions you like. But at fifty, I'm inclined
to keep it."

"Let's meet in the middle. Sixty-two fifty."

Slader settled a mildly aggrieved look on his face. "Sixty-five cash and it's yours."

Because Slader remembered the old-school days when book scouts carried around tens of thousands hidden in a hollowed-out smuggler's Bible or, like one guy he knew did, tucked inside his cowboy boots, he wasn't particularly surprised when the dealer excused himself, left the room briefly, and returned with the money in hundreds. Even though it was an all-cash deal, Slader, comporting himself as professional to a fault, insisted on providing his contact information in the unlikely event any issues cropped up in the future regarding either volume. He was between residences, he averred, so gave his colleague both an old address in Hamden, Connecticut, along with his new one in Old Saybrook, neither of which towns had Henry Slader ever set foot in or intended so much as to visit.

"My condolences again for the loss of your wife," the man said, shaking hands.

"Good of you."

"And thanks for thinking of me with these books, truly. I'm always interested in buying material of this quality."

Slader assured him that he'd bear it in mind for the future, knowing this was the last time he would ever hustle or even lay eyes on the guy. Why take the risk when there were so many other marks out there whose natural greed made them eager to be scammed? The forgeries were clean, even if the Poe provenance was pure Alice-in-Wonderland. Who was to say that the Egremont dealer wouldn't turn right around and ape the same story to a collector, using, as Slader himself had, the *Tamerlane* auction result as encouragement?

Like a predator after a successful kill, Slader returned to his lair where he would rest, out of sight of other, more lethal predators. His earlier bluesy loneliness behind him, he would lie low for a while, stay away from Connecticut and its false addresses, be in touch with his new partner, Nicole, as needed, step aside from the busybody world. He would allow one day to bleed and blister into the next while he recuperated in earnest from his wounds. Maybe he'd even get himself in to see a physician, now that he could afford one.

S trange to walk the long exhausted corridors of Heathrow again at the start of the new year. My last visit to London, I was a naive art lover, a green pilgrim come to England for the sole purpose of standing before the originals of paintings and antiquities I'd only ever seen in books. The National Gallery, Tate Modern, British Museum were cathedrals, and I was a kind of aspirant—though wearing Jacks, not Mary Janes—ready for my first communion. Now with my innocence long since lost, I entered the country with a very different purpose in mind. Instead of cherishing its heritage, I proposed to forge a not unimportant part of it, reshape it to my own fancy.

Once I'd checked into a modest hotel near the Thames in Pimlico, I found my way to Chester Square, where, in a classic white four-story townhouse on the northwest side, Mary Shelley had spent much of the last five years of her life. Here I lingered, read the blue plaque that had been installed above the entrance in recent years, strolled around the grand square with its uniform white facades and black front doors, studying the architecture that observant Mary knew well even during her declining years before she died of a brain tumor. The sky was low and dirty white, just as it might have been on the February day of her death, and the air was damp. I knew I was reaching for impressionistic straws, but still summoned some feelings from the stones beneath my feet and facades that surrounded me. I made no sketches. Took no notes. All I wanted was to be near what she'd once been near, to view what vestiges remained of what she viewed.

By the time I got to the cemetery that interested me most—even more than Mary's own burial site in St. Peter's Churchyard in Bournemouth—small flecks of snow had begun to wander across the London skies. They wafted sideways and flurried upward as if unwilling to meet the ground where they would instantly melt. These gravestones in the churchyard of St. Pancras, colder than the grasses or trees that surrounded them, did accommodate the snow, however, forming white skeins on their granite pates. Fog caught the bright red and silver flickering lights of the traffic and commuter trains that ran nearby. And yet, even hedged in by these noisy machines, the cemetery was charged with a kind of magical grace. The timeless ignored the temporary.

It took me a while to find the precise spot where Mary Wollstonecraft Godwin had been interred in 1797. I knew that her and her husband's remains had later been exhumed and reburied in Bournemouth, where, separated in life, mother, father, and daughter were finally reunited in death. When I did locate Mary Godwin's original grave site, I was overwhelmed by the vision of Mary Shelley, kind and decent Mary, visiting her mother in every season. During the close heat of green summer, when she would have spread out a blanket to sit on, maybe more than once in her lover Percy's arms. In autumn, when the leaves of the forebears of these very trees would come sailing down and land on a notebook in which she was drafting a poem. Under an umbrella as a spring shower passed through, awakening the croci and daffodils.

Was it true that she'd first declared her love for Shelley where I now knelt? True she had lost her virginity to him on her mother's grave? Yes, please, I thought. Even if we might never know for sure, I'd make it so in my imaginary letters—

Which broke my sentimental, indulgent reverie. The reason I was here had less to do with eroticism or poetry or romantic fantasies than objective illicit business realities. Aside from the hours I looked forward to spending with Renee, my presence here was that of a skilled drudge. A gainfully shamefully employed laborer. I needed to remember that.

After a quiet meal at an Indian place near my hotel, I stayed up late reading Mary's published letters, absorbing her prose rhythms, her locution, her favored turns of phrase. Up early the next morning, I took the tube to the British Library to view an original manuscript of hers under glass in its permanent display. South Kensington's Fulham Road was next, where a lively-eyed, shaven-headed bookseller in an elegant, unpretentious steel-blue suit, whose family had been in the rare-book trade for half a century, took me at my word when I told him I might be in the market for an original letter. One might have thought, given my youth and a bit outré appearance, that I would be shown to the door. But collectors these days, as Will had told me, weren't all cut from the old mold of tweedy white males with a taste for cigar bars, cognac, and incunabula. Odd fashion and grooming—mine to a fault—implied wealth as much as it did pennilessness anymore. I was given the benefit of the doubt because, well, why not? I was serious and had come to his bookshop with very specific wants.

It was all I could do not to faint when he showed me to a table in an inner-sanctum second-floor office that looked out on an old walled Jewish cemetery across the way. That being said, I maintained the facade of professional curiosity and calm when I was allowed to hold in my hands several original letters Mary had written to friends. He also had in stock first editions by both Shelleys, which one of his colleagues, a tall young man with shoulder-length silken brown hair who looked not unlike Percy Shelley himself, fetched down from a glass-fronted bookcase. Both men, it occurred to me as I held one of the handwritten letters up to the light to study its paper—wove, no watermark—might have stepped out of an engraved illustration in a nineteenth-century novel that Mary herself could have read. More Austen gents, however, than Dickensian barristers.

They allowed me to take photos with my phone, provided sophisticated descriptions of their cache of materials, offered me terms if I decided to buy any of the letters, and when I left their treasure-trove shop I couldn't help but feel euphoric at having touched paper that Mary herself once handled. At the same time, I knew that the booksellers would have considered me pure poison if they'd discerned my real purpose in visiting Fulham Road. Maybe, I mused, when this nightmare was over I could sell my paintings and Conan Doyle pen—anything but what was left of my soul—and return to acquire what unsold Shelley letters they might still have, or others new to stock, and donate them anonymously to the British Library as a small act of repentance. Yes, I know. Silly me. But, still.

Next I made my way to the London Fields Overground in the East End to visit Atlantis, an art-supply monolith that carried my much-preferred Kremer Pigments, used both in historical restoration work and by upstart purist painters like myself. With the dark-brown-black hue of Mary's ink fresh in mind, I picked up a medley of bone, mineral, and plant blacks—Mars, ivory, vine—along with some burnt umber from Cyprus and Italian raw sienna. I also bought the basics for making iron gall ink from scratch. Oak gallnuts for their tannin. Ferrous sulfate, which turns the gallic acid from brown to black. And gum arabic, whose resin binds the solution and helps with the flow of ink on the nib. If when mixing up my ink I found that my palette needed different pigments, I knew where to get them, though the selection at Atlantis wasn't as exhaustive as at my local Kremer shop in Manhattan.

What I now had in hand would do, though. It would work.

Back at the hotel, I stashed my haul in the closet, grabbed my Rhodia notebook, and returned to the same Indian restaurant as the night before, where I sat at the same corner table beneath the same über-kitschy Vishnu painted on faded cream velvet the color of *ras malai*. I'm not so superstitious that I felt obliged to order the tandoori chicken again, but I knew I was going to need a consistency of focus if I was going to pull off this gambit, so I did anyway.

Nothing is quite like the solitude of dining by oneself in a mostly empty restaurant in a foreign country where you know no one and nobody knows you. As soft sitar music droned, I began making notes about themes Mary would expound upon in her letters to her mother. Aloneness was certainly at the top of the list. But also her desire to be worthy of the sacrifice her mother'd made when giving her life. To have Mary confess she'd made love with Percy on the grass above her mother's decomposed body, the imaginary missives would have to date to summer 1814. And for her to describe that evening in a villa on Lake Geneva when Lord Byron made his challenge to the assembled writers to compose a ghost story, she'd need to have scribed some of her letters post-*Frankenstein*. Maybe the unsent letters could come to an abrupt halt on the day Shelley died, in midsummer of 1822. The day poetry itself died, Mary believed.

Those eight years seemed like a good chronological arc. Intermittent and written only when matters of grave or tender or memorable importance broke across young Mary's life. Which of course meant mixing up slightly different shades and densities of iron gall ink for various entries, which had the benefit of creating a more visually dynamic document, one that would

more easily beguile and deceive whoever might eventually study
it under a reading lamp or, more forensically, an ultraviolet light.

I ordered another glass of malbec, and when my waiter
brought it, he asked if there was a problem with the tandoori.
Seems I hadn't touched the dish.

"No, no—it's delicious," I said, dutifully cutting a slice and
eating.

He left and I took another bite, because it was indeed delicious, just not what interested me at that moment.

As I swiped through the photos I'd taken of Mary's letters
at the antiquarian bookshop, pinching out the images to get a
closer look at the variations of thickness in her downstrokes and
initial letters, comparing minute permutations in her approaches
to the letters *a, e, t, s*, as well as how she dotted her *i*'s, I felt a
mix of guilt and gratitude toward the booksellers who allowed
me such access to their holdings. Why, I wondered, hadn't Will
or Slader or, for that matter, Atticus, chosen a path on a similar
higher road? Was it that much harder to make a living on the
up-and-up? Will was trying to, of course, though his past had
him in its clutches. Atticus must once have been idealistic, an
honest broker before greed or some other flaw seduced him
into dealing literary counterfeits. And what of Slader? Most
people who loved books enough to make them their lives and
livelihoods were ethical actors.

Taking a deep drink of the wine, I turned my thoughts to an
idea that I'd been mulling during the weeks before coming to
Ireland and now England. It was an idea that would make my
forgery project far more difficult but profoundly more satisfying. While it wouldn't free me from complicity with Slader and
Will, it would be a small gesture toward contrition. An act of
dishonor among thieves.

I would forge as authentic a suite of Mary Shelley letters
as possible, but at the same time encrypt a message in them
that would, when read by the right decoder, prove beyond a

doubt that they weren't the real deal. Somebody I might never meet, someone deep in the future maybe, would read past the pareidolia of Maryness to discover another author lurking right there in the cursive. Done properly, it would be as if the man in the moon suddenly started talking. And what he would say was that he wasn't a man after all. Just a ball of igneous rock, some iron, silicon, magnesium, oxygen. Bunch of craters and mountains and dust.

After a long day, I was far too tired to work out what my encoded confession would be or how I'd fit it into the language of a precocious nineteenth-century girl. But I was galvanized now. False art was going to be converted into true art. Like my first forgery in Henry James's *In the Cage*, I was going to create something exquisite that would be rendered worthless by strokes of the same pen.

The romantic in me would have loved to take a train to Bournemouth, about two hours away, but the light pouring in when I woke up from an overlong sleep was too perfect to waste on sentimental travel. Mary's final resting place would be there for me to make my homage after my project was completed. My hotel room, deliberately booked on a high floor with a large desk and resplendent southern exposure, was where I needed to hunker down for the next foreseeable days.

Slader had provided me with not quite a hundred leaves of vintage paper, sourced from God knows where, that looked much like the letters I'd seen on Fulham Road. I candled several blank pages against the morning sun and saw just the same wove finish and opacity as Mary's stationery. Using a hot plate I'd gotten at a local supermarket and filters that were provided with the coffee maker that came with the room—room service had already brought up a fresh pot with toast and jam—I began the process of mixing my ink.

Inappropriate as it may have been, I felt happy.

Now if Gertrude Stein's eccentric calligraphy had been hard to mirror, Mary Shelley's was more demanding yet. For one, Mary's word-spacing was a little less regular than Stein's, and Stein's wasn't all that predictable. Mary's ligatures varied. The dots over Gertrude's lowercase *i*'s flew above her words like birds, while her uppercase *I*'s looked like halves of hearts. Mary's ascenders and descenders could be different as her phrases progressed, sometimes with her letter *d* whipping back upon itself at the top of the stroke, like a streamer on a stick in high wind, other times curling forward like a cane. They shared a penchant for making cross-outs and corrections in their searches for the right word.

Both women had scalpel-sharp intellects, followed passions that led them into then-radical relationships, and imaginations that were, to use a Maisie word, *wikad*. But where I admired Gertrude, since early youth I'd adored Mary. *Frankenstein* had been my gateway drug to Poe and vice versa. I always fancied similarities between Mary's monster and Edgar's Usher, each of whom was human yet not human. In the past I'd spent plenty of time pondering Roderick Usher, drawing and even painting him. Now was the time for me to submerse myself into his precursor's world, I determined, as I opened a bottle of commercial black ink while my own iron gall concoction steeped.

Back in his less-than-legal heyday, my father used to buy old blank notebooks that came up at auction in the UK. Some dated back to the eighteenth century, though most were from late Georgian to Victorian times. They came in a variety of sizes from octavo to quarto, often bound in vellum or powdery sheep. Not overly expensive, they'd been perfect for his purposes as most of their leaves were free of writing, their handmade paper unpressed, their deckled edges untrimmed. It wasn't hard to detach unspoiled sheets from their bindings and, voilà, he had period pages for forged letters and manuscripts. The blank books I'd figured my father was least likely to find missing from the studio were from the early nineteenth century, which I'd packed at the bottom of my suitcase. Even if Irish customs had uncovered them in front of all to see, my excuse would've been that I wanted to make watercolors on antique paper. But they remained safely hidden, wrapped in my clothes, along with my stash of pens and writing nibs.

I fitted my favorite wooden shank with a medium nib, dipped it in the ink, and drew circles, waves, the alphabet, a field of poppies populated with scarecrows and ghoulies in one of these books. I could only imagine how that young longhaired book dealer would cringe watching me doodle away on the virgin period paper. But my mind was focused on what was before me.

Even before catching the flight with my family to Shannon before Christmas, I had resolved that Slader's prompt was inspiring, in its own forbidden way, as well as plausible. Lost manuscripts and correspondence by famous authors were discovered all the time, and Mary was no exception. Her children's story "Maurice, or the Fisher's Cot" was unearthed and first published the same year I was born. Just four years ago an academic named Nora Crook happened upon thirteen unknown letters by Mary to her friends Horace Smith and his daughter Eliza while researching a completely different novelist of the period. Dating from 1831 to 1849, they portrayed Mary as bewitching, given to whimsy, a touch vain, self-aware, and terribly proud of her only surviving son with Percy—although she did wish he were just a little bit taller.

Stuff happens. Why not this lost clutch of letters I was about to create? Letters that Mary's wily and jealous stepmother could well have hidden in a trunk and, hesitant to burn them out of spite, shipped to relatives in France in the hope they would never see the light of day. And that was merely one possible scenario for a provenance which would be, in any event, Slader's headache, not mine. Encouraged, I began my historical immersion—the technicalities of forgery were, for better or worse, second nature—by reading and rereading Betty Bennett's three-volume edition of letters; Feldman and Scott-Kilvert's *Journals*; Emily Sunstein's biography *Romance and Reality*, not to mention what I found online.

I already knew that Mary, as a girl, used to spend hours at her mother's graveside, reading books and daydreaming and communing with her. But that she learned the alphabet by tracing the letters incised on her mother's gravestone came as a surprise. Pathos incarnate, I supposed, but also endearing. I could easily imagine doing the same thing if my life had taken a similar tragic turn and I'd grown up knowing that my mother's death was so intimately linked to my own birth.

Absent parents, so often at the heart of fables and fairy tales, weighed heavily on the lives of some of their greatest creators. Wasn't Poe, like Mary, a motherless child? Eliza Poe was at best one of these absent parents, a star of the theater in Richmond, Virginia, who performed while baby Eddie slept backstage in his makeshift bassinet, having sometimes been sedated with a thimble's worth of nip. She passed away when the boy was almost three, succumbing to tuberculosis, just like his thirteen-year-old cousin-bride, Virginia, would in later years. And since Mary Wollstonecraft survived her daughter Mary's birth for just ten short, painful days, baby Mary never knew her maternal namesake. It was Maisie's good fortune, I thought as I paused my practice strokes, to have known her own birth mother long enough to have at least a few memories of Mary Chandler, dead of cancer when Maze was six.

Motherless children. Mary, Edgar, even Maisie in her way. Each marked by a gaping absence, each forced to grow up differently from most.

Here was the heart of forgery that I admit to finding compelling, even addictive—the imperative of getting into the mind and the spirit and soul and even body of another person. Technique and historical knowledge about calligraphic styles, chemistries of mixing and aging inks, the understanding of cultures and their papers were crucial. Still, these were mere finite things I had learned and adapted. But my flesh-and-blood hand becoming, for a weird alchemical moment, theirs? This was the only way to produce a counterfeit document that was also authentic, a new reality that equaled or bettered an old reality, joined it, became one with it. Here was how forgery could be a way of telling fresh truths.

In my letters, Mary would confess how much she missed knowing her mother, how essential her mother's writing and philosophy were to her when growing up, how her father was never the same after his soul-mate wife's death. They would consist of fragments of dreams, scraps of ideas for novels, admissions about her grinding animus toward her stepmother, Mary Jane Godwin—so many Marys! They'd be a palimpsest of poem scraps, sketches, copied-out bits, whatever came to mind that she thought her mother might like to read. She'd confess to her progressive feminist mum how on a Sunday in June she declared her love to Percy Shelley while the two lingered by her grave, but omit mentioning whether or not she lost her virginity to him there on that same day. And because these imaginary letters would never have been posted, it saved me the impossible task of trying to counterfeit vintage envelopes that were red wax–sealed or franked with anachronistic Penny Blacks from the 1840s.

My own confession? I found all this shamefully exciting. Yes, I was a novice at supervising my own atelier of sorts, my own *Bateau-Lavoir* for outlawed art. Yes, naive in so many ways. And yes, it would be a maiden voyage without my father at the helm helping me navigate and trim the sails. Before this, I was more a steerage passenger called upon to lend a hand topside when the weather got blustery. Now, I set my own course.

I felt a kinship with Mary and her mother in a way I realized I never quite did with Poe, much as I was his lifetime devotee.

Poe was so flawed he was a saint. Mary was a girl ahead of her day, who, audacious and adventurous, mixed it up with poets, philosophers, romantic weirdos far older than she. Because she was something of a forever outsider, I embraced her. It was an honor to imagine myself dreaming on her grave what she might have dreamt on her mother's. Not to mention there was something Frankensteinian about my forgery arising from a nightmare scenario, and its being forced into creation by an assignment. Not that Slader was Byron any more than I was Shelley, of course. But rather than despise the monstrousness of my work here in London, I had somehow to find the magic, even the joy, in it. And any unsavory motives behind it were best disregarded in order that I stay immersed and creative.

I wrote and rewrote, my days running one into another. I tried, failed, tried again to get the look of the cursive and the flow of words to synchronize, using every square inch of paper at hand. People who think that forging is a straightforward practice that simply involves imitating somebody's handwriting and getting a string of plausible sentences together are, in a word, cretins. Easier to walk up a waterfall than make the humblest credible forgery. When we sit down at a table with pen and paper, and write down our thoughts, the calligraphic ways those thoughts form themselves on the physical page say as much about us as the verbs and nouns and articles and adjectives do. The semiotics of penmanship in action?

Once I started to hear the music of Mary's sentences and thereby her voice, the physical act of writing her imagined sentences became incrementally easier. I'd had an opening line in my head for several days, and though it varied every time I thought about it, there was no reason to stall any longer. I took a deep breath, flexed the fingers of my writing hand. Then I dipped the nib into my pot of homemade obsidian ink, took a deep breath, and gave it a go with the words *Revered Mother, I take up my pen in the fervent hope that by some miraculous means you might comprehend my words in that Other World beyond the grave, & that I may enjoin you to hear your daughter, who loves you as the bird's wing loves the zephyr—*

I was no Mary Shelley. Yet I felt more confident at that moment than I had at any time in the past days and weeks since Slader had proposed the scheme. Who knew but that it might fly, like that wing lifted on its fanciful wind.

Buoyed by finally having some money in hand, and the real prospect of freeing himself from his personal quagmire, Slader spent October into the new year mostly holed up in his Airbnb. The days passed with unusual calm. He enjoyed reading his way through the shelf of Ray Bradbury paperbacks a former tenant had left behind. He ate simple meals, took rural morning walks. Bided his time with glacial slowness until one afternoon, having not heard from her for a while, he texted Nicole to ask when she'd be free to talk. Though he made it sound like a business call, he really just wanted to hear another person's voice, hers in particular. Given the secrecy necessary for their conspiracy to succeed, he no longer called her without settling on a time when she'd not be within earshot of her family. On this day, she wrote him back right away, saying now would be fine, was just hanging with a friend in Brooklyn.

"Who's the friend?" were his first words.

"How is that any of your business? And hello to you too."

"They don't know about our deal, right?"

"Wouldn't matter if she did," said Nicole. "She's my best friend and we have lots of each other's secrets on lockdown. But, to answer your question, no. I asked her for privacy."

Not knowing what else to say, Slader moved on, asking about progress on the Mary Shelley forgery.

"A bigger undertaking than either of us thought, so I've been buried in research. It's one thing to float the idea—a sublime idea, don't get me wrong—another to make it a reality."

Slader felt sheepish, and Slader didn't like to feel sheepish. "What do you need from me besides paper?"

"Patience," she said, hearing the unusual tentative tone in his voice.

"Never my strongest suit."

"Don't worry, I'm all over this. I'm going with my family to Ireland in the middle of next month, like I think I mentioned. Then off to London in the new year by myself to finish the work. I hope to have it wrapped up before the February deadline."

"Hope?"

"Totally will. Better?"

"And we stay in touch how?"

"Snapchat, I figure. Our messages will disappear the moment they're opened. No trail of word crumbs that way. You'll need to download the app. You know how?"

"I'll sort it."

"I assume you still haven't gotten any medical attention, have you," and went on talking with him for another few minutes, more as a colleague than a distressed subordinate. When he got off the call, Slader felt uneasy that the technology of communications between them lay so largely in her hands, indeed so much of his future did. And yet, he knew his was the upper hand when it came to her father's fate, her whole family's. Besides, he had come to trust the girl. She wasn't some snake in the grass, but rather a misguided martyr for a cause not worthy of her sacrifice. He, of all people, was in no position to tell her any such thing, so he kept his avuncular concerns to himself.

When he did finally give in and pay his visit to a small rural clinic in northwestern Massachusetts, his ID easily passed muster with the receptionist. He who had always considered gratitude a fool's game felt grateful not to have suffered permanent damage during his assault and interment. Even his (tall) tale about taking a tumble down an unfamiliar staircase at his (fabricated) brother's (imaginary) house in Vermont—he now ditched the fake car accident scenario to avoid nonexistent police reports—was delivered persuasively enough that it didn't generate questions from the young physician who examined him.

"Typical direct-impact injury," said the lanky white-jacketed doctor as he flashed a medical penlight back and forth in Slader's eyes, directing him to look up, down, left, right. "So you say you're not experiencing confusion or headaches, brain fog of any kind—"

"When it first happened, I did. But no longer."

"No nausea, vertigo, dizziness?" as he stepped back, studying his patient's balance. "Any falls?"

Slader shook his head.

"Your pupillary light test is normal. Vestibular function seems fine. And you're not experiencing fatigue as you did initially, you said?"

"To be sure," Slader answered, encouraged by the diagnosis. "My problem now is less about tiredness than insomnia."

"Traumatic brain injuries can cause a pretty wide variety of symptoms, but nine out of ten people resolve within weeks or, at the outside, a couple months. Looks to me like you're one of the lucky ones, though if this ever happens again, you're going to want to get yourself to a hospital immediately rather than risk waiting around like you did."

"Lesson learned," said Slader.

"Good man," the doctor said as he wrote a prescription. "I'm going to order a CT scan of your brain so we can rule out bleeding or a stroke. You can take this scrip to a facility in any larger town around here you want. If your symptoms worsen, any fainting or dizziness, you'll want to get to an ER right away."

"So I'm okay to go?" Slader asked, taking the piece of paper and cramming it into his pocket as he eased off the examination table with its crackling paper tearaway sheet.

"Before you do, I couldn't help noticing your fingertips. Did you want me to take a look at them?"

After Slader had completed work on his forged identification docs, he'd moved ahead with ruining, or at least disrupting, the central pattern area of his fingerprints. Hoping to avoid pain, he'd tried using Nicole's naphtha. But his prints were too stubborn for such a sissy half measure. So he resorted to ten torturous applications of hydrochloric acid to strip off the ridged skin on each fingertip and both thumbs. Over a month had passed since he performed this caustic self-mutilation, but the affected flesh was still a sickly blood-orange color even though he had used liquid bandages—liberal amounts of the stuff—to keep the wounds clean, as well as further distort his prints.

"Burned them pretty good at my brother's. Barbecuing isn't my forte."

"Sounds like you might want to be more careful when you visit your brother," said the physician, aware his patient's story was suspect but having no interest in prying. He was a doctor, not a detective.

"Right you are," Slader agreed. "I'll get this scan done on the double," he added, fully aware he had no intention of doing any such thing.

A few days afterward, Nicole reached out to him to set up a meeting in person—*IRL*, she'd snapped, which to his chagrin he'd had to look up. They were going to make one last stateside exchange before she went abroad. For her part, she had some new forgeries for him. For his, Slader had received the package of paper from Mallory Paperworks after negotiating with his deceased friend's associate at the plant, a guy he'd known almost as long as Cricket, a fellow who neither knew nor cared why Slader fancied overpaying for the oldest overstock they had in storage. Paper worthless to most anybody else.

They met at an Italian restaurant on the outskirts of Hudson, where they had lunch after handing each other their parcels. Slader ordered the blue-plate special of homemade spaghetti and meatballs, which, to his companion's amused disgust, he seasoned with ketchup.

"Your friend Mary would approve of the decor in this joint," said Slader, glancing around at the dancing silvery skeletons, witches' hats, and honeycomb paper pumpkins that still festooned the place though Halloween was long past and any Thanksgiving decorations were, it seemed, still in their boxes somewhere.

"This I doubt. She was a lot more than some spooky horror writer," Nicole said. "Not like she didn't write all kinds of other work besides *Frankenstein*. Mary was an unusually complicated woman."

"What woman's not?"

"Well, I don't think I'm all that complicated, for one," she said, tongue very much in cheek.

"If you say so."

"That aside," she continued, with a suddenly serious look on her face, "I do have a sort of complicated question, which feel free not to answer."

He said nothing, waited.

"What was my uncle Adam like?"

This did take him aback. He could dodge the question by asking her why she wanted to know. But the question was asked in gentle sincerity.

Looking past Nicole at a menagerie of black plastic bats and furry spiders by the cash register, Slader offered his answer in a similar spirit. "He was complicated in interesting ways, like you. I think you two would've gotten along. He loved books as books, as well as the words inside. Loved music, art. Shy, bit of a pessimist, soft-spoken but had an occasional temper on him. Could be a gourmet cook when he felt like it. Way too fucking dependent on your mother. Hated swimming, a terrible insomniac. What else. He smoked Gitanes, drank Tanqueray martinis dry with cocktail onions. Along those lines," and with that Henry Slader stopped talking.

Seeing he wouldn't, or couldn't, go on, Nicole thanked him. "I really appreciate that more than you can know."

Their conversation stalled, they ate in silence for a time. Averting her eyes when she sensed he was quietly studying her, she found herself convinced utterly and without any doubt that Henry Slader had not murdered her uncle. No way, nohow. Nothing could have been plainer.

After visiting the restroom to wash his hands, Slader returned to the booth, where, with a pocketknife, he opened her parcel of books and approved of the high quality of her Stein, Bowles, and Hemingway forgeries. He even smelled the pages for traces of a fresh ink scent, but the work was beyond pro, and he told her as much. She didn't bother examining the paper he'd given her. She accepted that it would be top drawer.

As they stood to go, Slader brought up the Shelley letters one last time and she assured him that she was on the case.

"Don't forget," he said, unnecessarily. "Natal day's your deadline. No extensions, mind you."

"No worries, mind you," she countered, noting how careful he was not to expose himself further to her. Sadness was not the man's style. Or, that is, showing sadness.

After they parted company—Slader picked up the tab—he reflected again on how crazy it was for him to like this young woman as much as he did. Everything reasonable suggested they'd hate each other, but this just didn't seem to be the case.

That squared, Slader loitered in his Airbnb for a couple more humdrum weeks before deciding the time had come for him to decamp temporarily so he could offload these new acquisitions. And, also, to make a couple of unavoidable personal visits up north. On the off-chance the heat came to search the rental in his absence, he swept, scrubbed, and wiped down every surface in the kitchen, bath, and two rooms. Not that he had fingerprints to leave, but washing the towels and sheets, essentially erasing himself, was for the best.

In Worcester, he bought new wheels—a nondescript second-hand Acura—and from there drove to Cambridge, where he sold to another dealer he knew the Gertrude Stein and Paul Bowles, along with a signed copy of *To Have and Have Not* in a decent jacket, without maneuvering for the last possible dollar in the deal. From there, driven by instinct as much as mindful planning, he set out toward his childhood home in Fall River, uncertain whether he would present himself to his estranged sister. He rather enjoyed this being-dead routine and the wicked freedom it afforded him of lying his arse off wherever he went. But he also knew that the seventy or so thousand in forgeries wrought by Nicole, should she fail in her Shelley commission, wasn't going to provide him with a civilized lifestyle in Tangier or Avignon or Cabo or wherever he might decide to disappear himself forever off the grid.

Slader hadn't seen one cent of family money after the death of his mother, who'd inherited a substantial portfolio from her second husband. Disappointed to her core by what had become of her once-promising son, Charlotte Slader-Givens had fully cut him out of her will during his stretch in prison. He now hoped that if he promised to stay out of his sister's life, let her consider him as dead and gone, she might see her way clear to giving him a token from that inheritance. Help her only brother,

her sole sibling, her hapless flesh and blood who was in need. Bethany had never married, had no children of her own. She could easily afford it, even though he imagined their mother's last wishes forbade such a gift to him.

Dubious proposition. But he still remembered from childhood that the loser motto of Fall River was "We'll Try." And so he would.

When Bethany opened the heavy door with its brass dolphin knocker, she no more recognized her brother than he did her. The street where she lived, once prestigious and affluent, seemed to have fallen on rough times. Slader could have sworn he saw a group of drug dealers working the downhill end of the block when he drove past to park in front of her house. While he himself didn't look threatening, especially in light of his new milquetoast wardrobe, she was leery of this stranger.

"What do you want?" she asked, peering from behind the door.

The day was overcast, gusty and bitter, and the salt scent of the eastern shore of Mount Hope Bay was carried on the fickle air. Slader knew this smell, recalled times when he used to bike alone down to the mouth of the Taunton River to see what there was to see, which wasn't much aside from shorebirds and local boats. Kept him away from kids who taunted him did the Taunton, he thought, remembering his old chestnut.

"You don't recognize me?" he asked.

"I'm sorry, but should I?"

She looked poorly, his sister. However pampered, life hadn't been kind to her. She'd gone sallow and plump since he last visited her aeons ago now, and was dull in the eyes, her voice froggy. If he didn't know better, he might have felt sorry for her.

"Bethany, you know me because I'm your brother. For richer or poorer," he added.

"Henry?"

"That's still my name."

"You look, heavens—really different."

This gave him direction. He would present himself as reformed. A wiser, kinder, and better person than she had witnessed in any of his prior manifestations.

"I hope that's a good thing," he said, trying to widen his smile though it hurt a bit. "I'm very happy to see you."

She stared him up and down.

"Are you going to invite me in?" he added. "I've been on the road all day."

The rooms had a kind of mausoleum timelessness and reminded Slader of the more upscale but equally staid atmosphere in the home of Mrs. Abigail Fletcher, from whom that *Tamerlane* was borrowed. Well, stolen. An artificial Christmas tree crowded with worse-for-wear ornaments, some of which he recognized from their childhood, stood disconsolate by the fireplace. That its twinkling lights were on during the daytime he found depressing beyond all reason.

"Why are you here, Henry?"

"I was on my way to Providence to see a friend and thought it was high time to stop by to say hello to my sister," he said, moving his gaze from the tree to her with another of his bony smiles.

Bethany did not return the gesture. "Now that you're here, I have a question. Both Mommy, bless her soul, and I want to know why you attacked that poor man. From what we read, it wasn't in self-defense. So what happened?"

Unexpected, her directness, though it shouldn't have been. And, please—*Mommy?* Bethany was always the unpolished of the siblings, the one who never learned the niceties of couching unpleasant statements in civil language. Words that cushioned reality. Slader uncrossed his legs where he sat on the mohair sofa, leaned forward, and set his forearms on his knees.

"How much time do you have?"

"How much time do you need?"

"Well," said Slader. "This man murdered my closest friend. This man has spent much of his adult lifetime trying to ruin my business. He thinks of himself as a decent fellow, but just because he has a wife and two nice daughters doesn't mean he isn't a thief who's cheated me out of everything he owes me. My bad that I reached a point of such frustration and anger that I struck out at him. If Mom had lived long enough so I could explain things to her once I was released, I'm sure she would've understood. Not like she didn't reach a breaking point with dear old Dad—"

"Yes, but she threw him out, divorced him. She wasn't crazy enough to—"

"She was a far better person than I'll ever be, all right. I agree. But you asked me a question and I'm answering in full faith," which, he realized, he truly was, if only as a way of keeping his sister at bay.

"She was," said an unmoved Bethany.

"Right. So this man has broken his promise to pay me for a job I did with him and as a matter of fact I'm now destitute while he's riding high."

An unreadable expression passed over his sister's puffy face. "You're telling me that after what happened between you two, you went back into business together again?"

"He felt guilty about my incarceration, to tell you the truth," Slader lied. "And so we decided to do one last business deal together, so I'd have enough money to get back on my feet and move on with my life. But I should've known that he'd find a way to cheat me in the end and abscond with all the profits himself." Funny how these mistruths felt more believable than what had actually transpired.

"And now you're here because you want me to give you money."

"That's not why I'm here," said Slader.

"Then we're back to my first question."

"Still the same old Beth," he said.

"Consistency isn't the worst thing," she countered, unmoved.

"'Hobgoblin of little minds' was what Emerson thought."

"Please don't quote at me from some stupid book."

An exchange, Slader realized, straight out of the pages of their quarreling youth.

"Please let me respond. I would never in a thousand years ask for money if I didn't need it, and I am doing my best to stay on the right side of the law. If Mom had known why I did what I did, I have to believe she'd have taken care of me in her will. At least given me some seed money after such a traumatic upheaval."

Bethany's turn to lean forward in what was clearly her favorite armchair, covered in damask. "Did you hear what happened to your old buddy Cricket?"

She might have appeared to him at first a bit stupefied or exhausted by her lonely life, but Slader was thrown by this wily switch of topics.

"I haven't heard that name in years" was the comfortable falsehood he offered her.

"Really now."

"What happened to Cricket?"

"He was found dead last summer. Murdered is what I heard. Over in the Hudson Valley. Which makes it kind of a mystery."

"How's that?"

"Because Cricket was a stick-in-the-mudnik like me. He never liked going outside of Fall River."

"I remember that about him. My question is, why go get himself killed elsewhere when he could've just stayed in the town where Lizzie Borden took an axe and gave her father forty whacks?"

"You're still cold, Henry. As ice," she said. "Do you know that before they caught the murderer, I wondered if yourself might not be involved. He told me you were doing a bit of shady business over the years with your reproduction stuff. And I warned him to stay away from you."

Ignoring her criticism, Slader asked, "You say they caught the murderer."

"Why do you sound so surprised? Of course they did. All these people eventually get caught."

"So who did it?"

"How should I know?" she said, raising an eyebrow. "Main thing is he's off the streets."

Bethany's long-lost brother sat on her sofa for a minute, listening to her mantel clock ticking away—how is it that all people hear ticks and tocks when there are only truly ticks or tocks? He probably shouldn't have come. She now knew he was alive and could say as much to authorities should they ever come knocking, after whoever was wrongly accused of Cricket's murder was released on lack of evidence.

He finally spoke. "If you're not going to see your way clear to helping me out—"

"You know I would. But Mother's wishes can't be broken."

"On earth as it is in heaven," he mumbled. "All right, then. Could you at least give me a glass of water and let me see my old room upstairs before I go on my way?"

Slader marveled at how painful it was for her to move on arthritic hips and crippled knees to the kitchen to fetch him the water. Meantime, he quietly flew up the curved staircase to the second floor, and ducked into the grand master bedroom where he used to tiptoe in at night to watch his mother and stepfather as they slept, marveling at how vulnerable they were in their canopied bed, dreaming. He easily located a dark blue satin jewelry box with floral inlay, and emptied its glittering contents into his jacket pockets. Next he searched her dresser for the underwear drawer where his mother always kept an envelope of cash, knowing his sister would have carried on the tradition, having no better ideas of her own. And, eureka, there it was, and quite thick at that.

"What do you think you're doing?"

Startled, Slader realized how badly he had underestimated how long it would take her to climb the steps. Before he could respond, she threw the heavy glass of water at his head, grazing his shoulder as he pivoted to face her.

"I'm taking my inheritance is what. Because I know you'll use Mom's will to keep it all for yourself."

As he spoke, Bethany flung what looked to be a Lalique owl at her brother, chosen from a small collection of such clear-glass sculptures on a table by the door. This time her aim was truer, catching him on his neck. Unprepared for this, Slader strode directly at her, hoping to push past and flee this house forever, but she blocked the way, screaming as she reached for another glass figurine. When they collided, Bethany lurched backward and her unsteady knees buckled. She fell hard, hitting her head on the landing, where she lay on her back, softly moaning words Slader couldn't understand. As her brother tiptoed over her, she tried to grab his pant cuff but he yanked himself free and double-stepped down the stairs and back to the entryway, a stale neoclassical foyer that had been painted back in his stepfather's day to look like some scalloped candy box in Wedgwood blue and white.

Here Slader halted, coughing as he rubbed his hand against his neck. His breathing was jagged, his face flushed. He struggled with a rare, uncomfortable sense of culpability. Rather than fleeing, as normally he might do, he steadied himself against an ornate pilaster and listened. Hearing nothing but the ticking of the carriage clock, he decided to walk himself through the living room to inventory what he might have touched. But then it dawned on him. He had no fingerprints to leave behind.

Part of him yearned to bolt, but the silence at the top of the staircase—no further moaning was heard, no crying, nothing—troubled Slader. He knew the wiser play was just to get a move on. Walk away and never come back. But maybe he should check on her, he thought, apologize somehow, give her back her gaudy jewelry and content himself with the wad of hundreds he'd absconded with.

Her eyes were wide open where she lay, paralytic but breathing. At least she was still alive. Sentient too. He could tell because her eyes followed him as he stepped over her broad supine body and returned to the bedroom, where he carefully put back the expensive watches, bracelets, rings, and other bangles he didn't want the hassle of trying to pawn after all. The glass she'd thrown at him lay unbroken on the carpet and the Lalique sculpture—it was maker-marked and probably worth a lot—had landed on her bed. He washed both items, leaving the glass on the bathroom sink and setting the owl back with its parliament. The envelope of cash he would keep for his efforts.

Kneeling beside Bethany sprawled on the landing, he said, "You're not going to like to hear this but what happened just now is as much your fault as mine. I'm sorry for my part and want you to know I've put everything back where it was. Your brother's no common burglar. I got carried away, all right? I should never have come here."

If she had been able to speak, she likely would have responded with a string of self-righteous epithets. But she wasn't and didn't.

"All right, so. I'm going to head out now. You're going to be just fine. Just lie here and rest a little and you'll be all right."

Her eyes were fluttery and nystagmic.

He placed his palm on her forehead, which was cool to the touch.

"No fever, good," he whispered. "So what I'm going to do is leave you here, where you're safe and sound, and you'll never see me again, I promise. Just think of me as dead because that's the best for all involved." He rose to his feet, glanced back into the bedroom to reassure himself that things were just as he'd found them, tiptoed around her body, and walked down the stairs two at a time.

Unhappy about the rotten mess he'd made, yet curiously sanguine about his prospects of getting away unscathed, he strode through the foyer and down the front steps to the curb. On quietly climbing into his car, he decided to drive up rather than back down the hill in order to avoid being seen again by the candy men on the corner peddling their addys, their Mollies, their chunk. For a brief flash, he fantasized about being an invisible wraith and what a useful magical gift that would be. But the hard fact of it was that unless some neighbor on this ghost block of once-stately houses, bygones of a lost era, happened to see him on those stairs or took note of his Acura—why on earth would they?—neither Henry Slader nor his body double Henry Edgar Wadsworth might ever be accused of setting foot in this place.

And in the week ahead, even if they had indeed observed that Bethany Slader welcomed a visitor into her house for an hour on an overcast day, they'd surely imagine that nothing out of the ordinary could have happened in such a short time. Nothing whatever. Bethany was, after all, known by the locals to be a bit of a recluse, a nice enough lady but one who preferred to keep her own company. Not a single soul on her block would consider it at all curious that she failed to appear outside her Victorian hermitage, or that when darkness fell over the neighborhood, none of her windows were lit.

Unavoidable, the encounter. I should have seen it coming. After holing up for a haze of days and nights in my hotel, fully focused on my growing Shelley manuscript, I needed fresh air, some comfort food, the company of strangers. Renee would be joining me soon enough, so I had to press ahead with my forgery before she did. But I had to stay fresh, and getting out of my room for a stretch was just what I needed. First, I took a long walk along the rain-wet sidewalks of the area, toward Vauxhall Bridge and along Grosvenor Road by the river, then returned to my Indian restaurant, where I was greeted like lost family.

"We miss you. Where have you been?"

"Out looking for myself," I said, invoking a bit of Maisie's Emily Dickinson banter as I was seated in my corner table beneath Vishnu.

"Find what you're seeking?" asked the headwaiter.

"Not yet."

"You will," he said with warm conviction. "Tandoori chicken, yes?"

My hair and face were damp from the stroll, so I went to the loo to dry myself off. When I returned to my seat and glanced around the dining room, my eyes locked on Pollock, nonchalantly drinking tea and eating khari biscuits—did the man ever eat anything besides cakes and snacks?—seemingly oblivious to my presence. Rather than wait for him to fake any ludicrous surprise at seeing me, I got up and walked over to his table.

"We have to stop meeting like this," I said, with not a trace of humor in my voice.

He removed the napkin from his lap and began to stand.

"Please don't trouble yourself, Detective."

Already on his feet, he extended his hand, which I shook.

"One of my favorite writers once said that the inevitable is no less of a shock just because it's inevitable," I told him. "I'm a little shocked you continue to follow me, even though it seems to have become inevitable."

"Won't you sit?" he asked, pulling out the chair next to him.

"I'm over there, and I've got food coming."

"Well then, if it's not an imposition, may I join you?"

"It is an imposition."

Without betraying a bit of annoyance—perhaps he wasn't annoyed—Pollock sat again and told me, "I have news I think you'll find less an imposition to hear from me than finding out some other way."

Vintage bait ploy, yet nothing in his demeanor or voice suggested frivolity. I may not have known the man very well, but I could see he was earnest and even concerned.

"Well, so what is it?"

"Has Henry Slader been in touch with you? He may be using an alias now, but have you spoken to him, whatever name he's going by?"

Grasping now that this exchange ought to be conducted in private rather than near the front of the restaurant, I signaled my waiter over, apologized, and asked if he'd mind moving my "friend" over to my corner table. Once resettled—literally cornered, it occurred to me—I told Pollock I hadn't heard from Slader. Which was the truth, and might've been concerning except I knew he was doing his own thing while fully counting on me to finish the Shelley archive for delivery next month. His temporary disappearance from my life was more a reprieve than a burden.

"So what is this news?"

"I was straight with you that my investigation has come down to two, actually three, possibilities. Slader, Will, or random."

"Your amateur investigation, you mean."

"In the old sense of the word *amateur*, maybe, something that's done out of devotion. You're the literary one, not me. *Amare* out of Latin, I believe. Means to love. So I'll take your put-down as a compliment."

My tandoori arrived. I thanked the server but didn't respond to Pollock. Wasn't in the mood for etymology.

Once we were alone again, the detective said, "I learned that Henry Slader's sister was found paralyzed, barely alive, in her house around Christmas. None of her valuables were taken, nothing was stolen or out of place. Seemed she'd tripped and broken her neck, maybe fainted, it was unclear."

"I'm sorry to hear it, but why are you telling me this?"

"She was in a coma. Came out of it a couple weeks ago and has been trying to communicate," he said. "Even though there's no forensics to back her up, she's claiming her brother pushed her down and robbed her."

"And you know this how?" I asked, hoping my face wasn't betraying how disturbing, how terrifying, this news was.

"Networks are networks. That part was easy. But the police want to bring Slader in for routine questioning and can't locate him. Her story doesn't square with the physical facts, so all they're looking to do is rule him out."

"If she fainted and fell, why would they need to rule him out? Makes no sense."

Pollock suggested I should eat before my food got cold, although any appetite I'd had was ruined by this news.

What he told me next was, in its way, more distressing than his story of an accusatory sister with no evidence. The descendant of a multigenerational paper manufacturer in Fall River, a John Mallory, was murdered in late summer, and the suspect who'd been arrested, arraigned, and was awaiting trial turned out to have a sound alibi that put him in a different location from where this Mallory's body had been found near our family house upstate. Because, as it happened, Henry Slader and John Mallory were longtime friends, Slader's name vectored into view again.

"Likely coincidental," Pollock reassured me. "But at the very least, it's concerning that the one person who knew both of these victims is currently nowhere to be found."

I leapt ahead. "So you're telling me that you're worried about my safety?"

"That, yes," he said. "And your family's."

Slader knew better than to bother my family when I was in the midst of forging his one-way ticket out of existence, though naturally I couldn't share anything about that. I assured Pollock my family could take care of themselves.

As if he were reading my thoughts, he asked, "It's none of my business, but what are you doing here in London?"

"You're right. All due respect, none of your business."

"Fair enough," he said, and rose from the table after setting down enough pounds sterling to more than pay for our food. "You have my cell. If Slader reaches out to you, would you let me know? If the spirit moves?"

"Will do," I told him, though I knew I wouldn't.

Another thing I knew for sure, as I watched Pollock exit the restaurant through crimson-and-gold-lacquered doors emblazoned with fanciful Bengal tigers, was that I needed to push through my Shelley manuscript as fast as possible and get it into Slader's hands. Naturally, I was curious and pretty alarmed about his sister's accusation, but was loathe to reach out to the man until I could deliver the goods we'd agreed upon. There was no need for us to talk—either he injured and robbed his sister or he didn't. And because I could imagine him admitting or denying it with persuasive conviction, I doubted I would ever know what had happened anyway. No need for more words other than those of my chimerical Mary Shelley.

I returned to the hotel after a scoop of decadent pistachio kulfi, and lay down on the bed, a little jazzed by the sugar, where I continued to read from a volume of Mary's letters that I'd bought at a used bookshop. The more I read of Mary, the more Mary meant to me. Her letters exhibited the broadest range of emotions and postures. She could be elusive and forthright in a single phrase. Sometimes formal and polite, she had the capacity to be self-deprecatory as well as unabashedly critical. She was melancholy, vulnerable, funny. She could lay out some insight or image with such breathtaking urgency that I found myself gasping with excitement. Above all, her missives were wicked smart.

In a note of fewer than a hundred words to Lord Byron in mid-December 1822, after making him a fair copy of one of his cantos, Mary wrote, "Your Lordships MS. was very difficult to decypher, so pardon blunders & omissions" and then offered a frankly tepid appraisal, "I like your Canto extremely; it has only touches of your *highest* style of poetry, but it is very amusing & delightful." Mourning the death by drowning of her young husband, Percy, just six months earlier, she told Byron, "It is a comfort to get anything to gild the dark clouds now my sun is set," and rushed the letter to an abrupt close with "But I will not scrawl nonsense to you." It wasn't a stretch for me to imagine she'd started to cry as she signed off, "Adieu Yours MaryS."

And this was just a hasty note. Longer letters to friends like Jane Williams Hogg, whose husband was to drown in the same

ill-fated boating accident at sea near Livorno that took Percy
Shelley's life; Edward John Trelawny, the man who'd identified Shelley's body that tragic July day; Maria Gisborne, who
had taken young Mary and her sister into her home after their
mother died; and others, not to mention Shelley himself, were
so enviably articulate and pitched toward truth-telling that my
own small enterprise here seemed beyond crass, truly execrable.
I knew I had to finish what I started, but it didn't make me feel
any better about myself.

After a nap, I saw it was dark outside and got up, washed my
face and hands, then continued to write out drafts of possible
letters to include in the final tranche. I wrote out these sketches
in a cheap modern notebook, scribing in Mary's hand when the
words came slowly, and in my own when sentences flowed fast
and her voice all but dictated to me what to put on paper. Not
every one of these candidates would ultimately make it into the
finished manuscript, but as my practice notebook filled up, it
became an incriminating document that I would need to destroy
at the end of the project.

At the same time, I continued to add final draft pages, vary-
ing inks and aging leaves in a hodgepodge of ways in order to
give the cache an appearance of having been written over the
course of time. One misty evening, I slipped into the cheap
raincoat I'd bought at a secondhand shop and carried some
finished manuscript pages outside to expose them to the elements. Fully knowing I must have been breaking some kind of
cemetery laws, or at least graveyard etiquette, I dug up a small
plastic bag's worth of St. Pancras Old Church dirt and absconded
with it to my room, where I evenly soiled several virgin leaves
of prized vintage paper. To compress this dirt—pulverized with
a mortar in my bathroom sink—into their surface fibers, I used
an improvised blotter fashioned of dead leaves from the Hardy
Tree. This ailing ash, an important landmark in St. Pancras that
dated back to Victorian times, was so named in honor of Thomas

Hardy, who back in the 1860s worked for the architect Arthur Blomfield, whose firm was tasked with the gacky job of unearthing people's remains to clear the way for the railway line that runs through there to this day.

Not that I anticipated anyone would ever view my work under an electron microscope. But if some forensics lab techs were ever to drill down that deep, maybe following up on a claim the manuscript letters were—God forbid—fake, well then, I figured the presence of highly specific local dirt and desiccated vegetable matter couldn't hurt an argument in their defense. Were the papers called into question by an institution or individual who was willing to pay a million for them, little shades of microscopic authenticity like this would, if not win the day, at least confuse matters. Muddy the waters of any allegation. I mean, what kind of forger would bother with such harebrained minutiae?

The days that preceded Renee's arrival were productive beyond my wildest hopes. Not only had I added a significant number of pages to the cache, but improved its quality with each new entry. Just as an example, I was intrigued by Mary's essay "On Ghosts," which appeared in *London Magazine* in March 1824. Even though her epigraph by Wordsworth threw cold water on her theme—

> *I look for ghosts—but none will force*
> *Their way to me; 'tis falsely said*
> *That there was ever intercourse*
> *Between the living and the dead—*

Mary wasn't having it.

She wrote beautifully, movingly about how our ancestors lived in a world of accepted myths, of fantastic fables in which the "empire of the imagination" and its "traditionary tales" of gods, giants, fairies, and witches were wholeheartedly embraced. Where ghosts reigned, "with beckoning hands and fleeting shapes," and did things both wondrous and dreadful. Now, she rued, that otherworldly world was dismissed as passé and worthy only of ridicule. She asked more than once, as if in pained disbelief, "But do none of us believe in ghosts?"

Anybody who's read the monster's—or, as Mary generally tried to counterbalance it, creature's—farewell soliloquy in *Frankenstein*, where he views death as the only condition that will bring him relief and even happiness, must realize how extensively Mary Shelley herself had meditated on death over the course of her young life. It dawned on me that I could reverse-engineer her finished essay on ghosts into source material for counterfeit earlier drafts and notes toward that same work. In my manuscript of Mary's—hers of mine? both?—I had to put aside my own thoughts about death and the idea of an afterlife. Before my near-fatal attack on Slader, I believed that death was death. When our brains stopped functioning, so did our imaginations, our memories, our characters, and we reentered the void. Whereas I couldn't bring myself to believe in the Bible's heaven and hell, and had serious doubts about reincarnation that frustrated my youthful embrace of Buddhism, I did find a line in Melville's *Mardi* that made sense to me in my late teens: "For backward or forward, eternity is the same; already have we been the nothing we dread to be." Slader's temporary death had made me wish there was some kind of hereafter. At least this way he would have had another chance and my own guilt might've been lightened. Thank God, so to say, he did live. This way I avoided being a slave to wishful thinking.

Now, as I fashioned a series of questions posed by Mary to her mother, I felt as if she and I were together crying into the dark from which she had a real expectation of answers, and I of just echoes. Since hers was a healthier point of view and hers were the queries, I leaned hard into her faith.

Does time exist in Death? I wrote first in my Rhodia pad and quickly, using another pen dipped in my iron gall ink, with conviction on my vintage paper, in as perfect a replica of Mary's holograph as I could, wrote it out again. I then added, without pausing to practice, *Is there a noonday when, as Percy believes, "Every little corner, nook, and hole / is penetrated with the insolent light"?*

With no thought as to whether there was any logical progression to my next question, I scribed a new line beneath Mary's quote from Shelley's *The Cenci—Can you see me sitting with you in darkness as in daylight?*

And pausing as the ink dried—I sometimes used a blotter, sometimes didn't, again as a way of making the leaves look different from one another, unpatterned, not simply banged out by some twenty-first-century calligrapher—I tried out another line in my Rhodia, liked it, and dipped my nib into the pot of ink once more.

Do the dead see ghosts, phantoms unreal or real?

Then, without a trial run, I wrote the words, *There is something beyond us of which we are ignorant. I have thought this many times, but are my thoughts yet another form of mere ignorance?* and feeling urgency and self-confidence, queried Mary's mother, *What has become of the enchantresses of the antediluvian world, with their palaces of crystal and dungeons where the sun with his chariot does not cast a glowing light?*

Seeing that I had nearly reached the end of a new page, feeling a little lightheaded and dizzy because I'd been unconsciously holding my breath every time I set nib to paper, it occurred to me that Mary could sometimes be a voluble woman and that even if she might never have experienced impatience in the composition of these letters to her mother, it didn't mean that I—I who realized I'd begun to hyperventilate—couldn't ask on Mary's behalf, *Will you ever grant me a visitation? Please do, dearest Mother. I will not be afraid and I will wait & wait for your beautiful spectre.*

A light knock on my door awakened me from a shallow sleep. Bolting upright in my chair, I saw that I had nodded off with my nibbed pen still clasped in one hand and my arm resting flat on the table where I seemed to have used it as a pillow. Afternoon sunlight had withdrawn from the room, so I knew at once that I had been dozing for several hours. My first conscious move was to switch on the desk lamp and make sure I hadn't accidentally smudged the freshly written sheet of questions to Mary Wollstonecraft. I was relieved to see that all was just as I'd left it when I laid my head down with the intention of resting my eyes for, like, a few minutes. Still drowsy, I heard a louder knock and a familiar woman's voice calling my name in the hallway.

"Holy shit, what happened? You look like a dropped pie," she said when I opened the door, taking me into her arms like a mother might a wayward daughter.

"You're a day early," I blurted, abruptly regaining consciousness.

"Better than a day late, no?"

"Right, yes, oh God—come in, come in," and we gave each other a proper strong hug and a kiss on both cheeks first, then on the lips.

"Was able to wrap things up early at the gallery, so I went to the airport, got myself listed on standby for an earlier flight. And, well, here I be."

For coming off a transatlantic flight and, knowing Renee, traveling not in first class but the cheap seats where you can chew on your knees if you're peckish, she looked radiant. At least in my eyes. I might have gushed but for my suddenly remembering that the room was in complete disarray, and that on every surface were forgeries either dry or drying, open books by and about Mary Shelley and her circle, a hodgepodge of raw materials for aging paper and manufacturing inks—a shady counterfeiter's lair on full, unadulterated display. My friend, who could never be accused of hiding her opinion, gently moved me aside with her hands on my shoulders so she could have an unobstructed view.

"So, my dear Squatch, what have we here?" she said, as I followed her to the table covered in manuscripts to the unmade bed that was arranged with jars of pigments. "Can't say much for room service in this joint."

When I stuttered out the first words of an apology, she interrupted me, "Do you mind if I use the ladies' room, or are you cooking chemicals in there?"

"No, yes—please do," I said, with such a broad smile it felt almost painful. "I'm beyond happy you're here, excellent Renee."

"Me too, excellent Nick," she said and before closing the door, added, "And don't do anything stupid like straightening up your mess. I'm keen to hear everything about what kind of crazy assery you're up to now."

While she was freshening up, I quickly changed out of my work shirt with its ink-stained cuffs and odor of sweat and sleep. I was as elated to see her as I was flustered that she caught me altogether off guard. Inasmuch as I'd given it any thought, which I really hadn't, I would have staged our reunion differently—with all the undeniable evidence that I was working on yet another forgery hidden away. I would've gotten around to telling her my situation, because of course I would. But over drinks in a semiprivate booth in some cool pub, not after being caught *in flagrante delicto*, so to say.

On the other hand, who cared? Her timing was impeccable. I needed her and here she was.

"So, sweet Nick," she said, her face still damp from washing up. "Don't get me wrong, you're beautiful as ever, but too damn thin, and pale as banana cream. How many nights has it been since you slept? Like in-a-bed slept?"

"Not sure. Maybe several," I ventured.

"Where do you eat dinner in this hood? You're famished and I could eat a horse. Plus we obviously need to do some serious catching up. For one, I never knew that Edgar Allan Poe had an affair with Mary Shelley. Or am I misreading the tea leaves here?"

"They didn't," I said, marveling at how observant she was. "And no, brainiac, you're not misreading the leaves. Indian good?"

"Indian's dope. And you can help me read the Darjeeling, my darjeeling."

"Laugh, laugh. Chortle, snigger. Let's do it," I said, as the weight of my anxiety lifted away and I felt, with gratitude, myself return to me.

Slader had taken no pleasure in leaving his sister incapacitated on the staircase landing. He wasn't some sadist, he assured himself. But neither did he like reading on his burner phone several weeks after the accident that an heiress who resided in the Corky Row district of Fall River had awakened from a coma claiming she'd been brutally attacked by her own brother and robbed of ten thousand dollars in cash. The fuck, he scoffed, do they mean by *heiress*? Just how was she *brutally attacked*? And what was this about ten grand, when he made off with only half that much? Would that she had gone ahead and met her precious maker, he thought, maybe a little sadistically, in fact, where she and their mother could ride on a fluffy sea of cotton-white clouds and reckon the ways Henry had gone to the devil. Hell, he thought. It would probably take them all eternity to tally the list of his trespasses.

He also took no pleasure in being forced to lie so low for so long. Sure, he'd been on the lam in times past for other illegalities, other transgressions, other crimes, plainly put. But back in the

halcyon days of his exploits with forged books and manuscripts
he at least had accomplices whom he could, if not turn to for
friendship, genially exploit in ways that kept his own exposure,
and loneliness, at bay. Honor among thieves and all that fooey.
But sitting alone now on a bed in an old-fashioned inn called the
Reynolds House, in a little Catskill hamlet, Roscoe, in upstate
New York, looking out his window at the tiny rural police station across the road, the Westfield Flats Cemetery adjacent with
its antique gravestones at severe angles in the bleak snow and
a white-clapboard, skinny-steepled Presbyterian church just
beyond, rapport among thieves was just what he missed. Or
something akin to rapport. That was gone now, if it had ever truly
existed. Now all he had was receipts, damning ones, that he could
use against Atticus and Will. To be sure, they had as many or more
on him. The three, at least for the churning present, neutralized
one another. A cobra, a mongoose, a tiger. Each ready to lunge.

What had brought him to this remote mountain village, popu-
lation five hundred max? A longing to withdraw even further in
the wake of one bad decision, or stroke of bad luck, after another?
As a trio of crows circled and landed in the town cemetery, where
they strutted, black on white, looking for all the world like they'd
flown there out of a winter landscape painting by Pieter Bruegel,
he reflected on this latest stretch of his fool's journey.

If it had been a disastrous idea to visit Bethany, it had promised to be an even worse one to drive straight to Providence
to see Atticus Moore. But Slader being Slader, that's just what
he did. The trip was under an hour by interstate. He knew he
wasn't welcome at Atticus's house, where his wife considered
Slader a bad influence. Indeed, a repulsive pariah. She had the
right to her opinion, Slader reasoned as he drove, but it didn't
change the fact that Atticus owed him his cut of the Poe given
that Will wasn't going to pony up.

He parked his Acura on an empty street near Baileys Lower
Cove on the Seekonk River behind an enormous bank of

rhododendrons. Nobody was out and about that evening as it
was raw down by the slow-moving water, so he took advantage
of the solitude to remove the license plates and fling them like
rectangular Frisbees far out into the drink. Bye, car, he thought
and headed on foot in the general direction of the university
that crowned the hill, where he hoped to find one of the Por-
tuguese restaurants in the area open. What he'd give for some
camarão alhinho with a side of fried cornmeal. Alas, he had to
settle for a burger and soda instead of his favorite dish of sau-
téed shrimp in spicy garlic sauce. As he ate, he swiped through
local news websites to see if anything else about his sister had
surfaced. After paying his bill, he checked into the first motel
he happened upon, not far from the deserted campus on winter break. Despite the day's craziness, he slept like death itself
while the hot radiator in his room clanked and hissed.

Atticus was best approached not at home but in his office.
Problem was, his hours were irregular, by appointment only,
and his business was in downtown Providence, where, Slader
figured, there were more functioning security cameras than up
here on the hill. After finishing a third cup of coffee, and having no better plan, he called his sometime friend and colleague
using one of his burners that at least wouldn't produce a display
identifying him on Atticus's phone.

"Atticus Moore," he heard, in a voice that was feebler than
Slader remembered.

"Atticus, Henry. Please don't hang up. I won't take much
time. We need to get together, talk for a minute." The other
end of the line was quiet, so he continued, "Not at your house,
obviously. Not in the office either."

"*Tamerlane*, right?" Atticus finally asked, after another long
silent lag.

"Right, Poe."

"Where are you?"

They agreed to meet, midday, on a bench near Manning Chapel, a stone-and-stucco replica of some Doric temple in Paestum or maybe Sicily. Which made a kind of sense, Slader thought. What better background for a forger and his fence to convene than in the shadows of a pseudo sixth-century-BC Greek temple erected in the early nineteenth? The sky was pale blue, no breeze, and the air was frigid.

Neither man appeared as he did the last time they were together in person, trading *Tamerlane*s. Atticus had aged, was fragile on his cane, his steps more cautious than Slader recalled. He'd shed weight, his cheeks were caved in and ashen. Still, he cut an elegant figure as he made his way toward his colleague, who rose to greet him.

Atticus shook his hand and said, without a smile, "Seems you've become a cross between a beatnik and a yuppie. I like the look."

"We all could use a remake every now and then."

"Especially if people are hunting for us, right?"

They sat on the cold stone bench and spoke, watching pigeons wheel around the naked trees on the commons, their wings clattering like sticks.

"Can you tell me what in God's name happened between you and Will? He pretty specifically told me you tried to kill him, took up a knife against him like you did in Ireland."

"Suffice it to say his daughter tried to kill me," Slader said, suppressing the urge to tell him it was a cleaver in Ireland, not a knife. "Almost succeeded. But no reason to rehash ancient history."

"You're right, forgive my curiosity," said Atticus. "Let's make this simple. After commission, taxes, hush money, all the rest, I can give you fifty thou nonnegotiable."

"What hush money?"

"The less you know, the better."

"I'd have thought I was good for five times that. Ten, given the result."

"It might have if you'd kept your wits about you at Will's."

"Yes, right, fine. Abject apologies," he said, frustrated that Atticus and Will believed it was fair to cut him out of their deal because he got unruly that once. Not like anybody got injured other than himself. "But I'm thinking that a third of hammer's closer to three-quarters of a mil."

"Fifty. And this is the last time we ever indulge in the joy of each other's company."

Slader wondered why pigeons were so disparaged by everybody. Flying rats, people called them. Soft wintry sunlight caught the sleek-feathered pearlescence of one that approached them there, perhaps hoping the men would toss some breadcrumbs in its direction. A beautiful bird, really. Didn't the Brits call them rock doves?

"Hundred."

"Sixty, take it or leave it."

"You have it now?"

"I do," said Atticus, who finally turned toward his companion and looked him in the eye after removing his designer sunglasses.

Slader didn't have the bandwidth to feel sorry for dying Atticus. Or, for that matter, himself. He knew he was being screwed but simply said, "Done."

"None of this ever happened."

"I don't even know you."

"Good luck with the rest of your days," said Atticus, satisfied, as his breath inscribed the air with a thin billowy veil. He withdrew an envelope from his breast pocket and passed it into Slader's hand. Leaning heavily on his cane, he struggled to get up from the low bench. Without giving it a moment's thought, Slader reached out and steadied the man, helping him to his feet. He watched Atticus find his balance, slide on his dark glasses, and slowly walk away without uttering another word or glancing back. Slader may have understood the weight of the moment, but didn't really give it much thought. He sat, unmoving, as the specter of his longtime partner disappeared into the distance and around the corner of a brick building of Victorian design that might well have been built in the Victorian era. But even if that were the case, Slader mused, it still looked like fake Victorian architecture, a travesty rather than an original.

With more money in hand than he'd had in years, it was time to acquire yet another new ride. Get himself sorted. For Atticus to suggest people were looking for him underplayed, indeed trivialized, his situation. Whether or not they knew it, authorities in three states had reason to be on the lookout for him, no matter what name he traveled by. Racketeering, breaking and entering, vandalism, fraud, burglary, aggravated assault, bribery— or was it blackmail?—not to mention forgery. Not pretty. And just imagine, he fancied, if bearing false witness was a felony.

He called a taxi and had himself delivered to a used-car lot on the outskirts of Providence. Here he settled on a dun-colored van, forgettable thing, but roomy in case he needed to sleep in the back rather than stretch the limits of his fake identity by checking into another motel along the line. After dropping into a strip mall, where he picked up a sleeping bag, two prepaid cells, an inflatable mattress, and other camping equipment at a sporting-goods store, he drove west. The sun set before him, an orange ball flattening into the horizon, as he migrated back to Millbrook, where he hunkered down again in his rented cottage that had become as familiar as an old shoe. Kept his head low, reread some books, counted his money and moved it from one hiding place to another.

Nicole hadn't been in touch since she'd left for Ireland with her family, so Slader thought he should check in, make sure she was on schedule. Maybe he was blinded by trust—that saccharine enemy of all rational beings—but he counted on Nicole's integrity and skill. She had no reason to trust him, indeed otherwise, but he had to believe in the girl, given the only relationship in his life that remained viable now, as far as he could tell, was his with her. Unbelievably, ridiculously, he sort of missed her. Still, vigilance is the price of knowledge, as some philosopher wrote. And knowledge is power, coined another. Santayana, Bacon. To his amazement, his memory was still intact.

Long time, he tapped, using his forefinger on the small screen, *hows baby doing? How r u? mama's birthday coming up on 5 right? want to celebrate & go our ways. best baby not travel I can join happy family where? will wait 4 news & invite.*

His trust in her was borne out by Nicole's prompt response. *Hello, long time yes. baby doing v well. Good health & growing fast. Hope you'll be as proud of her as mother is. Left Ireland now London but gone soon. Ms will be where MS rests.*

Canny woman. She would deliver the manuscript—*Ms*—where Mary Shelley was buried.

Got it. will light two candles, he texted back, watching a squirrel bound across the anemic grass in the yard out his window. He figured she would realize that he meant one candle of remembrance for Mary and another for Nicole's birthday.

Nice, was her response, which suggested she had. *Is this right # for future?*

Why he didn't verify his number was complicated. The number would change again, so why tell her until he knew what it would be. What was more, he preferred asking rather than answering questions, old habit, even if it was his partner of sorts making the query.

Till soon, he tapped.

Time passed, a cluster of days, then weeks that crept toward February. He continued to check his phone for news, but Bethany's story had faded from headlines to brief updates before disappearing altogether. This should have bolstered confidence, he knew, that her accusations had been shrugged off but, oddly, it only made Slader more jumpy. Though he was loathe to admit it, he'd grown wary, even spooked, as January dragged along. More often than before, lights from some car passing his Airbnb in the night were freighted with foreboding. Rustling in the boxwoods outside his cottage window was blood-quickening. Even the barred owls that barked under the moon frayed his nerves. It was ridiculous, even mortifying, but could no longer be ignored. And one winter-dark morning he realized the moment had come to roust himself. Charcoal-gray clouds blanketed the skies when he locked the cottage, slipped its keys through the postal slot in the door, and drove to Rhinebeck at day's end where he picked up the incriminating photos of Will he'd stashed in a bank on Mill Street. Ever cautious, he left the negatives behind. Time was growing nigh—couldn't come soon enough—when he would exchange them for Nicole's forgery. An idea occurred to him as he climbed into the van. Under the heavy overcast, soon veiled by full nightfall, he ventured west across the Hudson. If he drove carefully, not too fast, not too slow, he believed right now was the best time for him to be on the road. Darkness meant fewer speed-trap patrolmen making their quotas. Fewer police of any kind out and about. The make and year and color of cars either stolen or suspicious were harder to see.

He remembered going fishing once with his stepfather in Roscoe—among other faint childhood memories recirculating through his thoughts—and recalled how off the beaten path it was. Situated on the Beaverkill River, one of the most famous trout runs on the eastern seaboard, it would be in full dormancy this time of year. Offseason, no anglers. No summer visitors or autumn leaf peepers. None of the little businesses that depended on their tourism would be open. Just across the bridge and due west, then north up into the mountains, if he could find the hotel—two stories with a wraparound porch—where he and his stepfather had stayed that once, it would bring him some modicum of peace. At least enough to catch his breath.

The Reynolds House wasn't hard to find. Little had changed in all these intervening years. He parked as far off the street as he could, behind the inn. Had to wake up the manager, who was delighted to have a guest and put him in the Rockefeller room on the second floor.

"You know, John D. Rockefeller himself stayed here more than once in the 1920s," she told him, standing behind the front desk in a flannel nightgown under her overcoat. "His signature is in one of the old hotel registers in the parlor."

"I'm sure it is," he said, wondering if it was authentic.

"Complimentary breakfast in the morning," she said and handed him his key, directing him up the narrow flight of stairs.

The room was spare, tidy, quiet in the extreme. Not a room one would think baronial enough to accommodate the wealthiest business magnate in the world back then. But the man had come to fly-fish, and the Reynolds was the only game in town, so it made sense, Slader mused. He washed his face, avoiding the mirror above the sink, switched off the lights, and crawled into bed, feeling calmer than he had in months.

When he woke up late the next morning, he took a bath, shaved his head and trimmed the goat, examined his scars, which were blessedly fading, and then went downstairs smelling of lemon soap. The manager, now dressed in jeans and a plaid shirt, poured him a cup of freshly brewed coffee and asked what kind of jam he liked with his toast. They seemed to be the only people in the inn, which was fine with Slader.

"I noticed the police station is right across the road," he said, making small talk as a prelude to informing himself about how dangerous it was for the enemy to headquarter so nearby. On the other hand, keep your friends close, enemies closer?

"It is."

"Must make you feel pretty safe here."

"I guess," she said. "Never gave it much thought. That's the Rockland Town Justice Court building too."

"A one-stop citadel of crime prevention."

"Mostly speeding tickets and drugs."

Slader sat back in his chair and rolled out a platitude about how this mountain valley was too pretty for there to be much crime.

"And what brings you to these parts?" she asked, a question she'd probably posed hundreds of times over the years but which nevertheless caught him by surprise.

"Ah, well, thinking about moving up here. I have family a little farther north."

"Really?" she brightened. "Who, where?"

He gazed at an old photograph of the inn on the wall. "I doubt you'd know them."

"I've lived here my whole life, so maybe."

Hoping not to sound too curt, he paused before saying, "I really think you wouldn't. They're kind of hermits."

"I see," she said, unoffended, it seemed, that her guest had cut off their chat. "Can I get you anything else?"

"Thank you, no," Slader told her, with as big a smile as he could summon. "But tell me, is there a place in town where I could buy myself some warmer clothes? Silly of me, I hadn't anticipated a polar vortex. Not to mention so much snow."

"We're expecting more tonight. Roscoe's not *mountains* mountains, but we get our share of the white stuff," she said, and directed him to a store a short walk away from the inn. "There's an excellent Italian restaurant on the corner of Stewart and Old Route 17 near there for lunch if you don't feel like driving." Sleepy as the police station was, Slader thought it best to leave his van safely hidden behind the hotel, walk past the cemetery and church to the one-street downtown to do his shopping. Given he was in fishing-and-hunting country, his style was about to change again. Not the worst idea, he thought, as he made his way along unplowed, uneven sidewalks. On the road, he'd encountered many anonymous other people at gas stations, diners, rest stops, stores. If on the outside chance any of them had found him suspicious enough to offer a physical description to the authorities, his shot at a new life would be cut as short as the manager's chitchat about his nonexistent relatives somewhere up the winding road.

The shop was open and stocked with Carhartt, Orvis, and all manner of outdoor gear Slader would never have been caught dead wearing six months ago. He went for a drab, almost military look. Not camouflage, which ironically would stand out. But beige, khaki, fawn. A burnt-orange shirt and brown pants with innumerable pockets. Even his plaid scarf was sorrel and maroon. A pair of duck boots, which he wore along with the rest of his new clothes to the corner pizzeria, rounded out his new costume. He already had a watchman's cap from earlier chapters in his life.

Whoever would have thought the outlier craft of forgery would have led him to this, sitting in Raimondo's across from a fire station museum in a tiny Catskill burg, dressed like a mountain man, waiting for a pizza while a young cohort overseas was finishing a seven-figure fake Mary Shelley manuscript? He quaffed his self-indulgent local craft beer in a kind of euphoric trance and lingered over his lunch as afternoon clouds lowered themselves into the Parrish blue valley, obscuring the ridges along either side of the river. It began to snow. Gently at first, then in steady waves. Wasn't today the anniversary of Mary's death? Yes, he was certain of it.

He paid his tab, careful not to flash any of his hundred-dollar bills. Grabbing the large bag that contained his old threads, which were in need of laundering, he made his way along the icy walk past the church. The cloud ceiling was so low he felt as if he could reach up and touch it. It seemed, he marveled, as if he were inside a snow globe. At the cemetery entrance, with its black wrought-iron archway, he paused, then stepped inside to watch the white flakes spiral over these tumbledown markers. Many inscriptions on the older stones had been worn away by time and the elements. But he could make out the names Chapman and Ellsworth, and wondered, as the storm picked up, what sort of lives the men and women had led before they ended up just there, doubly buried beneath the ground and the growing blanket of snow. Maybe they prayed, to no obvious avail, in the church pews next door. Maybe they broke bluestone for a living. Maybe one of them took the life of a friend in a hunting accident. Maybe one had seven children and spent winter evenings like this making venison stew while a fire roared in the hearth.

Yes, of course, the alcohol fired his daydream, nothing more. But he couldn't help but wonder where he, who never did any of those things, would end up when his life fluttered out. This transient moment of being embroidered in snow, in an inn nestled on the Beaverkill flats between conifer mountains, was as close to happiness as he'd experienced in a long time. The quiet that surrounded his room was rich and soothing. Supper downstairs in the cozy dining room would be served in two hours and, although he was still full from the house pizza with its pepperoni, sausage, and anchovies, he looked forward to satiating himself again. If he didn't know better, he would think he was living a charmed life right now.

"Such an unusual time of year to be house hunting," said the manager, as she served him a plate of fried chicken, mashed potatoes, and peas. "When're you getting started?"

"First thing tomorrow," he told her, realizing he had no idea what day of the week it was. "Weather permitting."

"Supposed to be a dusting later in the day but otherwise good."

"Perfect," he said. "I know most people look at real estate in the spring or summer, but I want to see what things are like in the dead of winter. See the houses and neighborhoods undisguised by flowers and leaves. Prices in offseason are softer too."

"Hadn't thought of it that way. Makes sense," and with that she left the room so he could eat his dinner in peace and she could too, in the kitchen.

Slader admired that she seemed to have no deeper interest than engaging in easygoing patter about weather, food, local places of interest, hotel guests from a century ago. He appreciated that she so easily stifled her curiosity about his so-called relatives. She was a skilled country cook, a kind soul not many years younger than he was, a person, he sensed, whose past, present, and future floated along on an even-keel continuum. For a passing moment, he thought how nice it would be simply never to leave here. Become her permanent guest. Maybe help her with chores. Plow the snow in winter, paint the porch in spring, mow the summer grass, rake the autumn leaves. Marry her and sleep in separate beds. A peck on the cheek at holidays. Merge with her on that unperplexing continuum, grow old here, be buried across the way in that quaint cemetery. Life, and death, could be worse, could it not?

When she came back into the dining room with coffee, he noticed she was wearing a wedding band. He smiled at her and looked into her eyes just a little too long before thanking her for dinner and declining her offer of dessert.

Much as I wanted to fill Renee in on everything, sketch her an exploded-view diagram of the mess I was in, I held back. Instead, I described the Shelley forgery as an obligation to fulfill and refrained from confessing my father was a murderer and his nemesis was a murderer and I was an almost murderer trying to keep the former out of jail and the latter out of my life. And yet, before our mulligatawny soup and samosas had even been cleared and the entrées brought out, she'd intuited that significant pieces were missing from my puzzle-tale.

"So, wow, okay, all right," she said, folding her arms across her chest, draped in one of her colorful silk blouses. "Am I to understand that counterfeiting is your drug of choice from here on? Or have you forgotten what a kick-ass painter you are?"

"No, no. Rest assured I self-identify as a painter. Poe was just the alpha and Shelley's the omega of my nasty little detour into the world of forgery. Two and done for me."

"It's one and done, as you know," said Renee, an impish smile playing on her lips. "Two and screwed, dude."

Confident this was indeed my last forgery, I said, "If you want to know the truth—"

"Always."

"—I've been thinking how I might incorporate holograph letters and poems of famous writers and scientists and who knows who else into my paintings. Legit use of collaging this calligraphic stuff I seem to be so good at into the canvases."

"Like Cy Twombly? Or John Myatt?"

I adored her incisiveness, her limber mind. Twombly sometimes vigorously scrawled words into his paintings; Myatt's forgeries of Chagall, Matisse, and others were considered the "biggest art frauds of the twentieth century" by Scotland Yard, though my father believed Elmyr de Hory was the real art forger who earned that questionable distinction. De Hory's philosophy, Will liked to tell me, was that if you hang a fake long enough on a museum wall next to genuine great paintings, it becomes as real as the rest.

"Forget Twombly," I said. "And totally forget Myatt. I mean forgeries acknowledged as forgeries but that are so convincingly real-looking they might cause concern that I'm ruining originals."

"Interesting. So like who, then?"

"Like Nicole Diehl, of course," I said, maybe a bit more serious than intended.

"Nicole Diehl. Name's not familiar," said Renee with a straight face.

"It will be, because she's exclusively represented by the great Severn Gallery," was my comeback, feeling relieved when our dinner arrived and Renee, not unexpectedly, ordered another carafe of wine. How badly I wanted to switch subjects, gossip about Brooklyn or how her sister's new baby was doing, or just any other thing, but she kept on keeping on.

"Grasshopper, I love you," she toasted, and placed her glass back on the table. "But you're not telling me the juiciest parts of why you're making a million-dollar forgery and not keeping the million. I know you to be a kind and giving person, but charity has its limits."

When I started to speak, she shook her head and covered her ears with her palms.

"I know you, lady. So please do not lie to me," then reached her hands across the tablecloth to take mine. I found myself staring at her elegant manicured fingers interlaced with mine, which were stained with sepia ink and badly in need of a nail trim. "If you don't want to tell me everything, I'm good with that. But please just don't lie."

If my cheeks were already colored from the Côtes du Rhône, they now were a warmer rose red than before because her frankness needed to be returned in full. Being around liars, it occurred to me, made it so much easier to lie, though bending the truth was neither a habit I should blame on my proximity to Will and Slader, nor one that I wanted to continue.

During our wobbly walk back to the hotel, her arm on my shoulder and mine around her waist, Renee said, "By the way, I love love love your idea for paintings with expert-proof forgeries built in. Make the work. Let's cause a scandal, Diehl."

We stayed together that night. Drunkenly kissed a little— we'd closed down the restaurant after killing a third carafe— before falling asleep in each other's arms. Renee dozed off first, and I listened to her breathe for a while, inhaled her breath, our lips still touching. Before succumbing to sleep myself, I decided that she deserved to know everything about what was going on with me. She hadn't traveled all this way just to see the Klimt and Schiele retrospectives at the Royal Academy. Or to stare with me into Mary Shelley's large, knowing eyes in the famous 1830s-ish oil of her by Richard Rothwell in the National Portrait Gallery where it hangs. She had known, without my having said a word about it but in a way that the closest among us always know, that I and my kind were in deeper trouble than I'd let on. The distance between love and telepathy is immeasurably small, and I needed to open up to Renee, if only as an act of self-preservation.

The next day, after taking her into my confidence more fully than I'd ever done with anyone, Renee declared herself my silent partner in crime—no euphemism intended—and set herself to reading aloud letters from Mary to Maria Gisborne and others in Mary's circle, in search of material for me to work into my manuscript.

"You realize this makes you accessory to—"

"To you," she interrupted. "As it should be."

There was no dissuading her so I gratefully welcomed the help and, ardently, her companionship. This all was going to end well, I assured myself. Best get on with it.

As I sat at the table and continued to write, I listened to Renee's voice inhabit Mary Shelley's. Mary had such an open, even daughterly rapport with Mrs. Gisborne that it didn't seem so different from how she might have addressed her birth mother. Instead of feeling as if I were on the verge of cracking up, like I had before Renee got to London, I now felt something akin to inspired.

"'Rome,'" she was reading, "'is full of English, rich, noble—important and foolish. I am sick of it—I am sick of seeing the world in dumb show,'" and skipping ahead in Mary's letter of 9 April 1819, "'We saw the illuminated cross in St. Peter's last night, which is very beautiful; but how much more beautiful is the Pantheon by Moonlight!'"

"Let's go see the Pantheon by moonlight sometime," I said, impetuous, without looking up from my script.

"Why not the Parthenon while we're at it?"

Which made me smile. "The minute I'm done with this and Slader's out of my life, let's go straight there," I agreed, standing up from the table, pen in hand, to walk over to the bed where she was propped up on pillows and kiss her.

"No you don't," Renee laughed, gently pushing me away. "Get back to work, Bae. The sooner this is wrapped, the sooner we get to Greece."

While Renee and I had always been close, despite much of our time being spent apart, and had slept together before—as in spent the night in the same bed—we'd never been intimate. When she had awakened me that morning, kissing my breasts before fully taking me between my thighs with her tongue and mouth, I was startled at first, nervous and excited and a little confused before the length of my body shuddered and I let out a small cry. I lay there, feeling at peace for a passing moment, hearing the word *finally* again and again in my head. Afterward, she told me I was delicious, and kissed my forehead and my eyes, and everything felt different than it had before. The room, her mussed hair, the morning light, my life.

"What do I say?" I'd asked her.

"You're such a goose, *mon petit chou*." During lunch in a nearby pub, my phone buzzed and I saw that Slader had texted me using language meant to be cryptic to others but very decipherable to me.

"That him?" Renee asked without looking up from her plate of bangers and mash.

"Yep."

"Tell him we 'always consider it a black Monday when he does not write a little to us.'"

"Sounds like Mary," I said.

"I paraphrase. But I mean one to Marianne Hunt in or about 1819. An embarrassment of Marys, this world you've gotten yourself into, Nicky, but I'm sure you already noticed."

"I did," putting my phone away after a quick back-and-forth.

"What did your compadre want?"

"Same thing we all want. He plans on coming here to take delivery so he can move on with his life."

Renee looked me hard in the eyes before saying, in a low voice, her index finger pointed toward the floor, "Like here, in person? Here in London?"

"Didn't say that."

"Good, because that wouldn't be such a great plan, my dear. Outside China, London has more surveillance cameras than anywhere else in the world. Don't forget, Big Brother was an Englishman's idea."

"Point taken," I said. "I hinted Bournemouth."

"You a hundred percent sure you shouldn't just turn in both of these characters, keep yourself as far as possible out of harm's way?"

"I'm already very much in harm's way, Ren. Path I'm on is the path I'm on."

"All right, had to toss it out there," she said.

"You might want to rethink your own path, you know. No need for you to put yourself in jeopardy just because I have."

Without giving it a thought, she echoed me. "The path I'm on's the path I'm on. Has a nice Gertrude Steinish ring to it."

Renee took a second room in the hotel so that we could sleep together away from the ink fumes and books splayed every-where, and not risk damaging the drying holograph manuscripts by mistake when trekking to the WC in the middle of the night. My—now our—work went well. It helped beyond words, as it were, to hear Mary's sentences, their cadences and period ter-minologies, their politics and personal movements, their joy and melancholy, off the page and freed into the air. Renee's voice was strong and clear and held me in thrall as Mary's hand and my own began to merge. This was the big moment all forgers hoped for. When pareidolia and mimicry were left behind and a climax of authenticity rose up to take their place. When what was by definition *fake* became, as my father used to say, *Even better than the real thing*. My father whom, it occurred to me, I hadn't been in touch with directly since we'd said our goodbyes in Shannon.

I had messaged with Meghan and Maisie many times over the past several weeks and whenever my mother signed off, she always added that Will sent his love, asked that I stay safe, and wondered when I'd deign—no doubt his term—to return home. While I punted on his question, my exchanges with the women in my family were breezy. They asked where I had been and what I had seen, while I inquired about Maisie's violin lessons—her newest enthusiasm—and whether they'd seen our feral adoptee, Ripley, and to make sure to feed him if so and leave out a bowl of water even if they hadn't. After Renee's arrival, I wrote my mother to say we'd decided to venture beyond London's precincts and maybe make our way down to East Sussex to visit Monk's House, the sixteenth-century weatherboard cottage where Leonard and Virginia Woolf once lived.

When I wrote that, of course, I was fibbing in the hope of explaining away the length of my stay in England, and keeping my father in the dark. But now, who knew? A trip to see where Virginia wrote *Mrs. Dalloway* and *To the Lighthouse* might be the perfect farewell to Britain once the Shelley forgeries were passed along.

After a fevered couple weeks of work, punctuated by interludes to pick up more calligraphic supplies, spend some downtime in taverns, and sleep enveloped in one another's arms and legs, Mary Wollstonecraft Shelley's imaginary letters to Mary Wollstonecraft Godwin were nearing completion. My pace had picked up considerably since Renee'd entered the scene. As had my confidence and proficiency. I had produced about a hundred pages altogether, some of them full, others simply fragments of finished or unfinished thoughts. Some I had dated, most not. The stack of manuscript pages looked so authentic that I wondered whether those rare-book experts on Fulham Road might be taken in by them. Though, happily, they weren't the ones I needed to convince. Henry Slader alone assumed that role. He was the one who had to be satisfied. After that, the manuscript's believability was his problem, a problem I sensed he was equal to. Like most serious forgers, Slader was born with a gene that most of us—myself included—lacked. A gene that fostered profound self-confidence in the face of equally profound skepticism. He could precisely argue his way past any calligraphic flaws or biographical slip-ups, if they existed in my document. He might not get his full asking price. But he'd come away a richer man. One able to fade into the silent distance forever.

Which is not to say I'd forgotten to weave through the manuscript a confession, as I'd promised myself I would. My small gesture toward contrition, my encrypted message that would one day prove the letters to be fakes. I had taken my cues from *Frankenstein*, as its beleaguered and, to me, endearing creature was himself the ultimate forgery. Made from the flesh and bones of real, if dead and once-buried, people, Victor Frankenstein's monster was a fabrication, an approximation. A genuinely flawed pareidolian being, through no fault of his own. Frankenstein's creation was neither an automaton nor a real human. And yet, in some weird realm beyond the most brilliant forger's prowess, it was self-aware. It or, that is, *he* was also a deficient forgery, given that the experts in his day—in this case the country folk, the gentle townspeople with pitchforks and torches that he encountered—didn't believe he was one of them. At their own expense, they rejected his complex bona fides, his patchwork humanity. Even though he, unlike those more fortunate mortals, was fated to die not once but, since he was collaged together from corpses, twice. Poor bastard was often more humane than those who feared him, his vengeful murders aside.

From the first time the idea occurred to me, I had been
giving my "spirit line," as I'd come to view it, a lot of thought.
Ch'ihónít'i, it's called in Navajo—I looked it up—the deliberate
flaw traditional weavers patterned into their rugs so that their
spirits would not be left behind, trapped in the fabric, subject
to the depredations and bad dreams of others who would use
them in future years. Will had an old beat-up native rug on the
floor of the printing studio, and I'd always been fascinated by
its flaw line, which led from near the middle to its edge, a thin
cream line that traversed the reds and whites and pale browns.
For me, this flaw was as beautiful and necessary as the zigzag
design itself.

My personal *Ch'ihónít'i* would prove to be necessary too.
While I may well have willingly left some of my spirit in my
paintings, like little invisible numina who lived in the alizarin
crimsons and Prussian blues, no way would I want to leave
any part of me in these Mary Shelley letters. Instead, I would
pen pathways for Slader's soul—assuming he was possessed of
one, which I'd come to believe he was—to come reside in the
manuscript. The accomplishment of my toils, as Mary put it,
was his rich curse to do with as he liked.

Renee embraced my idea of writing a confession into the
manuscript. "Spirit line is an elegant way to think of it," she
said, "but if you'll forgive the businessy part of me, I'd call it a
product warning."

"Both," I said, with a laugh.

She continued with her recitations, though we'd by then
moved on from Mary's letters and essays to the complex narrative of *Frankenstein* itself, which is told in multiple voices
starting with the Arctic explorer Captain Robert Walton, who
sees the creature fleeing across the ice fields on a sledge; and
then Victor Frankenstein; then Frankenstein's creature, who is
allowed (by Mary—no one else would have) to tell us his own
tale in his own words; then back to Walton and Frankenstein

toward the end; and finally returning to the creature and his suicidal soliloquy. Postmodernist in design long before modernism was even born, I thought, a self-aware novel more widely read in the two centuries after its publication than anything by Byron or Coleridge or her beloved Percy or any of that male lot.

While Renee read aloud the Walton letters that began *Frankenstein* and introduced us to Victor, lost and near death on the polar ice while pursuing the creature, I tried my hand at patchworking words and phrases written to the captain's sister, to make my confession. In my Rhodia pad I jotted tantalizing lines like, "You seek for knowledge and wisdom . . . and I ardently hope that the gratification of your wishes may not be a serpent to sting you," which seemed apt. Or phrases like, "Such a man has a double existence" and "may suffer misery and be overwhelmed by disappointments." Elements of crime, duplicity, and failure were here and there. But nothing quite jelled for my purposes.

"Could you read me the last chapter?" I asked her.

"I could, I can, I will," she said.

In those bravura final pages of Mary's novel, after the forger Victor Frankenstein dies on Walton's ship, the creature unexpectedly sneaks on board to lament the lifeless form of his creator and share with Walton his life as an artificial man, his small joys and great sorrows. I couldn't begin to imagine what a fantastic state—high as a kite on pure imagination—the teenage author must have been in as she sat with quill and ink, alone in her room, and wrote this passage by candlelight. It was all too much for me to continue making notes, so I lay down my own pen and closed my pad.

" 'No sympathy may I ever find,' " I picked up where Renee let off, having climbed onto the bed, and leaned back propped up on pillows next to her. She laid her hand on my thigh while we both held the book, like a couple of mesmerized children playing at Ouija, our fingers touching the volume as if it was a sort of planchette. I continued reading aloud until Renee took over again at a natural place in the prose.

"'Once my fancy was soothed by dreams of virtue, of fame, and of enjoyment,'" she then read, as Mary Shelley channeled the daemon's words. "'But now crime has degraded me beneath the meanest animal.'"

"'The fallen angel becomes a malignant devil,'" I read next, and so proceeded to the last words of the book. "'He was soon borne away by the waves and lost in darkness and distance.'"

I had never thought of Renee or myself as sentimental. Just wasn't in our Buddha natures. But perhaps because we did think of ourselves as outcasts or weirdos or Others or psychic twins, we lay there together holding hands and stared outside into the snowy night. Not for long, but long enough to be overwhelmed by the beauty of the passage.

I spoke first. "No way will I use that. It'd be like a sacrilege."

"Not *like*," she said. "Would straight-up *be* a sacrilege."

"Pub break?"

"One pint, two max? Then back here till your disclaimer's finished."

When we returned to the room, still quite sober for having shared a third pint, my mind was made up that I would find my spirit-line text in the chapter where Frankenstein's monster first comes to life. Even people who hadn't read the book in a long time, or had only ever seen the exquisite black-and-white James Whale film version, or even Mel Brooks's whacked-out take, might recognize that passage. This way, I thought, my fakes might have a better chance of being flushed out.

As Renee read the fifth chapter, deliberately and slowly, I listened with my eyes closed, only opening them to write down a word or phrase that I sensed I could use.

"'It was on a dreary night of November,'" she began, the classic, unforgettable phrase that proceeded with elegant inevitability, "'that I beheld the accomplishments of my toils. With an anxiety that almost amounted to agony, I collected my instruments of life around me, that I might infuse a spark of being into the lifeless thing that lay at my feet,'" after which the horrified Frankenstein witnessed the fruit of two years' work, once his dream, but now his nightmare, open a dull yellow eye and gaze at its maker. The words Mary used to describe the aftermath of this resurrection were here and there perfect for my own creation. I wrote them down in a hand that was a confused amalgam of my own and Mary's. Among the terms that initially caught my attention were ones like *wretch, restored me to life, heartless, voyage of discovery, this horror, concealing, compose,* and *my disturbed imagination.* But I still couldn't see my way clear to piecing together my telltale letter even after a second, slower, reading and didn't want to test Renee's patience—though she brightly offered to recite the chapter yet another time.

Thing was, we were weary. It was midnight, that good old gothy hour, so we decided to leave my bedroom and head to hers. Renee kept a couple of bottles of super Tuscan, a *Tenuta San Guido Bolgheri Sassicaia,* that she, a fellow oenophile with even more underage experience behind her than I, had scouted for a decent if still-extravagant price at Vintage Cellars over on Churton Street. As I washed my face, hands, pits, and privates in the loo—we seldom bothered to shut doors at this point—I heard a cork pop in the other room.

When I joined her, she held out a plastic glass filled not quite to the rim and raised a toast, "Here's to disturbed imaginations."

"And to voyages of discovery."

The love we made that night was beyond my abilities of expression, then and now. After so many years of being a sworn loner, a decliner of dates, a solitudinarian homebody, a *cold fucking bitch*, as one pretty-boy alky called me in a bar in the West Village, I now—and in the midst of all this uncertainty—had found emotional equilibrium, a deep-felt home that would shelter me going forward. I told Renee I loved her, and she, without hedging or using any of her sweet nicknames like Squatch or Grasshopper or Bae, told me she loved me too. To say that all this felt as natural as a breeze in the branches of a flowering cherry tree on a spring day wouldn't do it justice. No sappy metaphor would bridge the feeling into words. We must have been in love for several long years and had lovingly danced around the truth of it for as many.

Before Renee was awake next morning, I quietly dressed and climbed the stairs back up to my room. The lines came to me fully formed, puzzled together from the scree of language I'd taken from Mary's novel, with every single word of my confession and declaration chosen from that fifth chapter of her masterwork, which, by then, I knew backward and forward. I took up my pen, dipped it in iron gall ink, and began to write my jigsaw confession.

To ease the load that's weighed upon my mind, and to restore me to a calm and serene life of reality and joy, I sincerely hope that these heartless employments, my words, can now be at an end and that I shall be at length free. My father and his enemy, an unrestrained wretch called Henry, fixed on me to undertake What I have created. They are the cause of all this. What was first a kind of pleasure turned to misfortune and, By very slow degrees, to bitterness and catastrophe. The different accidents of life are not so changeable as the feelings of human nature. How can I describe my emotions as the beauty of the dream vanished, and disgust filled my heart? I beheld the cause of all this with watery eyes, letter after letter, but the unbounded and unremitting attentions of my friend restored me to life. I felt impelled, in my own handwriting, to describe what I created. I feel the greatest remorse. Forgive me for the disappointment of which I have been the occasion.

Be in good spirits, I added as a postscript. *Henry will repay you entirely.*

Having noted that both patrol cars were gone from the station across from Reynolds House, Slader pulled out of the parking lot and headed toward the highway. He'd changed back into his blazer, white shirt, and chinos—needed to impress his make-believe real estate agents. The innkeeper had kindly packed a sandwich, chips, and an apple in a paper bag for his house hunt, but wouldn't have been able to see from the inn that when he reached the on-ramp he turned not north toward Cooks Falls, East Branch, and Fishs Eddy, but in the opposite direction, to Will's farmhouse. Careful to have left nothing behind in Roscoe that might incriminate him if she searched through his stuff—he doubted she would—he anticipated returning that same evening with a brand-new license and passport made in Nicole's studio. It being a Saturday in the dead of winter, he thought that Will, Meghan, and little Maisie would surely be in the city.

Turned out he guessed right. Not a soul was home. Using a spare he had boosted from the jumble of miscellaneous keys in a pantry utility drawer in September, he let himself in the back door and retrieved a shiny new brass key with a helpful little paper label attached to a ring, neatly marked "Garage Upstairs." Whether by negligence, overconfidence, cheapness, or the faulty hope that lightning truly struck just once, Will hadn't changed the house lock or installed a security system. Nicole's painting loft above the garage, however, where she kept her superior photography equipment, scanner, and other tech, boasted a new dead bolt on the door, which Slader now handily opened. Duck soup.

Daylight insinuated itself into the upstairs studio, a diffuse shade of tarnished silver, and he got right to work devising a new identity. Drop Edgar, done with Wadsworth. Erase Henry and Slader from his history and move ahead toward blissful oblivion with a name as common as a garden weed. He might have used the Roscoe innkeeper's ordinary-as-air surname, but he who could remember that Margery Williams's *The Velveteen Rabbit*, stacked with other children's books next to Nicole's bed, was dedicated to her husband, Francesco Bianco, and that inscribed copies were of utmost rarity, couldn't remember it. To think, only the night before he was daydreaming about her as his wife.

James, it occurred to him. What about the commonplace *James* that had reawakened him to himself? Sure, there were Henry James, James Joyce, James Baldwin, P. D. James. Great writers in their different ways, with simple names—excepting the latter's full name of Phyllis Dorothy James White, Baroness James of Holland Park—suitable for the recycle bin but for their literary accomplishments. Since there was nary a James among his personal acquaintances, James it was.

And why not add the male equivalent of Nicole? Nicholas James. No, James Nicholas, with a middle initial *S* clinging nostalgically to his own surname, like an S-hook on which to hang the shabby ghost of his past. *James S. Nicholas*. A stately inconspicuous name. The last one he would ever need.

That settled, he made good use of the steady, cloud-softened winter light to create a fresh driver's license that would work out fine if he was pulled over or carded for any reason. But when he scrutinized the homemade passport he'd altered earlier for Henry Edgar Wadsworth, he had to admit it was second-rate, wretched in fact. Sure, his headshot was digitally printed, as required. Page count matched the date of issue. But as for a proper chip, viably accurate holograms, correct perforations, and all the rest, this document was more likely to get him arrested than safely off to London.

Slader had enjoyed an unbroken streak of free movement for months by driving along a loose lazy-eight route that took him from the farmhouse east of Red Hook over toward Millbrook, up to South Egremont, thence to Fall River via Worcester, down to Providence and over to Red Hook, then west to Roscoe and back to his starting place. With the exception of those outings to the Poe auction and his rendezvous with Nicole in Hudson, he'd been moving in sketchy circles east and west since September. But here it was the beginning of February, and he was no longer penniless. In order to get to London and liberation, he needed some pro paperwork.

To avoid obtaining an ID on the dark web, whose crypto-currency and algorithms he distrusted, Slader settled on an acquaintance who operated out of a comfortable middle-class house in Hastings-on-Hudson, a pretty suburb north of Man-hattan, not far from where he too had lived once upon a time, in Dobbs Ferry. Might cost him ten, twelve grand, the passport. Nor did he expect a discount just because he was a fellow forger, didn't work that way. But even at full black-market retail it would be money wisely spent.

The passport counterfeiter's name was Jacek Czarny. Though Slader had his contact information written in the tiny frayed pocket address book he carried with him like a soldier might a Heart Shield Bible on the battlefield, he knew it was best to approach the man in person. Last time he'd visited Czarny was when he had trouble getting his revoked driver's license returned to him after his release from prison. Czarny had fabricated a beauty for him, using the name Henry Slader, sans Wordsworth, listing his mother's address as the home residence. He had even allowed his client to watch the magic being made. Observing the master counterfeiter at his bench that day was how Slader had been able to cobble together passable licenses in recent months. But, again, passports—*gateways*, as Czarny called them, *open sesames*—required an altogether different league of skill sets, equipment, contacts, and confidence.

Hearing his stomach growl, Slader gratefully ate his sandwich and potato chips while staring at the winter trees outside. After he finished, he chewed on the apple, which was a bit mealy, put its core into the chips bag, then tucked them in his jacket pocket. Next he wrote a snap to Nicole, having seated himself on the edge of her bed after washing his hands and thumbing through *Velveteen Rabbit* to check whether he'd been right about the dedication. He had, of course, for what it was worth. Closed the book, pulled out his phone, and typed, *Mary doing well I hope & u 2. soon on silver bird for yr bday.*

Removing his watchman's cap, he rubbed the back of his head where he could feel thin snakes of flesh, coral puckerings, and incidental pocks. They were mostly healed up now but would be with him for the rest of his days, a permanent reminder of Nicole, who, despite all and everything, was the only young person for whom he'd ever felt any hint of fatherly closeness. Shaking his head with impatience and mild disgust at his mawkishness, he tidied her studio, put everything where he'd found it, let himself out. After replacing the spare key exactly where it had been in the farmhouse pantry drawer, he relocked the house and split.

Afternoon sun was setting, a white ball inside ivory-gray layers of clouds lowering over the Catskills. Despite the calm anonymity Roscoe had afforded him, the fleeting sense of normalcy, it was a pointless destination. Nor did those cops across the road need to spot his van stowed again behind the hotel in midwinter. He could picture one of them strolling over, ordering a cup and cranberry muffin, shooting the breeze—they'd probably known each other since kindergarten—Hey, who belongs to that panel truck's been parked out back, just out of curiosity? Couldn't be a hunter this time of year. Nobody fishing. Town's dead as a bled buck. Anything she wanted to share about her guest? You know, like, out of curiosity?

Not so far-fetched a scenario, Slader concluded, ruing his having left some clothes behind. He would have to call her later, let her know he was tied up in Binghamton for a few days, not to worry. House search was going well. Please don't hold the Rockefeller room if she needed it for another guest, just toss his clothes in a grocery bag if it wasn't too much of a hassle. The last thing Slader needed was for the manager herself to walk across the way and file a missing person report.

While it hadn't been snowing back at Will's, the white stuff began to fall in bands as he drove south along River Road, past estates whose Currier and Ives acres softly rolled like painted utopias down to the icy Hudson. Was it absurd for him to be nervous about other cars with their bright headlights following him in the growing squall? Down through and past Poughkeepsie the flurries picked up, and back routes that connected to the Saw Mill River Parkway were slow going, dicey. The plows weren't out on the roads yet and his van, with its high center of gravity, fishtailed more than once as the snow began to freeze.

It was going to be too late to ring Czarny's doorbell this evening. Maybe he should've risked staying the night in Nicole's studio, maybe read her *Velveteen Rabbit*. Escapist lit for an escapist of sorts. But now it was too late and stormy to turn back. He would just keep going, call on Czarny first thing in the morning, and hope the counterfeiter wasn't in prison somewhere himself—though to Slader's knowledge he had never been accused of anything, let alone arrested and convicted. The man had forged himself an underground career while remaining publicly as pure as this very driven snow blowing against Slader's windshield. Testament to just how stellar, how unassailable his product was. And how low his profile.

Sleeping in the van under these conditions would be dangerous, but he had to find somewhere to overnight. His thoughts turned to the rooms he'd rented twenty years ago in the back of a red-brick two-story house on a residential lane in Dobbs Ferry. With neat houses set side by side on a block flanked by old oak and maple trees, it had been a lovely refuge back in the day. He'd lived there during what in retrospect were his golden years as a forger. Far off the beaten track, he had been productive beyond belief, not unlike Czarny. Made his money selling some true masterpieces to dealers and librarians. Many of his finest forgeries of Dickens, the Brontës, Frederick Douglass, Oscar Wilde, the crème de la crème, must still be out there, treasured and likely beyond suspicion. In commerce, in private collections, in climate-controlled inner sanctums of rare-book libraries they resided. In places accessible to scholars who pored over them and published their findings in peer-reviewed journals and pedantic books as they moved up the academic ranks in search of grants, awards, residencies, tenure. The whole donnish self-righteous parade of bamboozled experts, they all made him grin with keen satisfaction.

In the final analysis, as snow now shot through the twin cones of light from his van and he squinted over the steering wheel to get a better view of the road, didn't his own work mark a triumph that surpassed any by the arrogant professor friends his stepfather brought around for dinner at Corky Row? In heady moments he wondered if his accomplishments weren't comparable to those of the authors themselves. All had created genuine works of imagination. It was as if the writers cried out their words of genius in a valley, and he echoed them in return, a little altered, but faithful to the original sound and meaning. Like Echo and Narcissus—

Oh, cram a sock in it, he scolded himself. "Fuck me," out loud.

Having turned off the exit to Dobbs Ferry, he guessed his way up and down lanes that were blanketed in fresh powder until he found his old digs and parked across the street. Cut the lights but left the engine running for the heater. Headachy and eyes strained from the drive, he decided to rest in the gathered darkness. But for the storm, he lamented, he might right now be sitting in a cozy kitchen negotiating terms with Czarny. Might have spent the night in the forger's basement bathtub, as he'd once done many years back.

Instead, he gazed over at the house, which looked for all the world like a slack-jawed man lost in slumber, its stodgy facade and black front door centered between two tall windows. Evergreens edged its front as before, but thicker and taller. His landlady, who had lived with her mother and little boy, had probably moved away. The grandmother, who suffered from perpetual nosebleeds, surely had died long since, and the boy, whose name was Eric, would now be in his twenties and long gone. Slader always got along with Eric's mom, recalled being mildly attracted to her as he'd been toward the upstate woman, even though at the time he was carrying on an affair with Adam Diehl out in Montauk. And she always liked him, he felt, though he did disappear without leaving a forwarding address that summer after Adam died. How young they all had been.

He had the night to kill, probably in the van after all. Crazy, he knew, but he'd done crazier. As he listened to the radio, a classical station in the city that was playing some Mozart opera, Slader pondered just how little he had done in the years since he lived here. The life he was now so bent on leaving behind, using Nicole's forged Shelley archive as his ticket, hadn't really amounted to much, had it? Not to be morose but he wondered

what made him think that a future life, one that was freed of
having to make money, was going to be measurably better?
One of Einstein's maxims—Einstein whom Slader had forged
in a clutch of typewritten letters about the tragedy of the Trin-
ity atomic bomb test in Alamogordo, New Mexico—was that
the measure of intelligence was the ability to change. Slader
had always had a chameleon mind when it came to creative
problem-solving, to changing narratives as needed, pivoting
under duress. But for all that, wouldn't he carry the same baggage into a new life?

Sensing the answer was affirmative, he smirked at the house's
deadpan face across the street and, to his chagrin, it smirked
back.

The headlights of an approaching car woke him where he'd
fallen asleep sitting up in his van. Instinctively, he ducked. Seeing
its beams sweep across the back of his seat and disappear, he
peered outside to find it had parked in the driveway. A heavyset
man emerged from the driver's side, no one Slader recognized,
and on the other a short woman got out, not by any stretch his
former landlady. Automatic security lights illuminated the brick
facade as these strangers let themselves in the front door. He sat
there very wide-awake, stunned and disgusted by his sentimental
journey here and his useless regrets and worries. He needed to
focus, deal with the gravity of his present situation. Bundling
himself in his sleeping bag, he settled in for the balance of the
night, now and then turning on the heater. His breath fogged
up the windows, cocooning him in privacy.

Predawn roused him, along with its arctic air, to a classic
wonderland of powdery snow. Stiff from sitting still overnight,
he saw that his old neighborhood hadn't yet begun to stir, so
the blanket of bluish-white flakes was pristine under a clear
sky. Good, he thought, as he put the van into gear and slowly,
silently drove away, knowing he would never see any of these
houses, trees, fences, yards, ever again. He parked across from a

greasy spoon in Hastings-on-Hudson, sat at a corner table, and treated himself to a three-egg omelet. Just another anonymous early bird, Slader felt calmed by its atmosphere of strangers starting their days in separate booths, staring at their papers or phones, sipping their coffee, utterly indifferent to their fellow diners. He glanced around at the ceiling corners and over the counter and saw no security cameras, so had, like the very man of leisure he hoped one day soon to become, a second and third cup of coffee. Needed to fritter away a little time before finding Jacek Czarny's house and making his request.

Snow on the wet-black streets had already begun to melt. Back outside in the dazzling sun, Slader drove up and down several blocks in the part of town where the counterfeiter had lived, and found the house far more easily than he might've hoped. Place looked the same as years before. Hiding in plain sight. A woman answered the door. Walleyed, she seemed to look left and right at the same time, and thereby at nothing. He remembered her instantly.

"Good morning," he said. "Is Mr. Czarny in?"

Char-nee, his pronunciation flawless—a sign of respect.

She returned his smile, her gray hair up in a bun, like some grandmother out of a Brothers Grimm tale, benign but yet canny. "Who may I say is asking?"

"Henry Slader. I hope he'll remember me from a few years back when he did some excellent freelance fabrications on my behalf. He may recall that we work in similar fields."

"Henry," she said. "Slader," seeming to recognize him. "Just step inside, get yourself out of that cold, and I'll let him know you're here."

He didn't have to linger long before a short stylish man came into the entrance hall and warmly shook his hand. But for his cheeks and nose perhaps more deeply reddened by rosacea than before, he hadn't noticeably aged a day. Slader marveled that he was dressed in a gray wool herringbone suit on a weekend

morning at nine thirty. Neither annoyed the other with unnec-
essary pleasantries, although clearly Czarny remembered the
literary forger from before and vaguely asked how business was.
    "Can't complain," Slader said. "You?"
    "Still aboveground, still married, life is good. What do you
need?"
    After Slader filled him in, avoiding any and all personal
details, he explained this was a rush job and was prepared to
pay the fee as such.
    "Rush job as in today rush job? You realize it's a Sunday,
day of rest."
    "I'm sorry for the inconvenience but if it's at all possible."
    "This is difficult," Czarny said. "But doable."
    The two men settled on a fee with a surcharge, which wasn't
far off Slader's estimate, then made their way downstairs past
two locked metal doors, into the master's workshop. When
Czarny kicked on the overhead fluorescents and air purifiers,
Slader was as dazzled as he'd been once before when confronted
with the old-school magnificence of this studio. Here was an old
Hasselblad fixed atop a tripod flanked by umbrella reflectors,
a handsome Rolleiflex beside it on the floor, and several digital
cameras. There was a formal backdrop stand holding a large
long sheet of neutral paper, the door to a darkroom adjacent.
And elsewhere: engraving tools, high-end printing and mark-
ing equipment, laminator, metal trays of blades and knives, a
lifetime's worth of arcane widgets and implements of the craft,
and bankers boxes of lost or stolen passports, discarded driver's
licenses, diplomas, and the like. The one thing that had never
interested Czarny was fabricating money. Different sensibility,
he'd told Slader, without further elaboration.
    After having his photograph taken—his host provided shirt,
tie, and jacket—Slader was asked either to sit on the sofa in
the workshop or, if he preferred, to watch television upstairs.

To save time, Czarny would modify a relatively recent genuine passport, working as what was known as a cobbler in the trade. Because passports are scanned against a database, where they must match a corresponding record, Slader found himself with yet another name and thus added identity theft to his already impressive list of offenses. The work still went far more slowly than Slader—call him Joe Schmoe at this point—had expected. By the time he left, he had shared lunch upstairs with the couple, who kept strict hours, and grabbed a nap during the afternoon.

Owner of a brand-new-old passport, one of the most beautiful forgeries he had ever laid eyes on, Slader stepped out onto the street and climbed into his van. It was kind of Jacek's wife to give him supper while it got dark outside, though for twelve thousand five hundred cash he supposed it was the least she could do. As a crescent moon rose, the night now having gone crystal clear with stars winking like holiday lights in the grand leafless trees that sentineled the block, Slader drove away toward the Sawmill again with his destination in mind. One that had been right before him all along.

Friends close, enemies closer. Why not simply make this a round-trip, unlike his upcoming flight to England, and return to Will's? Like a silvery birch-bark canoe, the sliver of moon floated before him on the parkway in a sky as black as he'd ever seen it. Was it waxing or waning? he idly wondered. At least the roads were passable now.

Still no sign of life at the farmhouse. The heavier snow had been confined to south of Red Hook, as here even the back roads were only covered in a windblown dusting. Which was all for the best—no snow meant no tracks. Because it had worked so often in the past, Slader parked in his old hidden clearing off the road and returned to the house on foot, bringing food and his sleeping bag with him. He was careful to remove his shoes at the back door and crept in his socks to the pantry, where he retrieved the garage key. If he hadn't been leaving so soon, he might've had it copied in order to save himself extra steps in the future. Safely upstairs, the studio heat on but not the lights, Slader unrolled his bag on the floor, undressed, and climbed in. Peering out the window above him he saw the moon again and decided it was waning.

Renee and I took a train to the coastal town of Bournemouth in the south of England, where I was to hand over my Shelley manuscript to Slader in exchange for the incriminating photos he had of Will. Those and his assurance, contract or not, that we'd forever go our separate ways, and my family, particularly my father, would never hear from him again. What once seemed unimaginable—Henry Slader gone, along with any evidence that might send Will to prison for murder—was now within my reach.

After a month, give or take, mostly holed up in Pimlico, it was a dream to settle on a quiet Saturday afternoon into a grand hotel. The off-season rates allowed us to get a room overlooking a pewter-green sea with rolling waves of whites, deep blues, and sage—a sea that would be tough to paint, with its tertiary and quaternary colors, its citrons and slates. First thing we did, after depositing my unassuming sheaf of handwritten papers in the hotel safe box, was rush down to the beach and walk arm in arm in the opposite direction of handsome Bournemouth Pier with its

cheerful lights, away from others out to stroll, and find a secluded
bench from which to watch the sun set over the channel.

I was living my best life, I marveled, in the deep shade of my
worst. After the kind of sleep that only the lulling rhythm of
waves can induce, we breakfasted in the hotel's elegant dining
room, too shamelessly besotted with each other to feel embar-
rassed by our handsy behavior. One might fairly ask why Renee
wasn't able, just for instance, to feed herself the piece of toast
I had slathered with Seville orange marmalade and lifted to
her lips?

And yet, for all our personal happiness at the romance that
had overtaken us, it wasn't like we'd lost track of the life-and-
death nature of why we were here. Once breakfast was finished,
we walked together along Bath Road to Hinton toward a cemetery gate of St. Peter's Churchyard to check out where Slader
had proposed in a message that we rendezvous.

A blustery morning. The earlier sea mists had lifted and
the sky was bluing as gulls wheeled overhead. Sunday-morning
worshippers were making their way to services. On entering the
cemetery, we wandered past graves toward the elegant church,
the hum of nearby traffic in the air, until we found the modest
gray stone tomb set atop a grassy plot like a windowless long-
house. Fresh flowers had been placed by other visitors beside the
epitaph whose rooflike capstone was incised on both faces with
straightforward facts about who was buried beneath. Indeed, the
nearby oval blue plaque, like the one at Mary's house in London's Chester Square, was marginally more informative. Renee
and I held hands as we read: "IN THIS CHURCHYARD LIE THE MOR-
TAL REMAINS OF MARY SHELLEY AUTHOR OF 'FRANKENSTEIN,'"
along with her father, William; her mother, Mary Wollstonecraft;
her son, Percy; Jane his wife, "AND THE HEART OF PERCY BYSSHE
HER HUSBAND THE POET." Now and then we heard the cawing of
what sounded like crows. But when I glanced around to identify
them, none were to be seen.

Inconceivable, I thought, that baby Mary, who never knew her mother, who loved her father despite his remarriage to a woman she despised, who ran off at sixteen with a married man whose wife later committed suicide, who published at twenty a masterpiece of world literature, who married the widower love of her life only to watch two of her three children die before losing her husband to death by drowning, who raised her surviving son and championed the canonical poetry her spouse had written during his brief life, who herself carried on writing until she succumbed on the first day of February 1851—it was incredible to me that such a journey would end right where Renee and I were huddled together. Each of us laid a hand on the chill stone, thinking our own thoughts, saying nothing.

I felt so small just then.

Any earlier gaiety now gone, my eyes welled up. Guilt had been gnawing at me all along, though I hadn't wanted to admit it to myself. I had pushed ahead with moral blinders in place, seeing my goal while purblind to the very real people who once lived, breathed, loved, died, and ended as dust in this graveyard. The immediacy of what I was doing became as real as the tomb itself.

Who was I to taint this woman's story by weaving a bunch of fabricated ideas and words into its true narrative? Words intended to go out into the world as some great new discovery, private letters from Mary to her late mother, both of whom were buried—in cold, hard, plain, inarguable fact—right here? Even under duress, could I allow such fraudulence to enter literary history? Assuming, that is, the manuscript wasn't derided as a fraud right out of the gate, which, I'll confess, part of me hoped it was.

"I don't think I can do this, Renee," I whispered, my head on her shoulder after she'd seen I was crying and held me in her arms. "The Poe book was a whole other thing."

"Let's sit over there, why don't we?" she said, and we walked toward a bench down in front of St. Peter's.

Wiping my eyes, I followed her. "Sorry I'm being weak."

"Hardly weak, what you're doing takes some serious guts, either way you decide."

"Some serious madness, more like."

"That too, I won't argue," she said, close to me beneath the towering church spires, delicately turning my face toward hers and looking me in the eye. "So just how was the Poe different? I want to understand."

Good question, though not hard for me to answer. "*Tamerlane* was way less intimate than making these pages. With the Poe, my dad and I were just adding another copy of a known quantity—rare as a rooster's tooth, sure—but known. Matter of fact, there probably are more legit copies of the book somewhere. Remember you said at the time you thought it was a lark? This is more like a desecration."

"It's an imagined communication between two women. Three, in fact. Mary, Mary, and you. I'm not feeling desecration."

"Not so sure," I said, knowing what she was trying to do. "This is way more personal than the Poe. I'm presuming to bare Mary's heart. Besides, printing doesn't have the same almost sexual feel that writing does, where the hand embraces the pen, the pen touches the skin of the paper, the ink flows out—"

"I'm pretty sure you once told me that printing's a sensual act too," said Renee.

"Well, it's true that the printer's ink has to kiss the page—that's the terminology, not me being poetic—*kisses* the page in the press with just the right amount of pressure to—"

"You're besotted, lady," she half joked, though of course I was. "My question is, quite seriously, what are your alternatives?"

"That's just it. There aren't any. Not in the near term."

"Well, there's your answer, like it or not," she said.

"I've been thinking," I told her as a young couple rushed past us, oblivious both to me and Renee as well as the cemetery itself, which they seemed to be using as a shortcut to get from one part of Bournemouth to another, "that after enough time passes, I could write an anonymous letter, point out the *Frankenstein* puzzle confession, say in so many words that the cache is a fake."

"And hope they never find out who the forger was."

"Amen."

"This is your decision, Nicky, and yours alone," she said. "But I have to think a woman as radical, canny, risk-taking, unconventional as Mary Shelley was would kind of understand your situation."

Would she? If mine were Mary Shelley's story to tell, how would she compose my next moves? Absurd as that question was—and I didn't share it with my friend, now lover—I closed my eyes for a moment and silently asked, fully mindful I would receive no answer.

"Let's go back to the hotel."

"You good?"

As we stood, she took my shoulders and held me at arm's length, studying me.

"I'm good," I said.

"And so?"

"And so the letters are fiction," wiping my eyes on her sleeve and frowning as I settled on my choice. "They're notes toward a novel that'll never be written. Anybody who wants to look closely enough will see that. If Henry Slader wants to call the letters real, that's his choice. A forger of his caliber can't afford to care about history. His focus, by definition, must be on money and saving his own skin. He's a footnote with an asterisk."

Renee frowned. "You sure you're not letting yourself off the ethical hook a little easy saying that, Bae?"

"Can't disagree," I answered. "But right now, it's what I can manage."

"Good, done, finito, *pax vobiscum*," she said, a tender but determined look on her face. "Let's do this and no further misgivings. Sunday tea at the hotel for some hot Earl Grey with a nice strong dose of rum and dollop of honey?"

"Rum with a strong dose of tea sounds even better."

"Touché," said Renee. "Also, there's something I want to remind you about that I read in one of your Shelley books. Might make you lighten up on yourself to remember that Saint Mary of Somers Town was quite the hoaxer herself."

Several other couples, a single woman, and a family were seated in the spacious dining room when we returned. Must have been crazy crowded during high season if this group was off-peak. The handoff was scheduled for Tuesday, just before sunset. Which at this time of year was half past four or thereabouts. We had until then to pass time and hope everything didn't implode.

Renee, now wearing her androgynous half-glasses, had fetched a volume of selected letters from our room while I'd settled into a light-splashed table and ordered for us.

"So you recall," she said, now seated across from me, "that one of Mary's best friends in the late 1820s through the thirties was a young woman named Isabella Robinson?"

"I do, yes," and took a sip of my spiked tea.

"Remember how Isabella had an illegitimate child and needed to find a husband to save her daughter's chances at having any sort of life in polite society? And that, men being fucking men, nobody stepped up?"

"Right," I said, recollecting the story. "And with Mary's help another woman friend—"

"A dazzling cross-dresser named Mary Diana Dods, who published novels and translations under the pseudonym David Lyndsay—"

"—became Isabella's husband under yet another pseudonym, what was it?"

"Walter Sholto Douglas," she said without missing a beat. And as I opened my mouth again to question her, she went on, "Stay with me here. Mary Shelley damn well knew all along that David Lyndsay wasn't a man but she got herself wrapped up in, even partly stage-managed, an elaborate bunch of lies and deceits to help save her friend. May I?" as she turned to a page halfway through the book.

"Doubt wild horses could stop you."

"Okay, so. This letter to the publisher Henry Colburn—he's not mentioned in your pages, right?"

I shook my head.

"—reads in part, quote, 'A friend of mine, Mr. David Lyndsay, who is now abroad, has written to me, requesting me to propose a work of *his* to you.' Emphasis mine. She goes on to gush that his writing was highly praised in social circles and 'is indeed a production of genius' and that 'His present work is of the same cast.'"

Renee looked up at me for a reaction but, impatient even though she saw a smile of dawning recognition on my face, turned back to the beginning of the *Letters*.

"So, Nick. Mary was not only complicit in hiding Mary Diana Dods's gender—"

"Doddy, they called her," nodding.

"—but she took the lead in helping Isabella become the wife of, and let me get this mouthful right, Mary Diana 'Doddy' Dods David Lyndsay Walter Sholto Douglas. It was Mary Shelley who got them fake passports. Mary who secured letters of introduction in France, where the happy bride, she-groom, and Isabella's girl—bastardess no more—settled. Mary even stayed with them in France, where Walter seems to have become a real man-about-town among the Parisians."

I signaled the waiter and ordered two double whiskeys neat.

"Aren't we celebrating a little early, Squatch? Business isn't finished yet."

"We're not celebrating," I assured her. "I just need to raise a glass to one of the most modern women who ever lived. Her Frankenstein interest in coming back to life after death had a lot to do with her longing to meet her very modern mother. Show Mum what her baby'd learned from her feminist books and spirit."

Renee beamed. "I hoped this might help put things in perspective. Even your great Mary Shelley needed to go rogue sometimes, use some illegitimate documents—forgeries, to call a spade a spade—in order to get what she wanted, protect her renegade friends. I love it that she was out there like that."

When the whiskeys came, I finished mine in a single warm swallow, rose from where I was seated, strode around the table, and bear-hugged Renee from behind. I, who prior to these recent nights and days had pretty much avoided physical contact with anybody, was doing this unabashedly, in public? Just as you can never really know others, maybe you can never know yourself, I thought. Crazy time to fall in love but when is a sane one? We settled up and returned to our room, where, lying together on our shared bed, drowsy from the alcohol, I looked out the window over her bare shoulder and saw columns of slant rain unleashing torrents out on the horizon. Not a good day to be at sea. We kissed and soon enough drifted off.

Evening. Renee was still sleeping so I quietly got up, tiptoed over to the sofa, and sat crisscross applesauce like Maze might have done if she were here. With a pencil, I began to doodle some sea monster and kelpie sketches on a hotel notepad, now and then glancing up to look across that same channel where Isabella and her husband once sailed to France and a new life.

When I heard Renee stirring, I turned and asked, "You hungry? All we've had since this morning is tea with benefits."

We threw on our coats. Night had descended and a violet drizzle overspread the town as we walked to the restaurant where we'd planned to have dinner, the Bald Faced Stag. A girl at the hotel had recommended its chicken and leek potpie—and who were we, despite our worries, or because of them, to turn away from such medicinal comfort food as that?

Conversation over dinner moved to other things besides forgery and tawdry deals to cover up tawdrier transgressions. We spoke about this thing that had blossomed between us. Was it some odd strangers-in-a-strange-land fantasy, such that when we were back on native soil it would drift into a pleasant memory? We both knew that wasn't the case. Were we still going to be able to do everything we'd done before, but as a couple now? No question. We might even risk becoming inseparable, which wouldn't be the worst outcome. How would we negotiate a possible power imbalance if she were my gallerist and I came to the relationship with far less money than she?

"For one," said Renee, "the artist is essential while the gallery owner is useful. And as for money, I myself don't care. But trust me. With your gifts—used legally, Bae—it won't be an issue."

The irritating buzz of my phone interrupted us. A text from, of all people, my mother. And not written in a tone I was used to. *Do you plan on ever coming home?* it read. *Your father's threatening to go over there to kidnap you back to reality. You're not doing anything illegal, are you? Don't make same mistakes he did. You should know I'm at the funeral for Maze's biodad. Could use your support. Where on earth are you, Nicky?*

Floored that both Meghan and Renee, an ocean apart, nudged me in unison to play by the book, as it were, I texted, *So sad to hear abt death. Sad to hear you upset. Tell Will to calm down & stay put & that we're heading home very soon.*

Heard that before, she responded without missing a beat.

Honest, Meg. I mean it. Got to go but see u sooner than you think xxx.

A lot to take in. I felt stung by guilt. But no way could I let her in on where I was and why I'd been away so long. Someday, maybe; maybe never.

After I showed Renee the exchange, we debated whether we should move to another hotel, register under bogus names, pay with cash, go dark until the situation resolved. But since neither of us had done anything truly unlawful—even my fabricated Mary Shelley letters were arguably crafted for my own personal enjoyment, at least until I handed them over to Slader for him to sell as originals—we had nothing to hide and decided against it. That being said, I added, how would Will even begin to go about kidnapping me back to sanity if he didn't know where I was?

"You know what?" Renee announced. "It just occurs to me that I, not you, should go out to meet with whoever shows up—"

"That's for fucking sure not happening."

"Well, if you go there yourself, you go with an empty satchel. I can hold on to the letters somewhere close by, carry a bouquet of flowers with me. Since none of your Sladers or Pollocks have a clue who I am or what I look like, they'll figure me for a mourner if they even notice me. This way, assuming Slader meets you himself and everything's on the up-and-up, you just give me a signal and we'll take it from there."

I sat staring at my plate, then said, "We didn't talk about what to do if Slader bags."

"You're an obsessive about contingencies, girl."

"I confess to the accusation," I admitted.

Back at the hotel, I retrieved the manuscript from the safe, brought it upstairs to leaf through one more time. Although I knew better, and didn't share my shameful thought with Renee, I couldn't resist feeling proud of the masterful job I had done, if not of the work itself. Yes, my pride was appalling and preposterous. But as Slader himself had once said, when I asked him why he had stolen my copy of Henry James's *In the Cage*, even though it was flawed by my juvenile forgery, "Because it is very beautiful."

A feral scream shattered his sleep. Then another, muffled by panic. The girl who stood over this stranger lying in sudden brightness on the floor wasn't able to make a full-throated cry, but instead gasped for air and wheezed. At first the man didn't recognize where he was. He'd been asleep in comfortable darkness before she turned on the lights. But then he remembered, prompting panic of his own. Fully awake now, he gaped, blinking, past the girl and saw she was by herself. He tried to stand but found he was trapped in a sleeping bag. Casting about, he fumbled for the zipper and mostly freed himself. The girl remained tethered in place by fear, staring at his every move. A tremor ran through her as she held out both hands so her palms formed a tenuous shield of flesh and bone meant to ward off any assault he might make.

Slader hushed her, forefinger touching the tip of his nose.

"Please—stop," he said, his voice raspy. Dressed in T-shirt and underwear, he wished he had slept in his clothes on top of the bag. Would've left him less vulnerable and made for an easier escape.

Maisie cried out once more, or tried to, but now the noise she made sounded like a wounded animal reduced to soft moaning.

"Don't be afraid," Slader begged her, with a clumsy smile. "I'm your sister's friend. Nicole's friend. Everything's fine, don't worry."

Startled into tentative calm by the mention of her big sister, she took a step back.

Slader noticed the shift, moved ahead. "That's right, Nicole said to tell you I've got her permission to be here, okay?"

The girl dropped her hands and said nothing as she took another step away from him. Her cheeks burned, her lips were bleached and quivering.

"Maisie, you have to listen to me," he went on, trying not to show his frustration and swallowing hard as he found his voice. "Nobody's going to hurt you."

"How d'you know my sister?" she managed to stutter.

"Oh, we're old friends. She's in England right now, as I'm sure you're aware."

Soothing voice. Reassuring words. Slader hoped to project an easy calm, even get her to trust him if possible.

"Who told you that?"

"Nicky did, of course. I was just crashing here because she told me it was fine. She invited me. Even gave me the key. Look," fishing it out of his nearby rucksack and holding it up for her to see.

"How do you know my name?"

"Lots of questions. Let me answer with one of my own," he said. "How could I really be Nicole's friend, like I'm telling you I am, and not know your name?"

Still paralyzed by the shock of finding him in her sister's studio, Maisie coughed out, "That's a good point," a gesture toward getting herself out of harm's way while not making the man angry. "I guess she forgot to tell me you'd be here."

"Well, see, that's why she told me to tell you," said Slader, feeling calmer himself. "That is, if I ran into you. But she said you weren't around, so I wouldn't be in your way. Your parents must be here too then?"

"Course they are. My dad is, anyway. He had to meet somebody all of a sudden, and my mom's away so I came with him."

Hearing that, Slader's calm was short-lived. "They don't let you stay alone in the city, I imagine."

"Right, no," Maisie said. Her eyes were watery and her face wasn't working right. "Maybe I'll just be going."

"You know what, Maisie, I'm on my way to meet your sister," he extemporized, trying to buy time.

"She didn't tell me that either."

"Is there something you'd like me to take her? A birthday present? It's coming up, isn't it?"

She shook her head. "No, I'm good."

Slader had wormed himself partway out of the sleeping bag, enough to stay decent in front of the girl but able to vault to his feet if he had to. He sat up, bent at the waist, arms behind him, giving off as relaxed an impression as he could, feeling a fool.

"You know what?" he said. "Your father, Will, is an even older friend of mine than your sister."

"Really?" doubting him. "Why don't I know you, then?"

Slader smoothly answered, "Oh, we've met."

"I'm sure I don't know you."

"We only saw each other for a sec, so no need for apologies," he said elliptically, pleased with his gaslighting, as he remembered with clarity how he'd accosted her back in August while she rode her bike home in evening darkness. She'd screamed then too, at the top of her lungs, when he jumped out of the bushes and demanded she deliver a package to her father, a parcel that contained the stolen *Tamerlane* and a note instructing Will to make a duplicate, or else. The night her adoptive father was coerced back—blackmailed, more like—into the world of forgery, for one last hurrah. Maisie wouldn't have recognized Slader in the dark even if he hadn't been wearing a mask—which he had, a perverse mask of Adam Diehl's face. The ploy worked just as planned when she got home, terrified into tears, insisting the parcel had been forced on her by Meghan's dead brother. Will had recognized at once who was behind the morbid prank.

Here, now, the girl had no reason to apologize. So she shrugged off his words and glanced over her shoulder to calculate how many steps it would take to reach the door and fly down the stairs.

"Maisie, I know you're keen to get back to whatever you were doing. So why don't you tell me what you came for, and we'll get you squared away. Then I can go ahead and pack my stuff," he said, adding, "Glad you woke me up when you did, by the way. Else I might've slept right through my flight."

She found it dismaying how polite and reasonable the stranger was being. This wasn't how bad people were supposed to act.

"Don't need to do it right now," she insisted. "Seeing as you've got to get going."

"'It' what?"

"Just was going to grab some of my books."

"Like *The Velveteen Rabbit*, you mean?"

He was full of surprises, this man. "That's one."

"I loved *Velveteen Rabbit* when I was a kid. What a classic story. You remember when the Skin Horse says something like, 'Real isn't how you're made. It's a thing that happens to you'?"

"Yes," she said, wondering where this was going.

"You know what? I'm curious whether you're allowed to be in here when Nicky's not around?" he asked, knowing it was cruel but to build on his authority. "I thought this was her private space. I mean, I have her permission. Do you?"

Maisie was flustered; the man was right. What with her sister being away so long, her father so sullen and quiet, and her mother pretending nothing was out of the ordinary, the girl sensed something was very wrong and had grown reserved during the first month of the new year. While having outgrown children's books some time ago, it still comforted her to reread the familiar tales whenever she felt confused or lonely, and she'd brought some favorites here for solace. "I didn't think she would mind. Just I miss her, is all. Don't tell her I've been out here reading on her bed, please?"

"I'm sure we can work out a little deal between us."

Ignoring his comment, she said, "I gotta go. My dad's probably wondering where I am."

"We don't want him to worry," said Slader as he climbed to his feet, and swiftly dressed.

Averting her eyes, she looked in the direction of the nightstand where the slim books were stacked and said, "I'll just grab them and be on my way."

"That works. But about our deal. Like you, I've got a favor I need to ask."

She waited for him to go on.

"It doesn't involve you doing anything. More that you do nothing. If I don't tell Nicky about you being in here, can you do me a small similar favor?"

"I don't know."

Hands in his pockets, frowning at her defiance, Slader said, "You're not being very fair. You mean to say you can't do absolutely nothing for me? Nothing's too much to ask?"

"Maybe" was all she could come up with.

"Did I say maybe when you wanted me not to tell Nicky about you?" and explained, firmly and not untruthfully, that her sister and he were finishing a project together that would greatly benefit her father. But for reasons too complicated to get into, Will wasn't meant to know about it. And that being the case, it was of utmost importance Maisie say not one word to him, to anybody, about seeing Slader here today. "You think you can do that? For your sis and dad, if not for me."

"Since I don't even know you, I wouldn't do it for you anyway, right?"

"Sure, fine," taken aback by her cheekiness, yet respecting it. For all his bad history with Will, he had to admit the man had helped raise two admirable girls. "But for them you would, wouldn't you. Besides, all I'm asking is an even-steven pact. I don't tell, you don't tell."

"Not even my mom?"

"Well, I don't think that's such a good idea either, since we both know that she'll just turn around and spill the beans to your father."

Seeing no clear path out of her predicament, she agreed to Slader's demand.

"And as a way of thanking you for keeping our secret, I'd like to give you this," he said, pulling his wallet from his pants pocket and counting hundred-dollar bills. "I heard down the grapevine somebody wrecked your bike last summer and how upset you were about it. So I promised Nicky, again as a friend, that I'd love to give you enough to get it fixed."

She looked at the money first, then at him, then back at the money.

"There's five hundred there. You think that's enough to cover costs?"

"It's too much."

"Well, get it fixed and add a vintage night-light for the thing. Maybe a basket or a bell. I used to have a bell on mine when I was a boy."

"That's nice of you, but I don't think I can take your money."

Slader was truly impressed by Maisie. If only he'd had such integrity when he was her age—ringing his bell as he bombed through the streets of Fall River to annoy people and get their dogs to bark—or really at any time in his life. "Tell you what. I'm going to leave the money right here on Nicky's worktable. So if you change your mind—"

"Like I said."

"—when your sister gets back from overseas, she can give it to you. How's that sound?"

"So listen. I totally gotta go now" was her response, emboldened by his odd kindness toward her, a benevolence even he knew she oughtn't trust.

"Get your books then, and go in peace, Maisie."

"Thank you—oh, I don't know your name."

"No need. Nicole will tell you everything when she gets back from her trip. Wish us luck on our venture?"

"Good luck," she echoed flatly, clueless as to what he was going on about, holding the stack of a dozen picture books to her chest.

"And don't forget. Not a word about me being here."

Maisie nodded uncertainly, then walked—didn't run—down the stairs. As for Slader, he recognized the time had come for him to set his endgame plans into motion. Killing the overhead light, he tapped on his cell phone's flashlight, gathered up the sleeping bag, crammed it into its compression sack, slipped into his coat, looked around the studio to make sure he wasn't leaving anything behind. Next he needed to make a fast decision as to hiding the key to his safe deposit box in Rhinebeck where he'd left his negs of Will taken in the early morning hours the day of Adam Diehl's murder. Slader, who lied as readily as he breathed, had always told the truth about the cache of evidence that would prove Will's guilt.

And knowing that Will the forger, Will the murderer, was every bit as capable of violence as Slader himself, there was no way he'd have risked bringing his only bit of leverage to their doomed meeting last September. Slader had rightly predicted things could get nasty. The two despised each other. Both were angry at being pressured to do things they didn't want to do. Given that Will had the upper hand—money, homes, family, job, reputation—Slader had stashed both his safe deposit box and car keys under that rock before he went to demand an advance on the *Tamerlane* sale. Good thing he had. His imagination was dark, but he would never in a hundred lifetimes have guessed how wildly that evening would spin out of control, landing him in a grave, left for dead.

That was all in the past, however. Time had come for a new resurrection.

On Nicole's worktable sat a stack of drawing pads and notebooks. Propping the cell phone so the light pointed away from the window, he opened the thickest one, in which she had only filled the first pages. Moving quickly, he picked up one of her retractable Olfa knives and cut a square recess into the blank pages, a hole just deep and wide enough to place the safe deposit key inside along with a folded, duly signed document transferring ownership of the box to Nicole Diehl. If the bank refused her entrance because there was something amiss with the paperwork, so be it. And if she had to hire a lawyer or bring in the police to gain access, so be that too. Once he had vanished, it would be of zero consequence whether Will's terrible secret was kept under wraps or discovered for all the world to see. And for that matter, just because an innocent man was facing charges for the—his—accidental murder of John Cricket Mallory, presumably still in jail while awaiting trial, it didn't mean Slader's conscience was troubled enough to turn himself in.

It was what it was what it was.

He replaced the notebook, a burgundy hardcover with a black spine, in the middle of the stack, nimbly swept the confetti of cutout squares into his pocket, and made for the door. Before turning the knob, he looked over his shoulder and, seeing the five hundred on the worktable, decided to grab it. Not because he was some penny-pincher who'd changed his mind about the money. He truly wanted the girl to get her damn bike repaired. But because, if left there, it would confirm Maisie's tale when she inevitably told Will about her unhappy encounter.

Outside, dark as it was, Slader decided to cut through the woods on the near side of the road so the garage blocked any direct view of him from the farmhouse. Overhead, the sky was scattered with stars and a sliver of moon. Through the thicket of trees he could make out the field below the house, and did he possibly see eyeshine down there, a possum or skunk? Or maybe even the same cat he'd encountered months ago, a stray wise enough to shun human contact beyond the bare necessities of begging for food. Ripley, Ridley? Nicole had told him the cat's name at some point. Sage furry philosopher, mused Slader as he picked his way through the brambles, shielding the phone light, avoiding patches of unmelted snow. If you keep humans at a wide berth, you'll live your nine lives in fine fettle.

Looking down the road one last time from a hundred yards along, he saw a car parked in front of the farmhouse, illuminated by light from its windows. While this didn't alarm him—wasn't a patrol car—he did have to wonder who would bother visiting a man no more sociable than Slader himself or that mangy cat were, especially at this hour.

Back in his van, he crossed the Kingston–Rhinecliff Bridge and merged onto the southbound thruway. As much as the thing had cost him, persuasive as it was, he found himself growing wary of testing out his new passport against state-of-the-art security at Kennedy, LaGuardia, or Newark. The smaller Stewart International Airport in Newburgh and New Windsor—one terminal, two concourses, ten gates—seemed a far safer point of departure. Since he didn't have a credit card or a reservation, he would fly standby, pay cash. Good thing, he thought, that he'd had the foresight to buy a money belt after his exodus from Providence. It would hide, he hoped, the thousands extra he'd be traveling with illegally.

Fatigued and not a little cranky at having been rousted from Nicole's studio, Slader chucked caution to the wind and, seeing it wasn't yet midnight, ditched his van in as out-of-the-way a location as he could find and walked a mile to one of several nearby generic airport inns, where he crashed for the rest of the night in a clean bed. Better to go to fucking jail, he thought, than sleep like a frozen cadaver in that smelly bag again. Midmorning the next day, he showered and, after a visit to the continental buffet, took a free airport shuttle to the terminal building. A mammoth cargo plane lifted off from the military airfield neighboring Stewart's commercial traffic and tore its way upward into the air, its heavy rumble rattling his nerves as he got off the bus.

Easy, man, he chided himself. You got this.

Once inside the terminal, he checked the departure board for London-bound flights. The earliest available was routed through Reykjavík, Iceland. While he would've preferred to avoid the stopover, the sooner he flew, the better. His next move was to buy a respectable carry-on bag, kelly green, trimmed in nubby leather, and transfer his ditty and the all-important photographs into it before ditching the knapsack he'd carried them in. Then sundries from shops to fill out his bag, make it look more, what, valid. Finally he queued up to see what tickets were available without a reservation.

"Baggage to check?" the agent asked, with a perfunctory smile.

"None today," he said, adding for a lark, "My daughter's moved up her wedding date. So I'm in a hurry to get there."

She began typing, eyes on her monitor. Without glancing up, she told him, "If you're willing to fly business class, I have one seat near the front of the cabin."

"I'll take it," said Slader, realizing he ought to have asked the cost. Not that he cared, just didn't want to act out of the ordinary.

"Passport, please. What credit card will you be using today?"

He improvised again. "Wouldn't you know, in my rush to get here I left it home. But cash will be all right, I assume."

She counted the bills before calling over a supervisor who recounted the couple of thousand and scrutinized his passport. After comparing its photo to the man before him, he approved the transaction and said, almost as an afterthought, "You're aware you'll need to fill out paperwork if you're intending to carry more than ten thousand cash on your flight?"

Slader's heart sank like the proverbial stone. "That won't be necessary, thanks."

"You're all set then," said the agent, handing him his boarding pass and ticket, along with Jacek Czarny's counterfeit, which had easily cleared its first hurdle. "Congratulations to your daughter."

The decision made itself. Sickened and enraged by this unexpected turn, Slader knew he couldn't hazard filling out their gnarly paperwork any more than he could risk forfeiture of his cash—and, more to the point, his freedom—to some astute TSA officer using a Terahertz scanner. The situation was quicksand. *Fuck fuck fuck*, he thought. To get to the bigger money that lay ahead in England, he had no choice but to ditch his problematic stash. Back in the men's room, in the privacy of a stall, he removed his money belt, rolled it up tight, and wrapped it in lengths of toilet paper. Furtive, he tucked the mummified bundle into a trash receptacle. Some lucky janitor would become the ultimate benefactor of his hard work, he imagined, if he had the common sense to keep his mouth shut about the treasure he'd discovered before spiriting it home.

Boarding was at seven. Facing a drawn-out Monday afternoon, he inquired if there was a bar at the airport. Departing flights were upstairs, as was the cocktail lounge. Trying not to think about the past or future, as the former was too dispiriting and the latter too rosy optimistic, he decided that either things would go badly at security or they wouldn't. Unburdened by the belt and its chancy freight, he set a congenial look on his face, the epitome of a cooperative traveler.

A security agent inquired about the eight or so grand in his wallet and he retailed the same story as before. Dad off to daughter's nuptials. The money a wedding present. He passed through the scanning machine, relieved after all that he'd ditched the belt with its unregistered, thereby unlawful, dough. Didn't need to be more radioactive than he already was, he reasoned. His classy overhead bag warranted a cursory search but nothing in it raised suspicion. He was, to his surprise, golden. Still had to get through British customs but for now all was well. He found the bar, ordered a Bloody Mary with all the fixings. Marveling at his success thus far—maybe he wasn't fundamentally a bad man, maybe he could become normal in his new life—he watched a soccer match on the overhead flat-screen, brightly costumed men running to and fro on a field of green, kicking a colorful ball in a contest whose rules he neither understood nor cared about.

For a stretch of time Slader felt as oblivious and innocent as when he was first in college, away from home, keeping his own hours, reading banned books, making his own set of weirdo friends. Life was okay then, as it would be once more. Even after he had dropped out of school—he'd never been one for attending classes and passing tests—he still was just a young guy afloat in the world. Someone with a gift for mimicking movie stars' and other famous people's autographs, a talent he'd honed in a high-school drafting class. He worked all manner of temp jobs, disappointing employers who saw his promise too often undermined by a habit of messing up assignments. As well as his penchant for quarreling with colleagues.

Savoring a vodka-soaked olive, he reminisced about his first job at a used bookstore, from whose shelves he found it beyond easy to steal certain volumes and take them home, where he taught himself to forge their authors' autographs in them. A faint smirk on his lips, he recalled selling them to higher-end book-stores in Boston. Business—for soon it became a business—grew to the point where he got bored with filching unsigned second-tier books and instead began purchasing nicer first editions. Firsts that became blank canvases that he could elevate with faux inscriptions.

He met his future partner, Atticus Moore, at a rare-book fair in New York when, in a moment of purest audacity, he waved the dealer aside to inform him that one of his expensive offerings was "a magnificent forgery, totally plausible, but all the same a fake."

To which Atticus unexpectedly responded, "What, you can do better?"

Before answering the question that would change his life, he paused to think. It was a crossroads moment. "Why do you ask?"

Charmed days, those; high times.

From there Slader followed his destiny as Atticus's demimonde connection, making and losing money, getting in and out of trouble, journeying from there to here. Here in this airport bar. Everything, he reflected, the entire arc of his life, would have been fine had he never met Will Gardener. Will with the wholesome surname that Slader had never known until he stole his business certificate, intending to burn it in celebration one day soon. Will the dark gardener, whose life's very groundwork was overgrown with shady oleanders, fatally toxic and yet attractive to all around him. In so many ways, subtle to blatant, decades ago to now, Will had all the traits of a poisonous jimsonweed, a bitter nightshade, a mountain laurel, every kind of deadly flower. Will, who'd been the greatest blight in his life.

Slader ordered another Bloody, this time a virgin. More passengers congregated at the bar, anonymous and friendly, discussing the weather at their destinations, what they did for a living, the usual pother. Slader welcomed the distraction, enjoyed spinning autobiographies that left himself and his nemesis out of the narrative. He needed to pass time, and this was a winning way to do it.

Sometime during the lengthening day, he noticed an older man with scrunched shoulders, dressed in a corduroy suit, seat himself at the far end of the bar and order a stout. After taking a quaff, he nodded in Slader's direction, saluting him with two fingers and a nod. The man had about him a blend of world-weariness and old-school polish that gave Slader the impression he was a Brit on his way back to the old country. Turning away, Slader asked for a splash of vodka to spike the rest of his virgin, hoping it would help him sleep through much of the flight, as he'd need to be fully on his game after passing through Keflavík on his way to Heathrow.

Drink downed and tab settled, Slader got off the stool to head for his gate, which had been announced. As he passed the British gentleman, a look of curiosity swept over the man's face. "Excuse me," spoken in an accent distinctly not British, "but aren't you Henry Slader?"

Slader assured him he was mistaken and, with a forced hint of a smile, wished him a good day as he tried to squeeze through a group of drinkers.

"No, I'm quite certain," the not-Brit persisted. "You're the same Henry Slader I questioned in Montauk, how long ago was it?"

Standing all but eye level with the man now, Slader realized he was right, though the name escaped him.

"See, you remember now," Pollock said. "We talked about a friend of yours who met with a misfortune, great misfortune about twenty or more years back."

"I'm sorry but I have no such memory," Slader insisted, thinking that if others nearby overheard any of this they'd naturally assume the old codger'd had more to drink than he could hold. "Now I have a plane to catch, so excuse me."

"People do change their names these days, along with their identities and all the rest," Pollock continued, undissuaded.

Surprising himself and Pollock both, Slader halted and turned around. "So did you ever catch him?"

Gone were their patient manners, however labored.

"Catch?"

"You know, the bastard who butchered my friend all those years ago like a lamb in a slaughterhouse. Because I don't think you'd be sitting around an airport cocktail lounge enjoying a brew and spouting this crap if you'd done your job."

Here Pollock had Slader little more than an arm's length away, but with no authority to do anything about it. Slader wasn't, so far as Pollock strictly knew, guilty of a single solitary crime. Even the alleged attack on his sister in Fall River remained in question, she being an unreliable witness at best, and nothing had been developed that would point to anyone beyond the suspect who'd already been arrested for John Mallory's demise and let go. The retired detective had no jurisdiction, no proof of anything.

"I'll take your silence to mean you never caught the murderer, did you, boss," Slader pressed. "If you want my advice, I'd say keep your innuendos to yourself."

"So, Slader," said Pollock, unperturbed. "What's in your carry-on?"

Without a thought, Slader said, "A stolen Gutenberg Bible from the Morgan Library."

Pollock hesitated, frowned.

"No need to pout. It's not like they needed all three of the ones they owned. Besides, it's none of your goddamn business," and made his way past the crowd toward his gate.

M aisie's call wakened me in the middle of the night. Groggy, I pulled the cell from beneath my pillow and squinted at her name on the screen, brushing away a busybody dream like some sticky cobweb. Her hyperventilating words roused me into a fast crisp focus.

"Say again, Maze?" I whispered, trying and failing not to disturb Renee, who sat up in bed, as alert as if she'd not been sleeping, and asked what had happened.

"Don't know," I said, switching the phone to speaker, and telling Maisie, no longer in a whisper, to slow down, start over.

"There was a guy here, scary bald guy with scars on his head."

"Did he tell you his name?" I asked, but already knew who she was talking about. The fear in her voice was something I'd heard from her just once before, that time at Slader's prompting too.

"No, but he said he was your friend. That you told him he could sleep in your studio and he was on his way to see you."

"Shit," I hissed under my breath. "How'd he get in? No, never mind how, when was this?"

"Just now, before I came back to the house. He told me not to tell Mom or Dad, but didn't say not to tell you."

"Clever girl," I encouraged. "Why don't you take a deep breath and try to calm down. He didn't hurt you?"

"No," having inhaled and exhaled. "It was weird. He was superpolite in a creepy kinda way."

"Is he still out there?"

"Think he's gone. He seemed all of a sudden to be in a big hurry."

"Where's Will?"

"Downstairs with some old man I guess he knew years ago, but I'm not sure because he asked me to leave them alone. It's all pretty crazy, Nicky. That's why I went to your studio. Hope you don't mind."

"Of course I don't mind. But, Maze, this other man, you get his name?"

"Not his first name, but he said he was Mr. Pollock when I answered the door. Then Dad came out from the back and let him in."

Renee and I exchanged a glance, my heart sinking as Maisie's story became yet more convoluted. "Did you hear anything they said?"

"Well, I tried to listen in, but didn't want to get caught. I did hear them talking about you, though, where you were. What you were up to."

This was not happening, I told myself. Surely I was dreaming again, some horrible new nightmare. Seeing how upset I was, Renee stepped in, "Heya, Maze. Renee here—"

"Oh, hi Renee, how's it going?" By now she sounded almost normal. But that was my resilient little sister all over. Maisie knew how to bounce back.

"Going all right, girlfriend. Your sis and I plan on coming back to see you soon, so get ready for a big girls' day out on the town, all right? Just quickly, though. Could you take a look out the window and see if Pollock's car is still there?"

A silence on the line preceded her confirming he must have just left.

"Does Will know you're upstairs?" I asked.

"Dunno, why?"

"Because I want you to do exactly what the man told you. Don't say a word to Dad or Mom about him. I haven't got time to explain, and you know it's not something I'd normally ask, but could you just keep it a secret between us?"

"Sister to sister."

"That's right."

I heard Will's voice in the background calling her name. An urgency, a kind of impatient alarm tinged his voice even muffled and distant as it was.

"Where are you guys, in London still? When you coming home?"

"Bournemouth," I told her, without a thought, and gave her the name of our hotel, before I noticed Renee vigorously shaking her head.

"Bournemouth? Where's that?"

I swallowed hard, realizing my mistake. "But Maze, you can't tell Dad that either. Anyway, we're just here to do my birthday, then heading home. I need you to hang up now. Not a peep about this call, promise?"

"Pinkie promise," she said.

"Phone me again if you find out anything more about all this, but only when you're by yourself, okay? And be careful about—"

The connection dropped. I imagined Will had entered her room, and could picture Maisie hiding the phone in her overalls pocket, trying to look nonchalant, even though the news she had just delivered to me and Renee was perplexing, ominous. Pollock with Will at the farmhouse? Slader in my studio? Maisie, the little wren in the furze, unprotected from such treacherous men? Meghan away? I felt like the proverbial bird on a wire, akin to the wren, exposed from every direction, torn about what to do.

Skies were just beginning to brighten. Predawn turquoise and pinks of cirrocumulus reflected in the swells out past the beach. In a state of disconcertment, I pulled on my sweatpants, wrapped the chenille throw from the bed around me, and stepped over to the bank of windows, hugging myself. Down below, a sleepy dog walker bundled against the chill made his way along the beach behind a playful barrel-bodied lab retriever. In the other direction a pair of joggers were headed toward the Victorian-era pier, which jutted steadfast out to sea like a great millipede fixed in its tracks. Otherwise, the beach was empty.

"Shall I pop downstairs, see if the kitchen staff's stirring, try to get us some coffee?" said Renee, getting dressed, clearly wanting to give me time to myself.

"Epic plan, Ren," I said. "Thanks."

"Then we can have a think together, if you like," and softly closed the door.

I turned to survey our bedroom in her absence, so barren without her there, no matter how replete with its scent of our recently sleeping bodies. What a lame little monosyllable was the word *thanks*. Insufficient to the hilt as a way of expressing how grateful I felt for her companionship. I had come firmly to believe that I wouldn't have made it this far without Renee's steady presence, although I knew she'd laugh her ass off at any such notion.

Just doing what comes naturally, Squatch, I could imagine her retort. *Like breathing. You gonna thank me for breathing?*

Goes unsaid I would. When I turned again toward the shore, I was overcome by a fresh epiphany. Maybe it was some continuation of my dream? Maybe inspired by my mounting jitters? Either way, it occurred to me that this was the exact time of day when my uncle's life was terminated at the hands of a killer. Meg always described her older brother as a night owl who loved puttering around late in his recluse's cottage in Montauk— the family residence she and Adam inherited after they were orphaned by a boating accident—reading and tending to his literary treasures even as he fell behind on his bills. She never minded helping him out. When they also lost their alcoholic aunt who raised them to adulthood in Manhattan before succumbing to cirrhosis, leaving them deserted again, Adam became her sole surviving blood family, and she mothered as much as sistered him to a fault. All her overindulging, cosseting, doting, and catering to him left little room in her life for others. The siblings were, I had come to believe, emotionally inseparable, classic in their codependence. How had it never dawned on me until just then that Meghan might never have agreed to marry Will as long as Adam still needed her?

High-spirited Meg with her Pre-Raphaelite red hair had tried once, tried for her shot at independence by making an impulsive marriage with a man whose name she refused to tell me and who she declined to describe beyond the fact that they shared a love of music. None of her favorite Callas arias, none of his Coltrane jazz solos were going to save them, though. The marriage was good for a brief stretch of months yet doomed from the first, and ultimately overwhelmed by Adam's neediness and his sister's need for him to need her.

My epiphany grew darker even as the clouds outside continued to brighten. Watching two more runners set out on their morning routine, taking off in opposite directions, I thought through my father's motives to murder Adam. Will flat-out hated my uncle for his neediness, his narcissism. But even if he wasn't going to allow Adam to stand between himself and Meg, needless to say he should have found a sane path to what he wanted. I could see with bristling clarity that my father's fucked-up toxic brew of resentment—greed for Meghan's affections, yes, compounded by the belief that her brother was a rival forger—must have fueled his hostility for many months before he finally struck out.

Had Henry Slader not witnessed him at the scene that morning, my dad might've lived the rest of his life in a cocoon of deluded grace. A happy man, happily married to a woman whose tragic past was eased by the joys that came with her second-chance marriage and her daughters. I couldn't help but recall Pollock's words to me back on Wren Day in Dingle, when he said how it'd take a truly twisted sense of self-preservation to commit murder and then go ahead with living your life as if it had been some faulty fantasy, a bad dream best forgotten for everybody's sake.

"Coffee's here," Renee announced, scuttling my runaway train of thought.

Which was just as well. I had no further need to plumb the long hatred between my father and Slader that followed Adam's death. Forgery was only part of the picture. One of them had to lose his chance at love for the other to claim it.

"Troubled thoughts, methinks."

I turned to face her, shaking my head as if to rid myself of those very thoughts and said, "You know, I'm not sure we shouldn't just check out of here and take Mary Shelley with us."

"Really now," as she poured and handed me a cup. "Paris, anyone?"

I tried to smile, get with it. "Bhutan, more like."

"Bhutan's cool. I understand women are treated better there than in most places on our great big tumid patriarchal planet," she said. "I hate to point out the obvious, but you know the problem with Slader and your father will catch up with us wherever we go."

"Sad but true, true but sad," I agreed, as the sun finally edged above the horizon, the fiery pale disc that continued to widen as clouds picked up a prism over the sea.

"Well, since Bhutan won't solve anything, my dear, what's our action line?"

I wondered first whether Mary Shelley had seen sunrises such as this and second, what she might have done in similar straits. Neither question was hard to answer.

"Action line is we follow the original plan, let the flower bloom of its own accord."

"Good on you. But you know it could end up being a damned ugly flower."

"'O Rose thou art sick' kind of ugly?"

"Maybe worse," she said.

With my birthday approaching tomorrow, I hoped my transaction with Slader would be a fait accompli by day's end so that once the deed was done, Renee and I could bid him farewell—along with dear Mary, her revolutionary parents, and Percy's asbestos heart—and go back to London. Renee had got it in her head we ought to celebrate by splurging on a five-star night at Claridge's or the Ritz before we set out for parts unknown. Me, I just wanted to go on a pub crawl.

But no matter. Two messages on my cell a few hours later dampened our spirits about any such fantasy plans, high life or low. One from Maisie, *Yr hotel looks corking* ♥♥♥ *like a palace cept in Bornmth*. I rolled my eyes and mouthed "corking" to Renee before tapping over to a very different message that showed up on my phone not long afterward, a text instead of a snap, and from an unfamiliar number.

We still on? was the incoming question.

Still on, I wrote, my thumbs unsteady.

Remind me the time.

What was his problem? *Hour b4 sunset on bday u know.*

He came back quickly with a response. *Bournemouth still?*

Which floored me, as Slader and I had gone out of our way to be more oblique about details such as meeting places and plans. All things equal, I thought it best not to respond. He knew where we were meeting, knew when. It had been his idea in the first place.

Even as I decided to leave him in limbo, he came back with another text.

Nothing means yes?

Still seemed wisest not to respond.

After a pause he wrote, *Till soon, Nicole.*

His use of my name took my breath away. Since when, like never, had Slader used my name during any of our messaging?

"Renee? Something's wrong."

She pushed herself up on her elbows and yawned.

"Look at this" and held up my cell phone for her to come see.

Her chin on my shoulder from behind, she read the brief exchange. "Write him back. Ask him what the password is," as she came around and sat next to me.

"We don't have a password."

"Even better."

Whaz the password, haha? I typed, figuring if it was Slader writing for some reason outside our usual means of communicating, he'd know what I was up to and if, for some misfortunate reason, it wasn't, whoever was at the other end would reveal themselves. Hoary old investigator's trick, I knew, standard matinee movie fare. Who knew but that it would work?

Nothing further surfaced on my screen, however. Either my correspondent was Slader and he knew he'd screwed up and preferred not to acknowledge it—a strong possibility—or somebody else had stolen one of his phones—he'd been burning through burners—and was playing me. Bernard Pollock came to mind, but his modus was much more straightforward than being coy on some app.

Troubled, I speed-dialed Maisie but ended the call before she had a chance to pick up, for fear Will might be near. Always a looming presence in my life, he seemed to have withdrawn into himself after his clash with Slader and our place was vandalized.

Finding that spooky effigy in the woods only made him more disconnected. His auction, however corrupt, had been a triumph and gave him greater status in his world than before—a status I knew he never desired but had to bask in to avoid suspicion. I also knew, of course, that Slader wasn't pressuring him anymore, not since I'd picked up the slack. But even in Ireland my father hadn't been acting like himself, had aged, grown more bristly and suspicious of me, his sometime favorite. Which was why acing my upcoming meeting with Slader was imperative. Selfish or not, unethical or not, rational or not, I was still driven by the hope of saving my father from others, if not himself.

Rather than skulking around, we pulled ourselves together and spent the day walking the streets of Bournemouth. We lunched at the Hotel Miramar, a handsome Edwardian pile where Edith and J. R. R. Tolkien spent their holidays before resettling there from Oxford to escape the onslaught of admirers who descended on him after *Lord of the Rings* made him famous. Twilight we spent on a pier bench watching the gulls, cormorants, and gannets until it got too nippy, then back to the hotel bar to warm up. But for the fraught meeting tomorrow, it might have been a memorably mellow day for a couple of off-season tourists.

We were huddled at the bar when my cell rang. Surprised to see my mother's number on the screen, I excused myself while muting the phone, and darted to the ladies' room for privacy. Meg may not have been the last person I wanted to talk to just then, but she was close to it, if for no other reason than that she'd barrage me with questions—not without cause—and I would be forced to respond with half-truths or full-blown falsehoods.

"Hiya Meg, everything okay?" I said in as upbeat a voice as I could muster.

"You told me to call when I had some news," said Maisie.

"Maze?" I cried out, relieved nobody else was in the loo. "What're you doing on Mom's phone?"

"Mine's gone missing is why," she said, cool as cool could be.

Naturally, I wanted to hear the backstory, but she continued without a pause, saying she and Will had returned to the city the morning after Pollock had made his unexpected visit, though they'd planned on being at the house for a couple more days.

"Did he say anything about Pollock? What he wanted, why he was there?"

"Nope, nothing."

"Did you tell him anything about me?"

"Nicole, please," she scolded, then conceded, "Well, I did say you might be coming home after your birthday."

That wasn't good, but I was done with faulting Maisie. "Okay, so then where's Meg? What's this news? What happened to your phone?"

"She's back home from that funeral she went to."

The conversation was going in so many divergent directions, I was confounded rather than enlightened. "Some old book friend of hers died," she continued. "Mom kept staring at me when she got back. Kinda freaked me out. Told me about how nice it was, the funeral, I mean. Yech, since when are funerals nice, Nicky?"

Knowing it wasn't the right moment to discuss her relationship with that old book friend, I said, "Well, they can be quite beautiful and moving, you know, but—"

"I never want a funeral," she proclaimed.

"You may change your mind someday," I said. "But you called with news, you said?"

"Right, I thought you'd want to know that Dad's gone away on business all of a sudden. For the auction company, I guess."

I waited, impatient, as the signal was spotty and Will's going off to look at a possible consigner's collection wasn't anything unusual. "Right, and?"

"Well, um—" she paused, uncharacteristically hesitant—
"Meg told me he was heading to England. Don't think she was
supposed to say it, but it's what she said."

That gutted me. "When's he going?"

"Already left."

"But he doesn't know I'm in Bournemouth, so that's—oh,
no, Maisie. Your text, did you delete it?"

"I'm super sorry, Nicky," she said, her voice dropping to a
whisper. "I think he might've seen it."

I took a deep breath, dumbstruck as I tried to think through
what this meant.

My poor sister added, "I know I should've deleted it. Should
never have sent it."

Truth to tell, she should never have been put in the position
of having to worry about such things. "It's okay, Maze," I assured
her. "My fault and my problem to deal with. Now listen to me,
though. You need to get off Meg's phone, wipe the history right
away, and put it back where you found it."

I rejoined Renee and filled her in. Simply put, we agreed
that if we weren't going to flee—and no, we weren't—the sole
alternative was to water the ugly flowers in the garden we'd
inherited and hope they'd grow to be beautiful. We shared a
sticky toffee pudding for dinner like girls not yet Maisie's age
might, had a couple of brandies for dessert, and went upstairs
to crash.

My birthday morning was overcast and fog-clad along the
coast. Renee and I had agreed to celebrate it the next day, when
all this was behind us. Having heard nothing further from Henry
Slader or, for that matter, his shadow, Bernard Pollock, or anything from Will, we had a quiet breakfast in the dining room.
No rum laced the coffee, and our usual banter was dampened
by what lay ahead. Finished, we went upstairs to pack and made
online reservations for an evening train back to London. Renee's
profligate idea of setting up shop in a fancy hotel in Mayfair or

Piccadilly we ditched in favor of overnighting at less expensive lodgings in Soho. That way we'd be near the British Museum, where we could spend my belated birthday marveling at the Elgin Marbles and Rosetta Stone, one stolen from Greece and the other from Egypt, before catching the Eurostar from St. Pancras—forever in Mary's afterglow—to Gare du Nord in Paris, where we hoped to spend a few low-budget days before flying home. There would come a time, we imagined, when we might revisit these precious stolen artifacts after they had been repatriated to their rightful homes in Athens and Rashid. Girls could dream.

S lader remained hunkered in his seat when the flight made its stopover in Iceland. While many fellow passengers deboarded to stretch their legs or search for duty-free trivials, he leaned his forehead against the scratched window and watched a scouring wind send light snow racing across the tarmac. To avoid Pollock during the first leg of his trip, he had pretended to sleep. But after it now became clear that the *Ríkislögreglan*, Iceland's national police, weren't going to storm the plane and spirit him away in cuffs, he settled into a heavy slumber, only waking up hours later to gaze across the tops of large lazy clouds and vast stretches of the North Atlantic below. Squinting down some seven miles at waves that lay like threads across the silver water, he saw ships the size of poppy seeds making passage toward their ports of call.

No more prone to whimsical reveries than he'd been to the crying jags that afflicted him during those first blurry days after his concussion, Slader nonetheless mused on the lives of people aboard those vessels. None of them had led a pure life either, he reflected. From captains to shipmates, from honeymooners to retired vacationers on deck chairs bundled in blankets, every last voyager down there had screwed up over the course of their lives. Screwed up mightily, even monumentally. He wasn't alone in having botched things to hell and back with bad decisions kindled by greed, vanity, wrath, jealousy, and other vices only hinted at in the philosophers' books. More than likely none of them were literary forgers, but Slader was confident that each—no matter if they feigned otherwise—had taken damning truths and remolded them like soft putty into lies whenever it suited their purposes.

To live was to lie, he decided. Such was the price of being human.

In the end, all people were forgers.

As he drew down his window shade, he realized he could be as annoyed as he wanted that Pollock was on this same flight to London via Reykjavík, but there wasn't a thing he could do about it. They'd exchanged nothing further after he warned the guy to mind his own business at Stewart, and because he'd been among the first to board and Pollock the last, it wasn't like he could've bolted from the plane without drawing attention to himself—maybe from the airport police. The sometime detective had avoided eye contact when he'd edged his way down the aisle. Yet while there was no chance Pollock's moves weren't calculated, the reason they were flying together was opaque to Slader. No matter, he reassured himself. The old boy had nothing, nada, zip on him. And if he had, he certainly wouldn't have allowed Slader to go overseas.

The wizard Jacek Czarny's counterfeit passport didn't raise an eyebrow in Heathrow customs, and because Slader was able to exit the plane well before Pollock, he was cleared and quickly walked to the transportation area. Here he negotiated the fare with a car-service chauffeur to drive him direct to Bournemouth, some ninety miles distant, an hour and a half if traffic allowed.

Peering over his shoulder out the back window of the town car, he didn't see Pollock. Maybe he'd slipped the bastard, he hoped as he faced forward and reset his watch to local time. He would arrive several hours ahead of his meeting with Nicole. Plenty of time to get some fish and chips, knock back a couple of single-malt scotches. Take in the pure winter air of this seaside Dorset town before he started a new life.

Old life or new, however, he didn't realize Pollock had no urgent need to catch up to him. Not that morning, anyway. The detective already knew Slader's general destination and agenda. Certain that the situation was in hand and, moreover, was being captured by closed-circuit television as Slader made his way to Bournemouth, Pollock took a less expensive coach on a somewhat slower schedule. As a pensioner, even one with dark freelance revenue, he saw no need to waste money on some pricey limousine when public transport would get him to the same place for far less.

Nor did Slader know that Nicole and Renee's taxi let them off at Bournemouth Central railway station at about the same time he himself had been deposited there. The chauffeur's log would confirm the train station as his drop-off point, and at a moment that closely coincided with the date and hour stamped on the ticket the women were given when they checked their bags before setting out on foot toward St. Peter's Churchyard. When queried later, the driver would recall with clarity that his fare, after giving him an unusually generous tip, took off in a direction opposite the cemetery, toward a pub he himself had recommended for their fresh cod and eighteen-year-old scotch.

There was a possibility Slader caught a glimpse of Nicole and Renee at the station that day and simply didn't recognize them. He'd never met Renee. As for Nicole, her hair had grown out some since he'd last laid eyes on her and, more significantly, she emanated a kind of mature radiance that hadn't been there before. Curious to think how differently things might have gone

if either had noticed the other. The designated time and place
to exchange Slader's photographs for Nicole's forgeries would
have been rendered obsolete. The meeting might have happened a few hours early, right then and there, without a hitch.
Henry Slader, perhaps deciding to forgo his fish and chips and
his glass of Balvenie, could've engaged that same chauffeur to
drive him to wherever he contemplated going next—Maggs,
Quaritch, Harrington, Jonkers, Shapero, though none of these
rare-book and manuscript specialists were even remotely easy
marks—to try to sell his Mary Shelley trove. For their part,
Nicole and Renee might have said farewell to Bournemouth,
good riddance to Slader, and caught an earlier train to London,
where they themselves could venture forth into their futures.
And as for Pollock, he would have arrived late to find himself
adrift on the streets of the same town where Henry James once
resided while taking care of his invalid sister, Alice, and Robert
Louis Stevenson wrote *Strange Case of Dr. Jekyll and Mr. Hyde*.

This was not what happened. The conspirators had been
within a hundred yards of each other but were too preoccupied
to notice. Slader did walk to the restaurant, which, for all his
chauffeur's enthusiasm, proved to be only okay at best, and
offered no array of single malts as promised, but a lesser Whyte
& Mackay blend that would have to do. He was determined to
enjoy it anyway, and so he did, ordering a double neat. Despite
his distress over the nosy former detective, he was feeling upbeat
about what lay ahead. He'd begun to think of this as his personal
liberation day. How could he not be any less optimistic than
the two women who strolled north, hand in hand, to kill time
visiting St. Mary's Church at the cemetery?

Unlike from Heathrow, the drive to Bournemouth from
London Gatwick took closer to two hours, and Will, though
a little jet-lagged, felt comfortable driving a rental car on the
so-called wrong side of the road to the destination he'd mined
from Maisie's cell. How he wished he hadn't made the mistake

of forgetting to return the phone he'd taken from her dresser top where it was recharging. But he'd been in a rush to catch his flight, so packed and departed for Kennedy soon after Meghan returned from Atticus's funeral in Rhode Island, with his daughter's cell still in his pocket. Wisely leery of leaving digital footprints, well aware that he understood Vandercook proof presses far better than smartphones, he ditched the thing in a trash receptacle before boarding the AirTrain, keeping only the prepaid cell he'd used to text Nicole, posing as Slader. While he didn't know exactly what he would do once he reached Nicole's hotel, or whether her treacherous scheme would bring him into direct contact with his longtime nemesis, he did know in his gut that it was preferable others hadn't a clue to his whereabouts. His cyber breadcrumb trail would end in the garbage. Fitting, he thought, without a smile.

Now driving along the motorway, his plans crystallizing little by little, he found himself growing evermore angry as the miles ticked by. His daughter hadn't hidden her tracks as cleverly as she'd thought, and Will knew his fair share about hiding tracks. All those slender but revealing gaps on the print studio bookshelves? The reduced stack of period paper at the bottom of his stash? Her sudden deep-dive into *Frankenstein*'s author? And Pollock's report that he believed she'd probably handed materials over to Slader on at least one occasion, Pollock who should have been in Will's pocket by now but somehow seemed to be turning Nicole against him?

Maddening, in a word. He found himself gripping the unfamiliar steering wheel far too tightly and noticed he had sped up, so lightened his foot on the accelerator. No time to be stopped on the M3 for a speeding ticket, not when he had to get to Bournemouth to bring this all to an end.

Bournemouth. Will felt his stomach churn as he recalled a conversation with his then-teenage daughter about his ambitious idea to forge a clutch of letters from Mary Shelley to one or another of her relatives.

"Maybe back in the day," he had confessed to Nicole long ago, "but I don't have the hand for it anymore. And frankly, Mary Wollstonecraft Shelley's mind isn't one I could ever have easily entered. Not like Conan Doyle's, anyway."

"Not like a logical man's mind, you mean," Nicole had said. "Too much heart?"

She hadn't meant for her words to sting, but they did a little, because she wasn't wrong. And now it seemed she'd taken up the challenge, put her own hand and heart into it. But for Slader of all people. Will felt a reluctant admiration for her chutzpah, even envy, but more than that was outraged—enraged, finally—that Henry Slader had somehow arisen from the dead and, like some persuasive demon, twisted and manipulated her into a mockery of herself, blackmailed her into using her gifts for his own poisonous purposes. He knew he couldn't afford to get mired down in anger, however, and did his best to compose himself as he entered Bournemouth.

"Good day," he told the woman at the front desk of the hotel where Nicole and Renee had been staying. "I believe my daughter's a guest here and I'd love to connect with her, as I'm passing through town on business."

He gave the receptionist her name and was informed that she and her friend had checked out of the hotel not so very long ago.

"Did she by any chance say where they were going?"

The woman glanced at her male colleague behind the desk, dressed in a matching suit of burgundy wool with embossed gold buttons and trim, giving them both a faint military air. He shook his head and she turned back to Will with an apologetic smile. "I'm afraid she didn't leave information in that regard. I'm so sorry."

"Nothing at all? You see, I'm quite keen to locate her," he pushed, failing to conceal his desperation.

"I really am terribly sorry, sir."

"One other quick question, if you don't mind. Where's the nearest place that sells homeware goods or a hardware store?"

"That would be Wilko, up on Wimbourne Road," and she gave him the address.

Outside, the fine mist of rain was letting up. Sunlight shot through breaks in the fast-moving clouds. Will got into his car, watched its wiper blades scythe the water while he collected himself, then drove off in search of Wimbourne Road, wondering why he hadn't heard from Pollock yet. After Will had read Maisie's text and divined Nicole's whereabouts, he'd pieced together her plan and agreed with Pollock that if they were ever going to bring Slader to justice, they'd need to converge here in Bournemouth, confront him out of the blue. It was easy to imagine that when the bastard met with Nicole—at Mary Shelley's gravesite, Will presumed, knowing his daughter's goth inclinations—he would certainly be carrying his infamous Montauk photographs. And given the timing of recent events, they'd certainly have planned the rendezvous for Nicole's birthday. If all went according to plan, the images could finally be seized, confiscated, analyzed, and alleged beyond doubt to be doctored fakes. The weather on that bloody East End morning some twenty-two years ago—a faraway February on a faraway coast—would surely diverge from what was depicted in the photos. Or some Photoshop trick would come to light. This much Will had assured Pollock more than once. Today his claims would at last be revealed as the truth.

Pollock knew he'd broken every rule, resisted every instinct, in growing fond of Will and his family over the years, insofar as he was capable after a long career as a sleuth of liking anybody. He had also come to believe, however conveniently, that Slader displayed too many classic indicators of psychopathy not to be the unindicted perpetrator. It was time for Pollock to wrap things up so he could, unlike piteous Diehl, live out the rest of his days a completed, fulfilled man. And while it gave him no pleasure to admit to himself that he'd become what was known as a bent cop—not dirty, as such, like so many others he'd worked with over the years—he accepted Will's informal offer to hire him to solve the case, bring justice to bear on the guilty, and help offset a portion of his expenses, travel, and lodgings. Assured by his client as such of absolute independence in whatever conclusions he came to, the detective, funded now, set out to resolve the matter once and for all.

Will sometimes wondered, sleepless at night, if the money he'd given to assist Bern Pollock's investigation might be seen as bribery if viewed by authorities who didn't have much patience with tainted cops. He'd even wondered in recent months if he might have been better off sharing with Nicole, in utmost secrecy, that Pollock, whom he was aware had been tracking her, was on his side. Or was, presumably, leaning that way. But he had deliberately kept himself more and more out of touch with his daughter. Indeed, Pollock had urged Will to do so, in order that he himself might glean more about Slader's doings from the young woman.

None of this made Will happy. But what were the alternatives?

For Nicole's part, she felt her phone vibrate. A snap. *Here 4 christening. family pix in hand. who'd u tell abt baby?*

"What the—" and replied with a string of question marks.

"You all right?" Renee asked.

Old fossil dick tailing me, Slader went on. *Will ditch but this is bs & on mama, how else? be there with lil one or deals off.*

"That him?"

Stunned into silence, it took Nicole a moment to collect herself. Who the hell had alerted Pollock? Maisie wouldn't have made such a dangerous mistake, though it was true the girl had openly identified their location. Had Will somehow dragged the information out of her and passed it along to the detective?

All Nicole could think to reply to Slader was a lame *No idea who wd tail you but all set here*, and handed Renee the cell so she could read the exchange for herself.

"Look," she said, handing Nicole her phone back. "He's just nervous, who could blame him? Nobody's following the man. It's an honest mistake."

"Slader, honest?" and laughed, though Nicole sensed he'd been as straight with her as he was able to manage these last weeks and months.

"You know what I meant, Squatch."

"To be really and truly honest, I don't trust anyone right now except for you." They had earlier ducked out of the last of the drizzle into St. Mary's, the Gothic Revival structure where they'd gone in search of a window designed by William Morris, and toured the parish church as one might a museum, taking in art by greats like Edward Burne-Jones, Thomas Earp, and James Redfern, who had also carved some sixty statues for the Salisbury Cathedral, a mere twenty-eight miles distant. Back outdoors now, they found a mostly dry bench and sat listening to the water drip from ten thousand bare branches in the cemetery. Slader's next message soon enough came through.

Am here. ditched shadow. 20 mins.

"No change of plan, right?" Renee asked. "I'm holding the manuscripts until you give me a signal to bring them over."

"He needs my letters more than I need his photos."

"That's new," said Renee.

Nicole gave her companion a quick smile before looking away toward the headstones and grand tombs that glistened under an emerging wan sun. Her face settled into a look of resolve and wariness.

"Just trying to stay sane here, Ren, be pragmatic. Slader has to show his hand first or else game's over and he and my father can work things out by themselves. My priorities have changed recently, you may've noticed. Other things are more important than Will."

"More important than we ever imagined," she agreed, lightly touching Nicole's cheek with the back of her hand.

"Well, my blinders had to come off eventually," Nicole said, leaning her head into Renee's caress, not a little intoxicated by the heady perfume of the lilies they'd bought from a flower vendor on their way here. "Anyway, I still don't know if Slader really has any photos beyond the one I've already seen, so yeah, we should stick with the plan, see if we can't put the whole thing to rest—"

"—for once and for all. You got this, Bae."

As Nicole rose from the bench to walk toward the Wollstonecraft-Godwin-Shelley grave, Will did finally hear from the investigator colleague, whom he'd directed to the site. The meeting was imminent. Will himself, they'd agreed, would wait out of sight at the churchyard entrance on Iddesleigh near Grafton Road until Pollock could confirm that Slader had engaged with Nicole. For his part, Pollock—bent or no, partisan or not—was keen to get his hands on those photos. He still wasn't firmly convinced of Slader's guilt, and didn't want Will blowing up a delicate negotiation.

But Will Gardener wasn't about to wait. Believing in no one but himself at this point, he abandoned his car and walked, then ran, straight into St. Peter's Churchyard without looking left or right, heedless of drivers, who, in his wake, were leaning on their horns and shouting after him. Once inside the cemetery grounds, he dashed past a small clutch of mourners dressed in black near the church whose tranquil steeple had been shrouded in fog for much of the day. Yew trees, cherries, rhododendrons where drug dealers once used to ply their wares and users sometimes hid in shadows, flowerbeds asleep under mulch—these fell behind him on either side of the path, meaningless green-brown blurs, as he hurried past Pollock, who glanced toward the entrance from his own position in time to see a policeman direct traffic around the car that the detective understood must be Will's.

Slader might have wanted to give Nicole a hug when he recognized her standing by the modest rain-darkened memorial tomb incised with the names of the dead, surprised yet again by a resurgence of feeling that she would have changed his life for the better, saved him really, had she been his daughter. He wanted to tell her as much, but dismissed the idea in the same instant as it had overcome him. The look in her eyes didn't invite any such familiarity anyway. Hers was the countenance of a formidable woman who was here to do business. She had matured, he marveled. She had become beautiful. Wasn't the same girl—full of promise but unfledged—he'd met that autumn night in the parking lot of the Quaker meetinghouse on Bulls Head Road.

He spoke first, a shade more aggressive than intended. "Doesn't look like you have anything to give me. Mind explaining what's up with that?"

"Hello to you too," she said.

"Sorry. Hello, of course" and reached out his hand, which she shook. "But the Shelley manuscript?"

"Oh, I have it all right. And you're going to be very pleased. Just I need to see your photos first. Then we can trade."

"You understand I could take these"—and he patted his handsome new bag with its mahogany leather trim—"and go—"

"Straight to the police, I know. You've said all that before."

She was right. Time had come to show her the evidence he'd long been touting. Slader undid the latches on the bag, pulled out a tattered folder, uncoiled its flexible string ties, and passed the glossy photographs into her hands.

"You know, I was all but convinced these were a figment of your imagination."

"Your father and his lackey no doubt wish they were."

Nicole almost asked what he meant by *lackey*, but chose not to, in the interests of getting this over with. While she scrutinized the black-and-white images one by one, holding each print up to the light—the sky had gone pale blue, the storm having moved out to sea—before tucking it back in the bottom of the stack, Slader glanced around him. Against all odds, he felt at peace. Calmer than he had any right to be. His forger's road had been long and circuitous and messy, but was coming at last to an end. His life lay ahead of him, he thought as he noticed a woman who clearly was here with Nicole, based both on how intently she was staring at her and on something else he couldn't quite articulate. Her dovetailing personal style, her sophisticated face. Made him even wonder, just for a moment, if they weren't lovers. Breaking in on his own rambling musings, Slader asked Nicole if she was convinced now of what he'd been telling her.

She looked up at him, her arms dropping like dead weights to her sides, the series of photos clasped in one hand. "It's definitely my father in these," she answered, her voice tight, faint, resigned. "I see his hands are smeared with grease or maybe paint or, it's hard to tell."

"Blood, Nicole."

"Right, of course. And these date stamps? They're the day of?"

"The hour of."

Nicole felt lightheaded. She'd known all along, of course, but somehow had refused to admit to herself that it was the truth. Because, wasn't the truth what you made it? Wasn't that what she'd learned at her father's knee? With the long-promised evidence now in her hands, though, there was no more kneading reality into a more appealing shape. She leaned heavily against Mary's gravestone. Seeing this, Renee stepped up and slipped an arm around her waist to prevent her from falling.

"This is all of it, right?" Nicole said, willing herself to stay firm and businesslike. "Prints, negatives, everything, and no digital files anywhere?"

"As I've already told you, Nicole," said Slader, figuring he'd let her know about the safe deposit key in her studio later. "But it's time for you to hold up your end of the deal. I don't fancy being exposed out here with your friend Pollock following me."

And Will, Nicole remembered.

"How did the imaginary letters idea play out?" he asked, his eyes on Renee.

Nicole introduced them briefly, then answered, "Honestly? I don't even think of them as imaginary anymore."

"Don't say that. They're fakes, make-believe, illusions. You ought to know better," aware he sounded like some goddamn parental figure, but needing to say it nonetheless.

"I do know better," she countered. "Just I got ridiculously close to Mary and her mother doing them."

"Close how?" he asked, too curious not to, however impatient to conclude matters.

"You may think it's absurd, but spiritually close, emotionally."

"That is why you should never, ever in a thousand years, do another forgery. You're too human, for want of a better word. It's a job. Like a prisoner breaking stones. It's got nothing to do with human closeness, or spirit, or emotions. You're better than all that."

"I agree with the man," said Renee without any expression on her face, passing along the satchel of letters to their maker, who in turn handed them over to Henry Slader.

"So this is the manuscript that's been meddling with your soul?" he asked, hoping that his quaint advice, just now seconded by her friend—yes, plainly her lover—struck a chord with Nicole, even though he knew that it was precisely because she was so richly endowed with spirit that she was a master forger. Recalling the truism that it takes a lot of truth to tell a believable lie, he thought briefly that Nicole was full of truth, far more than he had ever been.

Before he opened the satchel to examine her labors, he glanced up and saw her eyes abruptly widen and now she was screaming "What, no no no, stop," as Will was upon Slader without a word or any warning, stabbing him from behind over and over, in his back and neck, wielding a chef's knife with such fury and quickness it seemed unnatural, not at all real although it was. Slader wheeled around in shock, flailing and shoving hard against his attacker while he blindly grabbed at the glinting air, failing time and again to seize the knife that sliced into his palms and fingers. If they were groaning or screaming or making any kind of noise, Nicole couldn't hear them over her own shrieking when she dropped the glossy prints on the ground and lunged into the fray to stop her father, stop this madness. Renee screamed, "Get the fuck out of there, Nick, it's not—" and, dropping the bouquet of lilies on the wet grass, succeeded in grabbing her arm and dragging her away from the fracas. The men, oblivious, staggered like a single thrashing beast over the grave and downhill to a walkway, where horrified would-be visitors to the Shelleys' resting place had converged, and Will, relentless in his assassination of Henry Slader, refused to stop stabbing the blood-soaked prostrate body even after the man was utterly dead.

When he climbed in a daze to his feet, Will was gasping like someone half drowned in his own blood. He was covered in violet and black gore, grievously injured by the same knife he'd so recently bought at the hardware store. Eyes darting about in terror, unsure he wasn't hallucinating what lay before and behind him, he caught sight of Pollock, who, pale as some incongruous liturgical vestment, staggered up to him and knelt beside his victim, desperate but failing to find a pulse in the man's neck or bloody wrists. He looked at the gathering crowd and shouted, had they already called an ambulance? And as Renee held Nicole close so she didn't collapse, the women, numb and mute, caught sight of police in blue-black uniforms who appeared on the nearby bluff before them and in the street below, both well aware what would, with crushing inevitability, next come to pass.

The Severn Gallery exhibit of my Mary Shelley collage paintings, *Mary to Mary*, was a success by any measure. The show
all but sold out at the opening, with those satisfying round red
stickers that indicate a canvas has been reserved adorning many
of the title tags on the wall adjacent to each oil assemblage.
Critics generally praised my multimedia approach, in which I
applied what appeared to be original Shelley manuscripts to canvases that were painted with Chagall-like whimsy to build narratives through image and word. The work was complimented
for its fluency of abstract-figurative painting with "undeniably
masterful" calligraphic ingenuity. Only one contrarian reviewer
deemed the Shelley manuscripts to be gimmicky, insisting their
incorporation into the paintings was, somehow, off-putting in
a manner reminiscent of Damien Hirst, who floated a shark in
formaldehyde and encrusted a platinum-cast skull with dia-
monds. I didn't get the connection, which, in any case, seemed
dated. Renee, however, assured me that the names Nicole Diehl

and Damien Hirst being linked in the same provocative article was nothing if not positive.

"Critic's an ass, but his comparison's badass," she quipped, adding, "And not to forget the wretched cliché, no news is bad news."

Even though my canny admission that the manuscripts weren't originals, set down in that letter I composed using Mary's own words from *Frankenstein*, was reproduced in the catalog and hung in the gallery so it was the first work visitors would see, many people thought the Shelley pages were indeed authentic. It didn't seem to matter that the confession was right there before their eyes or that I was obviously being artful about the source and history of the *Mary to Mary* letters. Viewers saw what they wanted to see.

The notoriety surrounding Slader's death and my father's arrest played its own part in the attention the show received. I remembered that unkind journalists had accused the young Agatha Christie of staging her disappearance to create an international sensation in the newspapers in order to promote her books. But really, I think she was nothing more or less than a jilted wife who ran away from her husband for a host of reasons, none of them having to do with commerce or fame. Like her, I never sought tabloid attention. I merely merged my painter's skills with my gifts as a reluctant forger who'd stayed deep enough in the shadows never to get called out. But it seemed that same wretched cliché about bad news was operative here as well.

As for the rare-book trade, a number of dealers turned up at the opening, some buying for collectors or resale, a handful shying away for fear—again, despite my disclaimers—that I'd used actual originals, which, had it been the case, would for sure have been scandalous. The two bookmen who'd shown me their stock of Mary Shelley letters when I was first in London were interested in setting up a show at their gallery the following spring. I'm not positive they recalled that I'd visited their Fulham Road shop, where they'd treated me with a kindness I didn't deserve, given the duplicitous game I was playing. But they did take me up on doing a part-trade, part-cash deal for one of their originals, a lengthy letter to Marianna Hammond, who was friends with Mary's stepsister, Claire Clairmont, mother to Lord Byron's daughter, Allegra—a nice artifact from the love-tangled Shelley circle. They even helped me arrange to donate it to the British Library, as I'd promised myself I would.

Renee and I never got to bed that night. Too much stimulus, too much everything. But when we finally returned to her apartment, we curled up together and slept well into the afternoon. On waking, she—a radiant ball of energy—showered and hurried off to the gallery for evening appointments with private clients interested in viewing works she'd reserved for them. As for me, I set out into the early evening in jeans, one of Renee's shirts patterned like marbled paper, and a black leather jacket, and wandered aimless and solitary along sidewalks filled with Labor Day weekend celebrants, past Brooklyn bars overflowing with lubricated noisemakers and others—couples, singles; old, young—just headed home for a quiet evening.

I had no deliberate plan, but found myself a bench in a poorly lit small park, where I sat undistracted to try and piece together all that had happened over the past year, the past twenty-one years.

My opening had been scheduled to coincide with Mary Shelley's birthday, Friday the thirtieth of August. And as fate would have it, tomorrow, the first of September, would mark the one-year anniversary of Will delivering Edgar Allan Poe's *Tamerlane* to Henry Slader. Without the latter, the former might never have happened. Could I loathe the past that landed me here and still be grateful for my present? Where's the rule says I couldn't? So much loss, though. I shook my head in disbelief. What in the world drives people to such lunacy?

There is a kind of black that is the blackest of all blacks. Known as Vantablack, it is a lab-grown superblack that absorbs all but the smallest percentage of visible light from every angle of its surface. Any three-dimensional object coated with Vantablack—say, a table or a chair or a tree—will be robbed of depth and look like a two-dimensional void. Similar superblacks occur in nature—the recently discovered Vogelkop Lophorina bird-of-paradise species found in the far western region of New Guinea is arrayed in plumage whose color absorption nearly equals that of Vantablack. During its courtship dance, the male bird-of-paradise flaunts a fan of electric-blue feathers that contrast with its black plumage, producing a dazzling, unworldly effect as it hops about in front of a promising mate. I have always found it intriguing that the females are tempted into the act of procreation in no small part by a color where light essentially goes to die.

The revulsion, the despair, the grief I felt watching my father get thrown to the ground next to his dead and bloody victim, arrested, taken away for booking, alone in a country far from home, as alone as I'd ever seen him in this world, was somewhere in this register of pure blackness. Slader's needless murder was a similar black, and its needlessness left me bereft in a different way. I felt inexcusably sorry for the man. When the detectives asked me what his name was—his driver's license gave it as James S. Nicholas, his passport as Travis Ainsworth—and I informed them I'd known him as Henry Slader, I knew they faced a thorny road ahead to untangle his true identity. An identity that might well forever evade them. The many thousands of dollars he was carrying only further complicated matters. They collected his photographs strewn everywhere but never saw my manuscript. Interviewed by them more than once, I stuck with the truth, mostly. The deceased was there to meet me to prove he hadn't been the murderer of a family member. My alibis held; my heartbreak was genuine.

Yet for all my grief over Will and sorrow about Slader, at the end of the day hadn't both men been manipulating me to their own ends? Wasn't it the case that neither deserved my mourning? Not, certainly, when I had so much of my own remorse to begin to work through for the rest of my days.

My mother would prove herself too much a survivor to wear the black of widow's weeds for very long. She'd stuck by Will through every unwelcome twist and downward turn, and when it was proven he had murdered her brother all those years ago, her feelings understandably changed. Changed radically. Still, she was much too willful a protector of Maisie and me to let on until years later how much she really knew about my father's sins, not to mention Slader's murder of his old friend Cricket, whose body he dumped on that dead-end road in her presence. None of her secrets much mattered now that the guilty were either imprisoned or extinct. That's how I imagine she lives with her memories, anyway.

As for dapper Pollock, these twelve years on, where I look out from a terrace at the Acropolis to celebrate my thirty-third birthday with dearest Renee, now my wife, he passed away not long after his cold case resolved itself. He was annoying, true, dogged beyond belief, shady in his dealings like so many cops. But as Maisie had said when she called me in Bournemouth, Pollock was also a "smiling old man." He knew loss, had his fair share of it himself. I bear him, in memory, no ill will, although I wonder sometimes about his curious methods and whether he mightn't better have lived out his senior years catching bluefish in the waters off Montauk. Either way, as I've already noted in these pages, dying is a difficult business.

The funeral that Meghan had attended back when Maisie encountered Slader in his sleeping bag and Pollock at the front door, had been for Atticus Moore. When later she revealed, per the signed agreement she'd made with Atticus, that he was Maisie's birth father and the girl was due to assume an inheritance from him on her coming of age, Maze was at first furious with me for not letting her in on the secret. But when I told her it had never been my right to say anything, I must've professed my innocence with such sincerity that she never questioned me again. Together she, Renee, and I took the oceanside train from New York up to Providence to visit his grave site—a stately headstone bore the words *Proud Father* amid the rest of the epitaph—and Maisie's reaction was as cold as the incised granite before her.

"Is it bad that I don't feel anything?" she asked me.

It wasn't, I assured her, sensing that an absence of feeling toward the man was better than rage or love or some other response she could have had, any of which might have led to distractions Maisie didn't deserve. Late in his life Atticus had grown a spine and developed a sense of responsibility toward his abandoned daughter, but the inheritance he'd provided for her on her twenty-first birthday was insufficient to provoke gratitude. Meghan had told me more than once that he never expected his daughter to love him retroactively, whether or not his blood was in her veins, his money in her bank account. Like so much of the business he and my father and Slader—and who knew who else—conducted, paying off Maisie for his own wrongs was right on brand.

In Providence, we paid homage to Swan Point Cemetery's most famous resident, H. P. Lovecraft. I also told the others that I was pretty sure Poe himself had visited this cemetery with a woman named Sarah Helen Whitman, whom he was trying to persuade to marry him. "Think that was in September 1848," I added.

"So did they? Get married," asked Maisie.

"Even if she had, she'd have become a widow right quick, since he died the very next year," and together we returned to the train station in downtown Providence and caught the first Acela back to Manhattan. Maisie has never once mentioned the name Atticus again, and neither have I. He was a Lovecraftian nightmare fantasy as far as we were concerned, a Poean question spurned, and though he looked like a Georgian-era gentleman with his stylish cane and suit the one time I saw him in front of the Beekman Arms in Rhinebeck, his image seemed a caricature now. One to erase and forget.

Paying a visit to Meghan recently in her by-now iconic little bookshop in the East Village, Renee bought me—insisted on paying full price—a copy of *To the Lighthouse*. First edition in a blue cloth binding, it was missing its Vanessa Bell dust jacket, which in any case would have sent its value into the tens of thousands. This was just after New Year's, and the city was swirling with polar-vortex snow the likes of which we hadn't seen for years, as winters had turned dry and too warm anymore for heavy coats and scarves. She asked one of Meg's shop assistants to wrap the volume, choosing a leftover holiday gift paper with gingerbread figures holding hands like paper-chain people. Looked like a retro design from the fifties, and pure Renee.

When we returned to our loft in Crown Heights, Brooklyn, she tucked the book away in her dresser drawer. Curious, I joked, "So you've decided to keep Virginia for yourself?"

"Naw, Squatch. Patience, you know. The virtue?"

I cannot remember whether I laughed, probably did, but afterward pretty much lost track of it. Life was busy. I was painting, as always, but also expanding into set designs for theater, dance, films, anything that fused narrative and visual arts. Maze, after a couple of post-college years living with a boyfriend in the Pacific Northwest, was back in the city, butterflying from job to job, a twenty-four-year-old with searching eyes and a kind of humane cynicism I adored. The two of us were close, closer, than ever, and I felt a deep need to be present for her, if and whenever she liked. Meghan was in negotiations to sell the farmhouse upstate, even though winter was deemed the worst season to make such a move. She wanted it off her shoulders finally, and who could blame her since none of us much stayed there anymore, and some frigging strung-out kids had broken in last summer and partied, stirring up bad old memories she felt were best left behind.

Then my birthday was about to come around. Forever destined to be bittersweet, since it was also a deathday, I leaned hard into the sweetness while always taking some quiet time to remember its bitter side. Renee and I planned to go back not to Greece or Italy or Curaçao but to London—staying a few nights at the Ritz this time and no arguing with her about it.

After the pandemic, our response hadn't been to rusticate in the country or to continue to isolate ourselves, but to follow, as Joseph Campbell put it, our bliss. Not that our little bliss needed following, as such. Yes, we had our noisy rows, yes, our disagreements magnificent and forgettable. But mostly our bliss was to be found wherever we happened to be, together. On any old street corner waiting for the light to change, swimming in the ocean, watching fall warblers in some park somewhere.

And in that spirit we are sitting here now, side by side in my favorite Indian restaurant, at my old corner table beneath that same flamboyant, mawkish, adorable Vishnu painting on faded cream velvet the color of *ras malai*, ordering tandoori chicken and Malbec. I can still picture the detective seated across the room by the doorway, eating his usual meal of tea and crumpets, and though my favorite waiter from years before isn't working here anymore—I have to wonder if the pandemic was the cause, or if he himself got married and moved on—the rest of the staff seem mostly to be the same faces as before, just older, like the rest of us.

After we order a second bottle of Malbec, the staff instead bring out a bottle of Krug Grande Cuvée with chilled flutes and a pillow-shaped red velvet cake with, for some reason, six candles on it. The inescapable birthday song is sung, in a delightful range of accents and voices, and I blow out the candles, which are mounted on an awesome pastry elephant with frost-white candy tusks, and everybody applauds and cheers.

"Damn you," I say through my smile. "You know I hate a fuss."

"A fuss is what you deserve, and a fuss is what you're getting, like it or not."

We lean over toward each other and kiss, and when I sit back up in the chair she produces two presents, one wrapped in plain kraft stock—the kind butchers use to wrap up a steak—and the other in gloriously busy wrong-season holiday paper.

After kissing her again and thanking her, I open the first gift and find inside, to my astonishment, my practice notebook from our Mary Shelley forgery days. Filled with drafts, sketches, roughed-out trial phrasings, some of which made it into the finished manuscript, some of which I'd abandoned. I had entirely forgotten about this artifact.

"I remember we were supposed to destroy this," I say, looking at Renee in confusion. "You volunteered to get rid of it, I think, no?"

"I did," she says, beaming with a smile. "Because, if you recall, you didn't have the heart to destroy it yourself, even if it could've been used as evidence against you if things got that far. But, well, I couldn't bear to destroy it either. It was too important a keepsake of those crazy times together for me to run it through a shredder."

"So you've kept it all this time."

"So I've kept it all this time."

I shake my head, tell her she's the best, and as I carefully remove the tape from the second package, say, "Think I know what's in here."

And yes, the first edition of *To the Lighthouse* is inside, though what I hadn't known before, because neither Renee nor Meghan had told me, is that the book is inscribed by Virginia to one of her Bloomsbury circle friends. I look up into Renee's beaming face, then back at the flyleaf. Not only was the ink mixed precisely to the purplish color the author favored, it was indeed used by Virginia herself back in 1927, since the inscription is without a question authentic.

Noticing me studying the autograph, she says, laughing, "No, none of your fancy-ass pareidolia in play this time around."

"It's perfect," I stutter. "How can I ever thank you enough?"

"You can't and you don't need to. Anyway, there are better things to do. Such as I want you to come along with me to pay homage to Virginia, who longed for her lost mother every bit as much as Poe did his and Mary hers," and reveals that she's rented us a car to drive down to Rodmell, Lewes, East Sussex, to see where the novel was written. How, I wonder, could she have guessed that the Woolfs' country home, Monk's House, was where I'd told my parents I planned to go with Renee before coming back home from England? It's not like I mentioned it to her.

Yet it all stands to reason, as my marriage to Renee is just that, a merging of minds, an intimacy of easy truth and honesty. A less starry-eyed explanation might be that in recent years I've been working up the idea of making another series of literary paintings in the same vein as my Mary Shelley, the Brontë sisters, Emily Dickinson, and Gertrude Stein manuscript paintings—this one, intended to be my final writer of the series, to be centered on Virginia Woolf. Renee, forever the practical romantic, hopes that our trip to the south of England will inspire me to push this to full fruition.

The most recent letter I receive from my father, now that we have returned home to Brooklyn, is written in old-school penmanship, a style of calligraphy that dates from the days when children were taught to form their letters one at a time on ruled paper with a dotted midline, or in a Big Chief tablet. While the schoolkids' longhand might have slanted more to the right or left than their teachers taught them, their capital letters taking whimsical flights at times with unwelcome flourishes like fiddlehead ferns or curly willows, the uniform nature of the letters, words, sentences, paragraphs, and pages assured them certain legibility.

Children now, of course, hardly know their way around a pen or pencil. Paper itself could one day go the way of all flesh, just as the forger's art may be doomed by artificial intelligence with a database of precise historical ink recipes and a bespoke autopen. Even if that's our fate—books on screens, manuscripts on memory sticks, hands-free AI forgeries—I find it painful to see that my father's handwriting, once so dangerously versatile, has degraded in prison to the bland anonymity of a five-year-old's ABCs. In his case, the homogenized dullness of the script, its deliberate humdrum appearance, suggests his spirit is broken. For all the bad he did in his life—transgressing against those who loved him as much as those who didn't—I hate to think of him as broken, as reverting to the conventional. Is such a sea change really possible? As I hold his latest *missive*, an antique word he always loved, in one hand, I brush away a tear with my other. Renee, who has been observing, sees this and gently asks me what's wrong.

Startled, I shake my head and continue to stare at the letter, not yet reading whatever he's written about—his news, his frustrations, his regrets. I imagine he'll have invented a bunch of clever details to protect me, or maybe even himself, from hard truths about his life inside. Be that as it may, while these rows of words written in blue-black may be my father's real handwriting, it looks to me instead like the crafting of an artful impostor. One who could at will, without the least difficulty or any practice, write the famous lines "The boundaries which divide Life from Death are at best shadowy and vague. Who shall say where the one ends, and where the other begins?" in the very hand Edgar Allan Poe once used when he wrote his story of premature burial. The right iron gall ink, the perfect period paper, and what's real becomes a matter of faith. Then, when Renee asks me again if I'm all right, my reverie comes to an end and I look into the eyes of the one I love, and tell her yes, I am.

ACKNOWLEDGMENTS

Great gratitude to my physician of many years, Dr. Eric Goldberg, for guiding me through the complex medical episodes that would follow a victim's suffering a concussion and being buried alive. Many thanks to my rare book dealer friends Pom Harrington and Sammy Jay of Peter Harrington Rare Books in London for reading several key passages in manuscript and providing helpful comments. I am grateful to Richard Kopley for his sage advice about Edgar Allan Poe and Mary Shelley. To my trusted early readers Christine von der Linn, Pat Sims, Tom Johnson, Jackie Douglas, Eleanor Polak, and Melanie Pflaum who offered insightful suggestions, my heartfelt thanks. I am grateful to Pip Franks for sharing his memories of Bournemouth, in Dorset, England and to Stephanie Neves who showed me around the historic Reynolds House Inn in Roscoe, New York. I'm honored that fellow bibliophile Nicholas Basbanes was willing to put his expert eyes on a late draft of this book. And to my former student who, during a class discussion about death, uttered what would become the opening line of this novel, thank you for allowing me to use your memorable words. *In libras libertas.*

Warmest thanks always to my agent, Henry Dunow, for his encouragement and support during the writing of the Forgers Trilogy—*The Forgers*, *The Forger's Daughter*, and *The Forger's Requiem*. Likewise to everyone at Grove Atlantic, my sincerest gratitude: Morgan Entrekin, Zoe Harris, Deb Seager, Sal Destro, Cassie McSorley, Mike Richards, Gretchen Mergenthaler, Becca Fox, Miranda Hency, Natalie Church, Judy Hottensen, JT Green, and Rachael Richardson. To Cara Schlesinger, as meticulous as she is insightful, my deepest appreciation for her evergreen support.